RUNNERS

RUNNERS BOOK ONE

TOBY NEIGHBORS

MYTHIC ADVENTURE PUBLISHING, LLC

Runners: Runners Book One

Copyright © 2021 by Toby Neighbors

ISBN 978-1-952260-22-3

Published by Mythic Adventure Publishing, LLC

Idaho, USA

Copy Editor: Aisha Matthews

ALSO BY TOBY NEIGHBORS

THE JOLLY ROGUE

Top down view

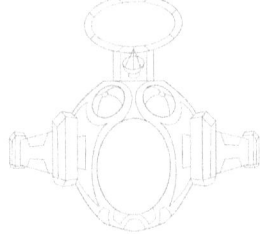

Front view

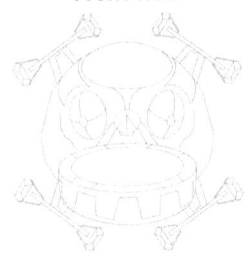

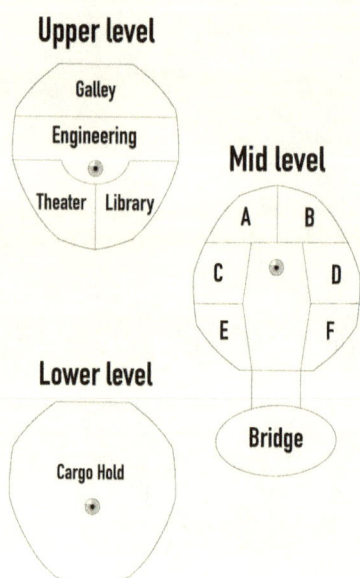

Upper level

Galley

Engineering

Theater | Library

Mid level

A | B

C | D

E | F

Bridge

Lower level

Cargo Hold

PROLOGUE

Are you a reader?

Do you have awareness of what other people are thinking?

Can you guess another's person's secrets?

Do strange, often inexplicable things tend to happen around you?

If the answer to any of these questions is yes, you might be a Reader. As a galactic citizen, you have the responsibility to report your telepathic abilities to the Galactic Authority. Even if you know someone that you suspect could be a Reader, your duty is to report them.

Help us make the galaxy a safer place. Hiding your abilities from the Galactic Authority is a crime. Don't be lured into breaking the law. We live in a free and just society where everyone is equal. If you're a Reader, or know one, don't wait, report it today.

CHAPTER 1

Colt O'Conner was, by all accounts, unexceptional. Perhaps the gift had always been there, lying dormant, just below his subconscious. Looking back over his sixteen years he could remember times when he acted on knowledge that he couldn't have known. And yet he had never consciously realized that he was a Reader. No outside thoughts had crowded his brain. He had never swam in another person's mind, and he certainly couldn't move objects merely by thinking about them. But when the change occurred, it was undeniable.

Fortunately for Colt, he had been home with his mother when the first echos of thoughts that weren't his own invaded his mind. His father was long gone, probably on a crew with no desire to return to the family he had abandoned on the primary spaceport in orbit over Helix Prime. It was the only home Colt had known. He and his mother lived in the pods. She was a sanitation professional, which was really just a fancy name for a maid. Her days were filled with ten hour shifts emptying the recycling collectors and cleaning the public restroom facilities near the port.

For most of his life Colt had gone unnoticed. He was average sized, well behaved, and fell into the common intelligence range. His second hand clothes were clean and well maintained, thanks to his mother. They didn't have a lot, but the two of them didn't need much. When Colt wasn't in school, he washed dishes for a pizza restaurant. It was a way of earning extra income and supplementing his meager diet, since there were often mistakes made on the pizza line that couldn't be sold. Colt was always game for free food, even if he didn't like the toppings.

His gift came to fruition in the middle of the night, and woke him from sleep. He was alone in the tiny bed nook built into the wall. His mother was below him in her own nook. Their pod was nothing more than a single room dwelling, with a video wall and tiny sanitation closet. As he lay in bed, wrapped in a tangle of bedsheets, he could hear the thoughts of the people in the pods around them. Many were asleep, the minds quiet, but others were awake. Some worrying about their troubles, others plotting their future, or fighting with their mates. It all came crashing into his mind suddenly and violently. He woke with a start and stumbled from his bed. The crash of his body falling woke his mother. She found Colt huddled on the floor, his hands over his ears, his teeth clenched as he fought to keep the sounds of dozens of strangers out of his head.

"Colt," his mother called out.

She was on her knees beside him in less than a second. Miriam O'Connor was not wealthy or proud, but she loved her son fiercely.

"What's wrong?" she asked.

"Make it stop," Colt begged through clenched teeth.

"What is it?" she asked. "Lights!"

The bulbs built into the pod's ceiling panels illuminated their tiny home. Colt was shaking, his face a grimace of pain.

"Are you hurt?"

"Stop the voices," Colt begged. "Please, mom, help me."

Her own worries and fears bled into his mind. *Is he having a seizure, or a stroke? Oh, God help me... please... help him!*

For three days he was unable to function. Miriam stayed with her son day and night, slowly coming to a realization that he wasn't sick. And he wasn't going mad. He was a telepath, a mentally gifted individual that was commonly referred to as a Reader, since many people with the gift could read minds. For Colt, it was like learning to think all over again. He had to learn to keep the outside thoughts from crashing into his mind and driving him insane.

We have to keep this a secret, his mother was thinking.

"I know," Colt said.

"What?" his mother asked. *Is he reading my thoughts?*

Trying as hard as he could, he still couldn't keep her voice out of his head. Her fear was like a neon sign, at times it was almost blinding. And every private thought she had was as clear to him as if she had spoken it out loud.

"I'm not trying to," he said.

"But you can. You can hear my thoughts?"

"Even when I don't want to," Colt admitted.

"Then you know what this means, don't you?"

"That I'm a Reader."

Another flare of fear, almost pure panic filled Colt with dread. It was strange to experience some else's emotions. He didn't want to be afraid but he had no choice. His mother's fear was so strong it flooded his mind.

"We have to hide it, Colt. We can't ever let anyone know.

Not ever," she insisted. "You know what they do to people with the gift."

Colt knew that Readers were hunted by criminals and government agents. A Reader, no matter what level, would never be free.

"They'll come after you," she continued. "If they find out." *And they always find out. They have people who track the gifted.*

Her fear kept slamming into him like waves from a malfunctioning repulser lift. It made him feel weak, and the cacophony of mental noise from outside their pod threatened to batter down his defenses. He pushed against her thoughts and emotions. It felt wrong to push his mother away, but he had to keep her at bay or might lose control again.

"We can't hide forever," Colt said.

"No, you'll have to go out again soon. I've been telling people that you're sick. But sooner or later you'll have to go out. Do you think you can handle that?"

"I have to learn," Colt said, ignoring her fear.

"If people figure out what you can do, Colt, if they even suspect it, they'll turn you in."

The truth was, Colt didn't know what he could do. All he cared about doing was keeping the thoughts of other people out of his head. He knew there were five levels of Readers, each one more powerful than the first. It was tempting to look up Readers online, but it might tip someone off. The GA monitored all online transactions. Nothing was secret anymore. Even just talking about what Colt could do in the privacy of their own home was dangerous. No one knew how deep the Galactic Authority's monitoring of average citizens went, but Colt knew they had the capacity to keep tabs on anyone.

"I can hide it," Colt said, glad that his mother couldn't read his mind and know that he wasn't sure he actually could hide his gift.

"It's really important," she said. "There are a lot of people who would do anything to get to you if they knew. Not just the GA, there are a lot of unscrupulous people in the galaxy Colt."

"I know," he said.

"And they can't find out."

It was her mantra, the thought that filled her mind. *No one can ever find out.*

And he knew it would be impossible to live his life without anyone ever knowing that he was different. He had already begun to act differently with his mother in the hopes of calming her fears. It wasn't intentional, but he knew what she was thinking and he didn't want her to worry. She had no idea how hard he was working to calm his mind and act normal. And no matter what he told her, he knew that it was only a matter of time.

CHAPTER 2

"Dropping out of hyperspace in three," the pilot said, "two, one."

Captain Wes Hanzor felt the transition. He'd heard it described many times, but never the same way twice. For him, moving from hyperspace to regular space felt a bit like a glitch. A missing step, or a skipped heartbeat, just strange enough to make him think that perhaps the transition wasn't as safe as the Space Transportation Union claimed. Not that he believed a word out of their mouths anyway.

"Status," he said from his station on the bridge.

"We have..." Stewart Price, their navigator said, his mouth working furiously to produce the next word, "... arrived." Getting the word out was a relief.

"All systems green," Di said. "I told you she would hold together."

"I never doubted it," Wes said, although in truth he had feared a complete breakdown halfway through the journey.

The *Jolly Rogue* was on her third hyperdrive and needed a complete overhaul, but that would have to wait. The crew was low on credits and pressed for time. Diana Silver, their engineer, had cobbled together a workable fix, but the hyperdrive would fail eventually and Wes didn't like thinking of that. If it broke down between systems, they would be lost. Hyperspace travel was the only way of moving between systems that were so far apart that even traveling at the speed of light it would take years to move between them. The *Jolly Rogue* could support the crew for a few weeks, but any longer than that and they would run out of vital resources. And if the entire mechanical system went down with the hyperdrive, they would freeze to death in just a few hours. Every jump they made between systems was a huge risk, but that was life off the grid.

On the ships large display screens they could see the space traffic moving toward the primary port. The Helix system was a major trade destination, which meant it would have a lot of the things the *Jolly Rogue* needed to get back into good working order. On the other hand, it would also be crawling with Galactic Authority agents who could make their lives extremely difficult. The GA didn't like independent vessels, and Wes knew they would have to tread lightly.

"How long to reach port?" he asked.

"Two hours, maybe more if they make us wait," Ilk Saide, the Hyborian pilot said.

"Di, get the lowband transmitter on. Let's see who's talking," Wes ordered.

"On it," the engineer said.

Wes glanced over and saw Di stand up from her station on the Bridge. She was big boned and looked stocky in her stained coveralls, but Wes knew that underneath the bulky clothing she was muscular. Following behind her was Zora Kaylee, who was Di's complete opposite. She was young, thin, with long arms and fingers. Where Di was outspoken and opinionated, Zora was quiet and submissive. She hardly ever spoke, and moved as silently as a cat. Yet Di insisted she was smart, with a knack for engineering. Together they kept the *Jolly Rogue* running.

They left the bridge just as the short range communication system lit up with hails from Helix Prime's flight control. Wes hit the button that opened the communication channel.

"Unidentified vessel," a bored sounding flight controller voice crackled over the ship's speakers, "please submit your STU registration, crew information, and manifest."

Wes wondered if he should bump up their communications gear on the ship's list of needed repairs. The *Jolly Rogue* was a good ship, but she had been around the galaxy a few times and many of her systems needed updating. He pushed the thought from his mind and punched the transmit button.

"Flight control, this is the *Jolly Rogue* an independent trade vessel," Wes said. "I'm transmitting our crew information and manifest now."

He hit a few keys on his console that would transmit the data requested. It took twice as long as it should have for the flight controller to reply. Wes knew the bored controller had taken the time to notify his superior that an off grid ship was coming into port. Hopefully, that was as far as the information went. The last thing they needed was an official GA inspection. Not that they were doing anything illegal. Their load of pharmaceutical grade magnesium wasn't a controlled substance and wouldn't land them in hot water. The ship's aging systems on the other hand could get them stuck in port until repairs could be made and inspections were passed. The *Jolly Rogue* and her crew lived from one job to the next. If they had to sell their load of magnesium in the Helix system the would only get a fraction of what it was worth on an Alliance world.

"*Jolly Rogue* this is flight control, you are cleared for entry.

Please follow the yellow guide to your berth in section twenty-seven, level D."

"You got that Saide?" Wes said, breaking the alien's last name into two distinct syllables, *say-ead*.

"Affirmative," the pilot responded.

Wes pushed the transmit activator on his console. "Roger that, flight control. *Jolly Rogue* out."

He got to his feet and stretched. Moving into a busy space-port like Helix Prime could be dangerous. There were hundreds of ships moving to and fro. One mistake could cause catastrophic damage to multiple ships, but Ilk Saide was Hyborian with the ability to link the ship to his neural synapse cluster, giving him complete control of the vessel. He could see everything and move the ship at thought. It was like the ninety meter freighter became part of his physical body. Taking the ship into port was as simple for Saide as walking was for Wes.

"Alright people, we're going in for a short pit stop," Wes announced, using the com-link built into the collar of his jacket so that Di and Zora could hear him. "In and out as fast as we can. I don't want the GA snooping around."

Di's voice came back over the Bridge's loudspeakers. "That shouldn't be too hard. With this many ships the GA should be swamped with more important matters. I can't imagine they would take interest in a little ship like ours."

"Well, as soon as we make contact with DeVoor we are shipping out. So be ready," Wes said. "Saide, you're in charge of resupply. Make sure we don't get any more of that GA experimental fuel. That crap nearly caused the fusion reactor or overload the last time."

The Hyborian grunted in reply.

"Where are we..." Stu worked through his process of

communication like someone with a mouth full of peanut butter, "going, next?"

"That depends on what DeVoor tells us," Wes assured his navigator. "I'll tell you as soon as I know."

"O... kay," Stu said without looking up.

Wes wasn't sure where Stu fell on the autism spectrum, but his ability to compute huge numbers in his mind was astounding. When Wes had first met Stu, he was living in a home for the mentally impaired and working at a factory checking the safety seals on bottles of energy drinks. It was, in Wes' mind, a complete waste of Stu's talent. He couldn't function outside of a controlled area. Busy places made Stu especially frantic. But the *Jolly Rogue* was an ideal environment for him. He thrived in the familiar surroundings, had no desire to ever leave the ship, and his mental computational abilities allowed them to function completely free of the Space Transportation Union's navigational network. Being off the grid was perfect for a ship taking advantage of the blockade between the Galactic Authority and the Alliance of Free Systems or AFS. The *Jolly Rogue* didn't deal in illegal goods, they just took basic supplies, like their current cargo of magnesium, from GA space, past the blockade, and into the planets that were under sanctions that restricted their trade. That was a crime, but one that Wes didn't lose sleep over. Every planet had unique resources, and he saw his job as making it possible for people to profit from those resources while also getting the goods to the people that needed them. It was a win - win situation for everyone except the GA, but they were suffering under the illusion that everyone in the galaxy should simply accept their complete authoritarian control. Wes, like the planets in the AFS, didn't want to be controlled. He enjoyed the freedom of living off the grid, even if it sometimes made things a little more difficult.

Stewart opened the lid to the antique digital optical disk player that Di had built into his work station. Music was one of the things that seemed to lubricate the gears of genius in Stu's mind. He put a CD into the player from the massive collection he had amassed over the years. Everyone on board made a point of picking up old music CD's for him whenever they came across one. He closed the lid and pressed the play button on his console. From the Bridge speakers the sounds of an electric twelve string guitar began to play. It the beginning of a song by the Nelsons. Wes thought they were the children of an even older musician. Stu had told him the story at one point, but he hadn't remembered it. The song was catchy though, he thought, as the vocalist began to sing: *Here she comes... mmm, just like an angel, seems like forever that she's been on my mind.*

Only one person had that kind of hold on Wes' mind. And one thing he knew for sure was that she was no angel.

CHAPTER 3

Colt didn't enjoy staying at home. He got out at the first opportunity, but couldn't stay out long because he felt like people were staring. It was difficult not to hear the thoughts of a person he was talking to, and even harder to keep a straight face. The spaceport was a busy place and crowded with people. It wasn't unusual to see aliens in the market, or when Colt went walking down the station's docking rings.

He loved to see the ships. The really big freighters and transport vessels were like buildings and not as interesting. But the smaller ships had style. Most were customized with upgrades. Colt and his friends often inspected the ships in port trying to identify the components. He had even been inside one. It was a space yacht that had seen better days. The owner had been trying to sell it and he let Colt in with a few of his friends so that it would seem like there was more interest in the vessel than there really was. Still, he remembered the cockpit with the massive nav computer and the engineering section with it's own fusion reactor. In a ship a person could be free, he thought. They could travel anywhere in the galaxy and still be home. Until his abilities appeared, he had planned to work in the dock yard or possibly on a freighter. His hope was that if he worked hard and saved his wages, he might be able to buy his own ship. He might even learn to pilot and make repairs himself. He could join the STU and see the galaxy if he played his cards right.

His plans for the future had taken a major and unexpected detour with the sudden onset of his abilities. And just taking a stroll through the station made it clear why the GA required Readers to register. He couldn't help but linger near a merchant's stall as the owner tried to sell a culinary processor to a Rangolian who was on leave from the freighter. Colt could hear the man's thoughts as clearly as if he were speaking directly to him. The merchant was peddling refurbished goods as new, and hoping the Rangolian wouldn't figure out how he could sell the culinary processor so cheap.

It was shocking to know the merchant's secrets and feel his desperation. At first Colt was shocked that the merchant would lie to his customer, but after a few moments the salesman thought of his sick wife and Colt was hit by a wave of fear. He felt like a cheat knowing the man's thoughts and emotions. And yet he couldn't seem to pull himself away from the merchant until a deal was struck. Colt felt the exaltation of the merchant and his excitement at making the sale, followed quickly by a wave of intense relief. The man had enough profit to buy his wife's medicine. He quickly closed up his little shop and hurried off to get what he needed.

Colt was left reeling. The power to know what other people were thinking was incredible and he didn't think he could hide his feelings the way the merchant had. He had never been good at telling lies. Even in school, his teachers could usually see through his weak excuses, even the Artificials that did much of the teaching once he was out of primary school. If he couldn't fool an android, what hope did he have of fooling a human. The thoughts caused him to hurry home.

"What's wrong?" his mother asked the moment he walked in the door. "Are you feeling okay?"

"I'm fine," he lied, feeling her anxiety like a blast of hot air.

"Did you have another episode?"

"No," he said. "But I don't think I can do this."

"Do what?"

"Hide it," Colt said. "I don't think I can lie to people, mom. Not when I can hear what they're thinking and feel what they're feeling."

"You just need time," she said. *They'll do horrible things to him if he's caught,* she thought, as fear radiated from her. *They'll take him away from me and I'll never see him again.*

Colt hated knowing her thoughts. He knew she was worried about him, about making their rent, about what might happen if it was discovered they were hiding his gift.

"It's too much," he said. "We're breaking the law by not reporting what I can do."

She sat down beside him in one of the two plastic chairs that was all the furnishing they had in their tiny apartment. His mother had always been able to calm him down.

"Colt," she said softly. "The Galactic Authority will take you away if we report it. They'll ship you off to who knows where and force you use your abilities in ways you won't feel good about."

"I don't feel good about any of it," he replied.

"But you will, in time. You have an amazing gift and you can use it to help the people you care about. You just need time. Soon, you'll learn how to really harness it and control it. There's no telling what you might do."

Her words were encouraging, but they were almost drowned by her fear.

"I have to go to work honey," she said. "I want you to stay home. Don't go out. Promise me."

"I promise," he told her.

"Okay, good. Just stay home and watch something online. I'll come right back after my shift."

She went to the bathroom and checked her hair in the small mirror. Colt felt almost claustrophobic. Not that he wasn't used to being in their tiny home, but knowing he couldn't leave made him feel trapped.

"And don't look up anything about your... gift," she said, but he heard her think the word *condition*.

He watched her leave and then thought about what she had said, and what she hadn't. All his life he had tried to make up for his father that left the two of them on their own. From a young age he had taken on odd jobs to help make ends meet. He always took pains to do as much around their little home so that his exhausted mother wouldn't have to. And yet after all his effort, he had become a liability to her. The last thing she needed was to worry about him, and yet he knew that she was.

Powering on his Personal Access device, or PA, he began looking for ways to relieve his mother of the burden he had become. There were jobs available, but it didn't take long to scroll through them and discover that he wasn't qualified for anything other than menial labor. He could push a broom or work a trash recycling machine, but those jobs wouldn't take him away from Helix Prime's space port. What he needed was to get away from all the people who might report him to the GA. There were solo assignments listed on his handheld computer link, but he didn't qualify for any of them. Those types of jobs had age, and experience requirements, plus applicants had to undergo full psychological profiles.

He wondered about turning himself in. That thought seemed to hold the most promise, except that his mother was worried sick about him doing it. He didn't like the Galactic Authority, and didn't know anyone who did. The government was a huge, bloated bureaucracy that seemed focused on controlling its citizenry. But if there were millions of people working for the GA, Colt had to wonder how bad it would be. He flipped over to the reading app and did a quick search for books. He didn't type in anything about Readers, or extra sensory abilities. Instead, he searched for conspiracy theory books. He found several that were about the Galactic Authority. Some claimed the GA was controlled by a tiny group of ultra-rich individuals intent on ruling the galaxy, others theorized that the GA was hiding information about the alien races. Most of it was too outrageous to take seriously, but a few books claimed to have been written by people who had worked in various clandestine GA programs. One was called *Erased: The Truth Behind The GA's Clandestine Service*. It was nearly forty years old, and written by a woman named Ermine Constance. Her bio said that after serving twenty years in GA secret programs, she found a way to get out. According to the book introduction, it was only after changing her name and making her way to a fringe world outside of the GA's control that she felt safe enough to share her experiences.

Colt didn't have a lot of spare funds, and couldn't afford to buy the book, but he downloaded the sample, which included the first two chapters. Soon he was completely engrossed in the book's description of Ermine Constance first job as an agent on hunt for unregistered Readers.

CHAPTER 4

"What's that all about?" Wes asked.

He was sitting with an old friend in a cantina near the docks. The entire space station was enclosed, and most of the establishments that served food and beverages didn't bother with an enclosed space. The cantina was a simple bar, along with a row of tables that ran beside the main thoroughfare. Across the plaza Wes had a nearly unobstructed view of the GA headquarters. Two groups of plain clothes officers had hurried from the building.

"Could be anything," Wes's friend said. "At least they aren't headed for the docks."

"Yeah," Wes replied, despite the fact that his internal stress was rising.

"Plainclothes is either detectives, or acquisitions squad. You got any illegals on that ship of yours?"

Wes shook his head.

"Then you ain't got nothing to worry about. How long you in port?"

"Long enough to meet with DeVoor," Wes said. "Then we're gone."

"Stop worrying, man, ain't nobody lookin' for you. And trust me, if it happens, you won't see it coming. Besides, we're all necessary cogs in the machine. You know that, and so does the GA."

"And yet here you sit, Dezi. You were the best pilot I knew. Now look at you."

"I'm still the best pilot you know."

"Well, you're not Hyborian," Wes said.

"Hyborians aren't pilots. It ain't the same thing, man, you know it."

"What have you heard lately?"

"Nothing new, not here. Out in the Persephone Arm maybe. That's where the Alliance is making their big push."

"And DeVoor?"

"He's still doing what he does," Dezi said, taking a sip of his drink. "Like I said, necessary cogs. When a vendor goes under or a ship like mine get's locked in the port for some trumped up charge, he goes in and buys them out cause he can afford to ship their goods to the fringe world and double his investment."

"So why hasn't he bailed out your ship?" Wes asked. "Surely he has the pull to get you out of lockdown."

"He does. I don't want it. I mean, I want my ship back, but I don't want to be in his debt. I'm too old to be pulling jobs that only young fools should be doing."

"So don't take them," Wes said.

"You think it works like that? Come on, man, once you owe a schemer like DeVoor you never get free. And you can't say no, or they take your ship. I'd rather it sit in the impound than see DeVoor get his grubby hands on her."

"I hear you," Wes said. "But you've been grounded a long time."

"Yeah, they charge interest and fines faster than I can earn. It is what it is. My crew moved on. I'm not sure if I'll ever get out of hock. But that's the game right? I'll find a score that works for me eventually."

Wes couldn't help but wonder if he would have the same attitude. His crew was capable, but came with their own baggage. They might not be able to just move on if he got grounded. But he understood that a man like Dezi wouldn't want to be in anyone's employee, not after he tasted freedom in open space. Wes pulled a universal credit chip from his pocket. Being off the grid made money more difficult to come by and keep up with, but most of the merchants he dealt with preferred universal credits that were completely untraceable.

"I've got the drinks," Wes said, standing up and looking back across the plaza toward the GA building.

"Appreciate it," Dezi said. "It was good catching up."

Wes' old friend looked tired, his clothes ragged, with deep wrinkles. There were bags under Dezi's eyes, and his hair was going gray, what was left of it anyway. Wes couldn't help but feel a pang of dread as he wondered if his own life was headed toward the same destination as Dezi's.

"It was, take care of yourself," Wes said.

He didn't have to turn around and look back at his friend to know that Dezi was pouring what was left of Wes' drink into his own glass. It was a sad state of affairs, but that was the life of a spacer. One wrong move could cost a person, and their crew, their lives. A careless word to the wrong person could bring the GA down on a ship. There were certain advantages to being independent like not having to log in every move he made on the

STU's Navigation Network. He didn't like the idea of someone knowing everything he did, even if it was just an Artificial Intelligence program. He didn't have to pay a percentage of every run he made either, but that meant he was forced to live and work outside the system. And the truth was that at any moment the Galactic Authority could pass a law that required all ships to be registered with the STU and his way of life would be over.

"Wes, Wes, Di," the engineer's voice came over the small speaker in his collar com-link. He quickly slipped the mono earpiece into his ear and gave it a light tap.

"I read you," Wes said. "What's up?"

"There's a power converter that will fit our hyperdrive for sale near the ship yards. Want to meet me out there?"

"Sure," Wes said as he suddenly changed directions and started toward the part of the space station where ship repairs were done.

"How much are they asking?" Wes inquired.

"They'll deal in trade. Zora and I are bringing the oh-two generator we rebuilt."

"Don't we need that?"

"No, the ship has one."

"You told me we need a backup," Wes said.

"Okay, maybe that's true," Di said. "But we need a power converter more. We get that and we've got another dozen jumps before we have to overhaul hyper drive."

"Fine," Wes said.

"You can trust me," Di replied, with just the slightest trace of humor in her voice.

"You're the only one I trust," Wes said. "And only so far."

"Don't worry, this is solid. As long as the power converter is in good shape, we'll make out like bandits on this deal."

"Bandits get locked up or dead," Wes said.

"Well, you'd know more about that than me," Di replied.

He caught sight of her coming out of the docking arm of the space station and was making his way toward her when he saw the men in suits coming out of several buildings. For a moment he thought they were after him, or worse after Di and Zora. Instead, they converged on a thin woman with limp hair in a custodial uniform. He stopped walking and moved against the side of a power charging station. For a few credits a person could charge just about anything, from a personal access device, to portable life support equipment. In space, as on most worlds, credit was king, but followed closely by breathable air and power. He leaned against the charging station and acted interested in his PA while the suits took the woman into a nearby building with no signage. It looked like a business that had gone under, but Wes knew that's just what the suits wanted people to think. It was an interrogation station, off the books, for the GA's clandestine services.

"What's going on?" Di said over the com-link. "I thought you were going to help us lug this oh-two generator down to the ship yards.

"I'm coming," Wes said.

"No you're not. I can see you by that charging station. What's going on?"

"Just checking something out," Wes said, pushing off the wall he had been leaning against. "Nothing to worry about. I'm on my way to you now."

"Anyone ever tell you that you worry too much?" Di said sarcastically.

"Everyone I ever met," Wes said, glancing over at the building where the suits had taken the custodial worker. The windows were covered. He couldn't even see any light from whoever was waiting inside. He felt a shiver run down his back. The last place he wanted to end up was in the hands of the suits that were working the back channels with no oversight. Whoever the woman was, he felt sorry for her.

CHAPTER 5

Colt had just finished the book sample and was trying to see if he had any credits that he could spare to buy the book. It was a fascinating depiction of a team of government workers tracking a rogue Reader. The book said their quarry was an L-3, which meant they could read a person's mind. No secret was safe with an L-3 Reader, which made getting close to one without their knowledge nearly impossible. The author claimed to have done it by pretending to have romantic feelings about the Reader. She was a new recruit to the secret government program who used acting techniques to get completely into character. With the subject's mind on her as she flirted shamelessly, the rest of her team was able to move in and subdue the subject.

The second chapter had laid out the GA's interrogation techniques. It wasn't pretty, but Colt couldn't stop reading. They almost had their subject talking when the sample ended. He was scrambling to know what happened and was so engrossed in finding a way to purchase the book, that he didn't know someone was outside the tiny apartment's door until they pressed the intercom button. The buzz took him by surprise and Colt nearly jumped out of his chair.

He set his PA down on the counter and walked over to the intercom. The camera feature was broken and had been for years. Colt pressed the transmit button.

"Help you?" he asked.

"Mister O'Connor? I'm Xavier Kine from the housing authority. I was looking for Ms. Hope O'Connor and her son, Colt?"

Colt reached out and pressed the transmit button again and was about to reveal his identity when he got the distinct impression from the man on the other side of the door that he was lying. A wave of excitement, danger, and a little fear came to him like the aroma from a bakery. He wasn't used to letting people into his head. Since the ability had blossomed a few days earlier, Colt had been working to keep everyone out. He didn't want to know what most people were thinking, but he could feel the deceit from the man outside his door and so he opened his mind, lowering the mental barriers for a moment.

Come on, kid, just open the door.

A bolt of blinding fear struck Colt. He could feel the hostile intentions of the man outside. And as he opened his mind he could sense three more men with similar intentions on either side of the doorway. They had somehow discovered him. He didn't know how, but any thought he had of going with them disappeared in an instant.

"I think you've got the wrong place," Colt said. "My name is Crane, Lavar Crane. I work nights at the port."

Colt wasn't usually so quick witted, but he knew Lavar Crane. He was a crass old man who cursed at Colt and his friends for loitering sometimes when they went out to the port arm of the station to look at the space ships.

A sense of confusion wafted from the men out in the hallway.

"Could you open up, Mr. Crane?" the man whose name almost certainly wasn't Xavier Kine suggested.

"I work nights," Colt said, feeling a rising sense of panic. He had no where to run to. If the men didn't leave he was trapped in the little apartment. "I'm not dressed. You've got the wrong place."

With his last statement he willed the strangers to believe him. Almost instantly he felt their confusion and eagerness to get to him vanish. It felt like someone had flicked a switch and he was hit with sense of total agreement from the men outside.

"Thank you for your time, Mr. Crane. We appreciate your help. Good day."

Colt stood by the door, his heart thundering in his chest, but he could sense that the men were leaving. In fact, he picked up one man's thoughts as they moved down the hallway. *I guess we got bad intel. Supervisor Synclair won't be happy about that.*

His legs trembled as he made his way back to the chair from the doorway. Colt had never felt such a sense of fear before. He had seen horror films and had nightmares, but nothing was like having men outside his apartment and knowing they were looking for him. Colt picked up his PA and typed out a quick message to his mother with trembling fingers.

— You busy? —

He waited. Normally his mother didn't like to text while she was on duty. It wasn't completely forbidden, but doing it too often would result in a strike on her employment record. But he knew she would want to know about the men at the door. And he guessed she would be more open to his message since his abilities appeared. She had missed two shifts to stay home with him when it first came on and nearly drove him crazy. Her worry would be enough to get her to respond, he thought. A moment later, the response came back.

— No, what is it? Everything okay? —

He started writing her back, telling her about the men at the door, but halfway through typing the message he stopped. There was no way to know how they knew about him and his new abilities, but he was certain the men that came to their apartment had been there to apprehend him. He didn't think he or his mother had shared anything over their PAs about his gift, but if the Galactic Authority knew he was a Reader, they were probably monitoring his texts. His thumb tapped the backspace arrow and he erased what he wrote. Before he could compose his next message another from his mother's account appeared.

— Where are you? —

He knew immediately that someone else was on his mother's account. She knew where he was, and had no reason to ask. It was as if someone had slapped him. He didn't reply. Instead, he left the PA on the counter and slid the curtain back on his bed nook. In the wall were several recessed shelves. He picked up a small box that his in ear speakers had come in. He used the fancy little box to keep his treasures. One was an old fashioned picture, printed on paper, of Colt and his mother from his birth a few years prior. They were standing in the observatory on top of the space station. Ships of all kinds were passing by and they both looked happy. He shoved the picture into his pocket, along with two twenty credit chips that he had saved over the years. Universal chips were hard to come by on the space station, and when he got one he kept it for emergencies. He dropped them both into his pocket and grabbed his jacket.

As a novelty, his mother had purchased an old fashioned ink pen and note pad. She enjoyed writing things on the pad and hiding them in his pockets occasionally when he was going out. He found the pad and wrote his mother a quick message.

Don't know how but the GA knows about me. Can't stay here. I love you. — Colt

He left the note on the middle of the counter. She would find it and know what had happened. He didn't really feel good about leaving her, but he couldn't risk getting her in trouble. And even though he didn't want to face it, the odds were good someone had already gotten to his mother. They had her PA, or at the very least had tapped into it. If she didn't know where he was she couldn't tell them and they couldn't force her to. He didn't like thinking about it, all he knew was that he had to leave. Getting out of their building was his only goal. Start moving and don't stop, not until he was sure he was safe.

He went to the door and opened his mind a little. There was no one waiting for him in the hall. That didn't mean there wouldn't be GA agents at the end of the hallway. Colt couldn't open his mind any more without letting in a flood of thoughts from people in the apartments around his, and from the floors above and below. If his gift could help him, he didn't have the time to develop it. Something he had done had brought the Galactic Authority down on him and he had one chance to escape. If anything was true it was that the men who had come for him would be back and he needed to be long gone when they did.

CHAPTER 6

Colt left the apartment and started down the hallway toward the emergency stairs. He didn't want to use the elevator where he could be cornered if the agents were waiting for him in the lobby. It was essential to raise his defenses and block out the thoughts that were coming at him from all sides. His head ached with the effort, but he could tell it was becoming a little easier to hold off the onslaught of thoughts and emotions around him. When he opened himself up, the voices in his head were loud, almost like people were speaking directly into his ear. And the emotions were like being in a crowd, the bodies pushing and shoving. He knew he could lose himself in the tumult if he didn't keep his defenses up, but it was tiring to always be holding back the telekinetic storm that was raging all around him.

The stairs were clear. He had feared there might be an agent stationed there, waiting for him. It didn't occur to the young Reader that he could influence the minds of the people around him. When he had willed them to believe his lie and leave the building, they had. Not because it made sense, but because his power had altered their thinking about the matter. It was the only reason his building wasn't being watched as he reached the ground level and slipped out the maintenance door in the back.

The space station wasn't exactly like a large city. The population was tightly controlled. Those who didn't have a job or reason to be in the space port were deported. There were no homeless people, but there were groups of people who spent a majority of their time wandering the streets. The spaces between the buildings were especially popular to the children of the workers who kept the space port functioning. Colt and his friends had explored all around the buildings where their pod sized apartments were located. And just as he expected, there were plenty of teenagers milling in the alleys between the buildings as he made his way out.

"Colt," a boy with bright red hair named Dirk said, moving toward him swiftly and followed by several other boys and few girls. "Hey man, where've you been, dude?"

"Sick," Colt said, not stopping.

He wasn't sure where he was going but he wanted to get some distance between himself and his apartment building.

"Wanna party?" Dirk asked. "I hear they've got some good stuff down near the ship yards. We just need some credits."

Colt had credits in his banking account, but his mother was counting on that money. Besides, there was no doubt that whoever was after him was watching his banking accounts. Colt didn't take drugs, and didn't really like to drink. He had tried it all, at different times with his friends, but he wasn't really enthralled with the idea. But the ship yards were on the other side of the space station. And if he could travel in a group he less likely to be spotted.

"Yeah, okay," Colt said. "I've got some credits."

"Right on, man," Dirk said. "Let's go."

The entire group followed the red haired boy and Colt slipped back into the group. He knew them all, but he had never heard their thoughts before. Most were typical teenage thoughts. Some were worried about what Dirk was getting them into, but they didn't want to appear afraid. Others were watching the girls, or just glad to be avoiding their parents. But a few were watching him and their thoughts about Colt surprised him.

... *he wasn't sick, just lazy I'd bet. Some people will do anything to get out of class...*

... *thinks he can just show up and we'll all go along because he has a few credits...*

... *what a dork. I would never be caught dead in that outfit...*

Colt ignored them. He didn't have the time to develop close friends and the people around him were classmates and acquaintances. He realized that if the government agents had found him and taken him away, no one would have missed him other than his mother. That thought sent a pang of regret through Colt. Of course he wanted close friendships, and he was definitely interested in girls, but between school and his job, he didn't really have the time or energy. And he didn't regret that he had begun working so early in life. He wanted to help his mother and not be a burden, but that meant he'd sacrificed some things.

"You feeling better?" a girl named Alicia asked. She was taller than Colt, with brown hair and bad skin. She hung out with guys more than the girls because she didn't like being teased about her size. Her height was less noticeable with the boys.

"Yeah," he replied. "A lot better."

He could feel the sadness she was projecting. She didn't look sad, but she wasn't happy. Her face was a mask, her attitude just camouflage so that people didn't look past the care free attitude she had affected.

"That's good," she said. *Wish I felt better. I hope we get something that makes me forget I'm alive.*

Colt felt a little surprised. He had no idea how bad Alicia felt about her life. Part of him wanted to dig deeper, to know why she was so miserable, and another part of him wanted to run away.

"Things will get better," he said. "They always do."

"What?" she asked, a wave of panic slamming into him from her.

Emotions were much stronger than Colt realized. Being so close to Alicia and feeling her panic was like being shoved. He nearly stumbled, but caught himself.

How does he know how I feel? He hardly knows me.

"I just mean, I'm better," he said. "You know, you get sick, you get better, it's no big deal."

"Yeah," she said.

Relief flooded over him like warm water. But there was also a tinge of regret, like a cold under current. She was relieved to find that her disguise was still in place, but the world was a little darker too, as if a spark of hope had winked out.

No one knows. No one cares. I doubt they'll even realize I'm gone.

Colt wanted to do more to help her, but he had almost make a mistake and let his secret slip out. He couldn't afford that. Not with GA agents searching for him. They walked in silence for a while, the other teens talking all around them. Colt searched for any signs of the men in suits that were looking for him. There was no sign of them at first. The space port was full of interesting people, from aliens to space mechanics, business professionals and tourists, all mingling together inside the space port which was a city in a bubble.

They were nearing the junction to the smaller ship docking

arm when Colt caught sight of his mother. She was surrounded by men in suits. They were all different, but all wearing the same type of clothing, and wearing glasses which Colt guessed were probably linked to their PAs. Colt was shocked at the sight of his mother. Her hair was down around her face and she was bent forward slightly. One of the men had a grip on her arm just above the elbow.

Mom! Colt thought.

Her head came up and she looked around with puffy eyes. She had been crying, that was obvious. Her make up had run and her hair was a mess. His mother prided herself on looking nice. She always took the time to put on make-up and fix her hair, saying that she never knew who she might run into. He had never seen her looking so disheveled in public before. She looked around, trying to find him, and he realized she had heard him. He immediately looked down at the ground, trying to blend in with his friends.

Colt, oh God don't let them find him.

I'm here mom, are you okay?

Where? Where are you?

Better not let them see you looking. What happened?

They know. Colt! her voice was clear as crystal in his mind. It was like being in a crowd of people, everyone talking. He could hear voices and thoughts but they blended into a kind of background noise. His mother's voice was clear in his mind, like she was right beside him, speaking into his ear. *They know. I don't know how, but they know and they're after you. Run, sweetheart. And don't look back. They're bad people. Don't let them catch you.*

Okay, Colt said, feeling bad. *Did they hurt you?*

Don't worry about me. Just be safe.

Okay, I'm going, he said. At that moment he glanced up and for a second their eyes met. Her's were red, puffy, and glistened with tears. She nodded at him, then stumbled.

Go! his mother ordered.

Colt knew she was pretending. Giving him the chance to slip by unnoticed. He was terrified by what she had said and angry that they had hurt her. But he knew enough to know that if they got hold of him they would do worse. And in that moment a plan formed in his mind. He knew what he would do.

"Alicia," he said softly, "I've got to take a leak. I'll catch up."

"Sure," she said as he moved past her.

He kept the group of teens between him and the government agents, then slipped down the corridor to the docking arm.

CHAPTER 7

"The Hapsis system, by way of Jurgen Downs," Kit DeVoors said, handing Wes a slip of paper with the instructions written on it in code.

"What's the key?" Wes asked.

They were in a booth in a dark restaurant that specialized in a greasy fish noodle that Wes didn't like. It was an acquired taste, but the Mergonians loved it. Luckily for DeVoor who owned the restaurant, the Mergonians had no ears and communicated through sign language. They had no interest in the humans conducting business in the corner.

"Backward minus eighteen," DeVoor said. "You have enough fuel to make that run?"

"Sure," Wes said. "We just topped off the tanks. We're ready."

"Good," Devoor said. "This one's on a time limit. You've got two days to get the Merconium at Jurgen Downs. My guy there's jumpy, so be cool."

"I'm always cool," Wes said. He hated the way DeVoor

talked, as if he had to tell Wes how to do a job. He wasn't an idiot and didn't appreciate being treated like one.

"Three more days to reach the Hapsis system. They have a processing station in orbit."

"You guaranteeing that price?" Wes asked.

"If you get there in time. You show up late, it will be less," DeVoor said. "So don't be late."

Wes lifted the small glass of old fashioned whiskey. It tasted horrible but he wasn't sipping it. He tossed the contents of the little glass down his throat and swallowed fast. It was like liquid fire, the heat spreading through him nicely.

"Thanks for the drink," Wes said getting to his feet.

"My people saw you with Dezi," DeVoor said. "I just bought his ship from the port master. Do you think he'll be a problem?"

Wes couldn't imagine losing his ship. It would be like someone ripping his heart out. He loved the *Jolly Rogue* more than anything. It was both a possession, and a life line. He needed it and the freedom it gave him. Being stuck on a planet or space station would be torture. And he was too old to be anyone's employee.

"No, unfortunately," Wes said, earning a strange look from DeVoor. "He's come to grips with it."

"That's good," DeVoor said.

Wes didn't like sharing information about his friends. He wasn't a spy and even if he were he didn't work for DeVoor. The man was a lowlife, a parasite that lived off the work and risk that other people took. But Dezi had lost his edge. He would never get his ship back, never make another run through the blockade. It was a shame, but it was no secret. DeVoor already knew as much, or he wouldn't have bought the ship.

Wes nodded at the man. DeVoor had his uses. He knew people, and could open doors for an opportunist like Wes. He didn't trust the man, and knew the feeling went both ways. DeVoor waved his hand in dismissal. It was another sign of disrespect, but one that Wes quickly forgot as he made his way out of the dark restaurant. As soon as he was out he tapped the activator on his collar that powered up the com-link in his ear. A moment later there was a beep.

"Stu, do you read? This is Wes."

"R-r-rog-roger," Stewart said.

"Jurgen Downs," Wes said. "Direct route. We're on the clock."

"O... kay!"

"Di, Di, Wes," he said as he walked toward the docking arm of the space port, his eyes scanning the crowds for GA agents.

"I read you, Wes," Di said. "We're on the clock. I only need an hour and I'll be ready to go."

"Good, I'm on my way to you now. Have Saide prepare to launch. I'll pay the docking fees on my way in."

"Already on it," Saide said.

"This crew is a well oiled machine," Di said.

"Let's launch as soon as I'm back," Wes said.

"Affirmative," Saide said

Wes had only taken a dozen steps when a woman in a business suit stepped in front of him. She didn't speak, just held one hand out in a gesture for him to stop. The port arm of the space station could be busy if ships were loading and unloading, but it usually wasn't as crowded as the rest of the port. A few people were nearby, but they weren't paying Wes or the woman any attention. She raised her hand and pointed to her ear. Then she pulled out her com-link and motioned for him to do the same?

"Do I know you?" he asked.

She raised a finger to her lips. It was strange and a little unsettling. The woman was plain looking. Her suit was like a hundred others, her hair was pinned up on her head, she wore no jewelry and had no distinctive features. Yet she moved with a feline grace that made Wes worry. She seemed mysterious and frankly, dangerous. The woman pointed to her ear again, then mimicked him removing his com-link. Wes didn't like not having the ear piece in, but he took it out anyway. He had a feeling that refusal simply wasn't an option.

"Okay?"

"Thank you," the woman said. "I won't take up much of your time, but I have a job for you."

"I don't need a job," Wes said. "But thanks for asking."

"You need this job," she replied. "Let's talk somewhere with a little more privacy."

She pointed to a customs booth. It was empty, as were the ones on either side.

"Alright, but I'm in a bit of a hurry," Wes told her, wondering if she were going to stab him and take his money. If so, she was in for a surprise.

"This won't take long," the woman said.

"What's your name?"

"I'm called Evon," the woman said.

Wes checked the handle to the customs booth. It was unlocked. The door opened to what was essentially a tiny office. He stepped inside, expecting trouble. His senses were on high alert, his body tensed for action, but the booth was empty. The woman came in behind him and Wes turned, still expecting trouble, but she didn't attack. She just closed the door and then touched a sensor that made the glass looking out toward the docking arm frost over. Light could still pass through, but no one could see inside.

"What's this all about?" Wes asked.

"We need you to find someone," the woman said.

"I'm not a bounty hunter."

"It's not a criminal," Evon explained. "I'm sure you've heard of Celeste Pierre."

Wes had heard of Celeste Pierre. She had disappeared when she was just three years old. Authorities on the planet Nouveau Lyons had suspected foul play but the body was never found and no one had ever been arrested. It was a tragic, but not uncommon story. What made it news was that Celeste's father was Guy Louis Pierre, a popular figure in galactic politics. In fact Guy Louis had risen to the rank of Under Secretary and some believed he would be the next Prime Minister of the Galactic Authority.

"Sure, but she disappeared twenty years ago," Wes said.

"The body was never found," Evon said. "And her family has never stopped looking for her. Recently, there was a report that she was living on Kellar Nine."

"What's that got to do with me?" Wes asked, although he could feel a cold sense of dread forming deep in the pit of his stomach. Kellar Nine was their destination, but it was an AFW moon in the Hapsis system. Getting there would be a violation of Galactic Authority law. He couldn't just admit they were planning to run the blockade, especially to someone he didn't know.

"You're going there," Evon said calmly, as she leaned against the wall and folded her arms across her chest. "You'll get a good price on that magnesium you've got on board your ship."

She knew too much. How she knew it was a complete mystery, but Wes didn't like it. Someone, somewhere was talking and the old sailor's adage was still true — loose lips sink ships.

"So while you're there," Evon continued, "you can find Celeste Pierre."

"How am I supposed to do that?" Wes asked.

"You're a resourceful man with a crew of very capable individuals," she replied. "How you find her isn't our concern. We want her back in GA space and we'll make it worth your while."

She pulled out a data card and handed it to him. It was glossy black with golden filaments connecting the nano chips.

"This is a universal pass for the Space Transportation Union. No names, no records, just open doors and no questions asked. Once it's activated, you can go anywhere and do anything. I'm sure you can see the benefits of something like that."

Wes could see the benefits. It was a license to haul whatever cargo he wanted to wherever he wanted. His mind automatically began to calculate the riches he could amass with such a card. No more questions, no more worries. He could take the best loads and charge premium rates. But there had to be a catch, there always was.

"What if she isn't there anymore?" Wes asked. "What if your intel is bad? I can't afford to go chasing a ghost."

"Once you report back we'll activate the card," she explained. "You come back with information we can use, we'll give you a year. You come back empty handed, we'll only authorize the pass for a month. This is a one time opportunity. Make the most of it."

"How do I contact you?"

"The closest GA space port to the Hapsis system is Gerber Three. Go there and I'll find you."

She opened the door and left him in the customs booth. He looked at the card wondering if he could believe it. It seemed too good to be true. All he needed was a little luck and their fortunes could change forever.

CHAPTER 8

Colt was looking for a ship that would leave the space station soon. He had to focus on his goal. Fear and anger warred inside him. He wanted to do something for his mother but he had no idea what he could do. And if he didn't get off the space port soon he would most likely be found. Once the GA had him, he wouldn't be able to help anyone.

Getting on board a ship wouldn't be easy, but he had worked it out in his mind. Sometimes when he had gone looking at the ships he imagined stealing aboard. The ships had airlocks through which people could come and go, but he couldn't just walk into one of the ships. He needed to hide somewhere inside, at least until the ship was away from the Helix system. The ships being resupplied usually had umbilicals that were connected outside the space port's artificial gravity. Water, fuel, and supplies were normally moved through the umbilicals which were really just collapsable tubes. If he was lucky, he might find one that wasn't being used. It didn't take long. Colt approached the view port to get a look at the ship. It was a Hyborian vessel, with four engines. The markings on the side said it was the *Jolly Rogue*. He looked around the docking arm, which was essentially a long, wide corridor. There were people working but no one paying him any attention.

The umbilical was still attached to the ship. It was just big enough for Colt to get into. He could see across the empty passageway to the ship. The *Jolly Rogue's* loading hatch was still open. He would have to be careful. If the crew was busy with the new supplies he would be discovered and sent back to the space port, most likely handed over to the port master who would then run his name through the admin system. It was a recipe for disaster, but Colt had to risk it.

He bent low and crawled into the tube. The umbilical was made of plastic, flexible material, but without any insulation the tunnel was very cold. He crawled for nearly two meters before he felt the gravity of the port begin to fade. A few more meters and he was weightless. He had lived his entire life in a climate controlled space station. It was always the same temperature and the closest he had come to the cold of the umbilical was when he went into the restaurant's walk in freezer to help load supplies. He shivered but kept moving. The tube was forty or fifty meters, but outside the gravity of the station he moved easily across the distance. When he reached the loading hatch, he found himself in a dark space. There were dim, red safety lights. He crawled into the ship and looked around. To his right was a huge tank that held the ship's water supply. To his left were several nozzles that were labeled in glowing lettering: Oxygen, Hydrogen, Nitrogen.

As his eyes adjusted to the dim lighting, he could see stacks of crates with cargo nets pulled tight over them. There were several chest freezers built into the floor near the water tank, and large metal locker. Colt could see through the openings in the sides of the locker that it was full of dry goods. He moved out slowly, keeping a watch for anyone that might be working in the cargo bay. Fortunately for him, it seemed empty. He moved across the deck, and ducked down behind one of the stacks. It wasn't long before a revolving red warning light came on over the loading hatch and someone started down the spiral stairs.

An iris hatch rotated closed just below the revolving light, cutting off the supply hatch. Colt felt a sense of relief that he had gotten on board in time. The person coming down the stairs was a girl. She was thin, and wore coveralls unzipped, the top folded down. The sleeves of the outfit were wrapped around her narrow waist and tied together. She had a white tank-top on that left her shoulders and arms bare. From his hiding place Colt saw that the legs of the bulky coveralls were tucked into boots that were too large for her feet. Her hair was short, shaved close on the sides and long on top, but twisted into rows and held together with elastic bands.

The girl walked to the loading hatch, her boots thumping on the metal deck. A large round door on thick hinges was open and she pushed it closed, then spun the locking wheel. It was the manual hatch cover for the loading space and the ship was sealed. She walked over to the locker, pulled open a door, and pulled out what appeared to be a package of nuts. She tucked the food into a pocket then went back to the stairs, never noticing that Colt was on board and watching.

A popping sound was heard when the electromagnetic seal of the umbilical tube was released. Then the whir of hydraulics when the port clamps opened. Inside the ship there was no sensation of movement, but Colt guessed they were leaving the port. It was his first time ever to leave the space station, and there was no joy in the occasion. He felt sad, and alone. Tears burned his eyes as he thought of his mother. It was impossible not to worry about her, but he had done what she said. He was getting away from the port and from the GA. All he had to do was stay out of sight and from the looks of things on the *Jolly Rogue* that wouldn't be difficult.

He stayed in the cargo hold, his jacket wrapped tightly around him, and hands stuffed deep into his pockets. The metal deck beneath him was cold and hard, but leaning back on the cargo net wasn't uncomfortable. He balanced the old fashioned photograph on his knee and wondered what was happening to his mother. It was impossible not to imagine that the government agents were doing horrible things to her.

Before he knew it an hour had passed and Colt felt a sense of isolation. At first he didn't recognize what it was, and when the realization finally dawned on him he stood up. The sounds in his mind were gone. He had grown accustomed to the roar of thousands of peoples thoughts. His mental defenses held them out, but the roar of them was always in his mind. The ship had obviously left the port and was moving away from the space station. There just a few voices left in his head, and with his mental barricades in place he could bask in the silence. For a while that's all he did, just stood listening to the silence of the ship. The *Jolly Rouge* made sound. The engines couldn't be heard in space, but inside the ship they gave a reassuring hum.

Colt moved around, exploring the cargo hold. It was a big space and the lowest level of the ship. There was one set of spiral stairs that led upward. Light shown down from the upper levels and while Colt wanted to explore the entire vessel, he knew better than to go snooping. He avoided the light, fearful that someone might look down and see him. There wasn't much to find in the cargo hold. Crates of Magnesium, if the labels on the boxes were correct, were stacked and held fast by the cargo netting. He found a neatly folded pile of nets that made a comfortable place to sit and was big enough that he could lay down on. Above it was a heat duct and the space was much warmer than where he had initial sat. There was even a gap between the pile of netting and the bulkhead where he could hide if the need arose.

He was getting hungry and was acutely aware that across the cargo hold from where he sat was a locker full of food. It was a wide, tall, sturdy looking container, and he thought it might be possible to eat a little without it being discovered. Still, he didn't want to press his luck and do something foolish. There was no way to know how the crew of the ship might feel about a stow-away and it might be possible to simply slip away at the first port they came to. He didn't know how he would survive with no identification and hardly any credits, but he could find a way. There was no reason to take unnecessary risks if he didn't have to.

After a while, he got sleepy. Perhaps it was boredom, or maybe the sense of relief that he had escaped the government agents, but when he stretched out on the netting he dropped off to sleep almost immediately.

CHAPTER 9

"Are we good?" Wes asked.

"Jump coordinates are... in," Stu said, his head twisting as he wrestled out the last word.

"All systems are green," Di added.

"Do it," Wes ordered.

"Jumping to hyperspace in three, two, one," Ilk Saide counted down.

Wes watched as the stars that filled the display screens winked out. Hyperspace was a deep darkness that was beyond even light. There were times when Wes felt like it was stepping into a dark closet in one place, and then stepping out in a completely new place.

"How long?" Wes asked.

"Nineteen hours and... twelve... minutes," Stu replied in his stilted cadence.

"Alright, we'll do four hour shifts on the bridge," Wes said. "Stu can go first. I'll cook dinner."

"That's good," Di said. "My shadow and I need a shower."

Wes glanced over and saw Zora. She didn't reply and though she was looking in his general direction she didn't make eye contact. Both of the females were streaked with grime.

"You're sure the hyperdrive is okay?" he asked.

"Absolutely. We could get even more out of her than I thought. That power converter was a perfect fit and beefy enough for all our needs."

"Good enough for me," Wes said.

"No dinner for me," Saide said. "I ordered food while we were still at Helix Prime. I'll take it in my cabin."

Wes nodded. Hyborians were carnivores who preferred raw meat when they could get it. Most of the time that meant small animals, even rodents. In space, there simply wasn't room for live animals. Wes guessed that Saide had a box of mice or rats or even a few plump guinea pigs. Watching him eat was not for the faint of heart.

Saide looked almost like a human in his flight suit. But his legs bent the opposite way, his knees faced the back. And where people had fingers, Saide had long, tapering digits that ended in claws. His teeth were pointed and spaced so that the top teeth filled the spaces between the bottom teeth. He grew the hair on his oblong head so that it covered and hid the neural clusters.

As Wes was leaving the bridge music began to play. It was a catchy song from a best of CD by an artist named Neil Sedaka. *I love my, love my, love my Calendar Girl, yeah, sweet Calendar Girl.* Wes remembered finding the CD. It was old, the cover was missing, and there was no way to know what songs were on it until you played it. When he had given it to Stu, his autistic navigator had bounced in his chair and clapped with joy.

Upstairs in the galley the strains of music could still be heard. The songs were catchy and Wes hummed along as he pumped water into pot and started heating it. Once the water was boiling he added salt, gave it a stir, then dumped in a box of dry pasta. The sauce came from a can, and they still had some frozen garlic bread in the galley freezer. He put a cup in the beverage dispenser and filled it with a fruity beverage that Di had insisted on. It wasn't bad but it was sweeter than Wes liked. He pulled a metal flask from the hidden pocket inside his jacket and added a little of the ardent spirits he liked. It gave the drink some kick and helped him to relax. The beverage went down with a sweetness that turned to heat as it sizzled down his throat and hit his stomach where it spread through his body and flushed the skin on his cheeks.

A few minutes later Di appeared. Her hair was wet and slicked back. Unlike Wes, she had a dark complexion and jet black hair. The bulky coveralls were gone, replaced with stretchy exercise pants that showed every contour of her muscular legs. She also wore a baggy sweatshirt that had the Freight Hauler's Guild logo on it. Wes knew she loved to wear the shirt just to annoy him. They were not members of the FHG and couldn't get certain jobs because of it. No one wanted the guild after them.

"Pasta eh? You're a predictable cook, Captain," Di said.

"Sorry," Wes said, pointing her toward a stool opposite him at the counter. "You want a drink?"

"Of course," she said.

He turned and got her a cup from their collection. Glass didn't do good in space, so they had metal cups with tiny magnets in the bottom and silicone covers on the outside. He filled Diana's with her fruity beverage and turned toward her.

"You want a real drink?" he asked, pulling out his flask.

"No, don't you ruin my drink with that swill," she said. "My body is a temple."

"I have news," he said as he moved around the counter and sat next to her.

"Good news I hope."

"I think so," he said as he pulled out the black card and set on the counter in front of her. "You ever see one of those before?"

Di picked it up and looked at both sides. She shook her head. "No."

"It's a universal pass," he said. "A GA waiver to go into any port and take on any load I want, regardless of standing with the Space Transportation Union or the Freight Hauler's Guild."

"That's impossible."

"No, it's legit. I mean, this one isn't activated, but I've heard of them before."

"And how'd you get one?"

"That's the news," Wes said. "It's a job. We're going to look for Celeste Pierre on Kellar Nine."

Di laughed. "Are you kidding me?"

"I was met by a woman named Evon," Wes said.

"I don't like where this is going," Di said, narrowing her eyes.

"On my way back to the ship. She said the Pierre family has never stopped looked for Celeste."

"Sure, because most people think her mother killed her," Di said. "She was crazy."

"True, but was she crazy before her daughter went missing?"

"That's the going theory," Di said. "This has to be some kind of con."

"I don't think so," Wes said. "This woman, Evon, she knew about us. Knew what we had on the ship and where would go to move it."

"She knew we were going to run the blockade?"

"Yeah," Wes said, getting up to go check on the pasta. He

gave the noodles a stir then slide a pan with half a dozen pieces of garlic toast into the oven.

"I don't like it," Di said.

"I don't like someone knowing what we're doing," Wes said. "But this could be our ticket to the big time."

"Don't do that," she replied. "You've got to think about this with a clear head. DaVoor probably put her up to it. He was the only person in Helix Prime who knew what we were hauling."

"He didn't know until I told him," Wes said.

"So then he told this woman. I don't think we can trust her."

"Maybe not, but it won't hurt to look around while we're on Kellar Nine. We aren't breaking any laws or taking unnecessary risks."

"Except for poking our nose into someone else's business," she replied. "And if Celeste Pierre is there, whoever took her obviously won't like that we're making inquiries. A person who will steal a child will do anything."

"Okay, okay," Wes said, pouring the pasta into a strainer and then back into the empty pot. He picked up a bottle of olive oil and drizzled it onto the pasta before giving it another stir. "I'm just saying we should think it through. A universal pass could radically change all our lives."

"You want to be on the grid?"

"I want to be above the grid," Wes said. "I want to make enough money that we can stop worrying about always making repairs and wondering what decrepit, old piece of outdated equipment is going to break down next."

"This ship isn't perfect, but you wouldn't want a new ship Wes," Di said, as he mixed the sauce with the pasta. She got up and pulled the toast from the oven. "They're all tied into the grid a hundred different ways. Everything is automated and when one minor system goes down the entire ship goes down."

"I'm not saying I want a different ship," Wes said. "But a new hyperdrive, yes. Enough surplus credits to refurbish the life support systems and have back up parts for everything."

"And that much junk would fill half the cargo bay," Di said.

"We have an empty cabin," Wes pointed out.

"You mean the junk room?"

"I mean we could clean it out and make it a proper storage space for essential ship supplies. For that matter, we don't need the library either."

"That's insane," Di said. "You love your old books."

"One person's preference shouldn't take up so much space."

"We all love that space," Di said getting out plates for herself, Wes, Zora, and Stu. "It's the one calm, quiet place on this old boat."

"I thought you loved this ship," Wes said sarcastically.

"I do, but it's not a spacious luxury yacht. Don't go filling it with unnecessary junk."

They fixed plates just as Zora came up the stairs.

"Perfect timing," Di said. "We're just making up plates."

Zora didn't reply. She picked up the first plate with a mound of spaghetti and two slices of garlic toast. Wes watched, a little surprised that she would take such a large plate of food. But she headed straight back downstairs.

"Is she?" Wes asked.

"Taking that food to Stu. She won't eat until he has."

"She's protective of him."

"He doesn't treat her like she's broken," Di said. "Maybe she relates to his struggles too."

"You still thinking of finding a good home for her?"

"I don't think I can keep the ship running without her," Di said returning to her chair. "She's a natural in the engine room, works like a slave and those little hands can get into the tight spaces that drive me insane."

After a few minutes Zora returned, took a plate with only a fraction of pasta that she had taken down to Stu, and began to eat quietly. Wes, his hunger curbed after the first few bites, leaned back and looked around. He loved the *Jolly Rogue* and wouldn't dream of getting anything different, but there were times when he felt that he was letting the vessel down. Obviously it didn't have feelings, but his feelings for the ship ran deep and he wanted to make sure she had everything she needed.

"You two should get some sleep now," Wes said once they finished their dinner. "I'll relieve Stu and Saide can take the dog watch."

"Fine by me," Di said.

"I want you with me on Jurgen Downs," Wes said. "DaVoor said his contact there is nervous."

"Wonderful," Di said. "Sounds like a proper date."

Wes wasn't sure, but he thought he heard Zora giggle.

CHAPTER 10

After cleaning up their dinner, Wes went down and informed Saide that he would have the last watch of the night. Hyborians rarely slept for more than four hours at a time and was happy to take a shift on the Bridge once Wes had finished.

With his other errands complete, Wes proceeded down to the cargo hold. He wanted to inspect the provisions that had been brought on board during their stay at Helix Prime's space port. He made his way down the spiral stairs and through the stacks of magnesium. He had the majority of their funds tied up in the mineral. Fortunately, if they could get past the blockade of GA ships intent on keeping worlds like Kellar Nine from trading with the rest of the galaxy, they could nearly double their money. Of course they would need to pick up a new load of goods to trade, and keeping the ship running and buying provisions would eat up most of their profits. Food, fuel, and water seemed to be at a premium no matter where their travels through the galaxy took them. They could rarely afford real protein anymore, and with the water processing unit only working sporadically, they couldn't afford not to buy drinking water. There were so many things on the ship that needed to be repaired he had lost count.

Opening the supply locker, he looked around. It was more of the same standard shipboard fare: bags of rice, beans, flour, and sugar. Boxes of powdered milk and powered eggs, canned goods, from stew to vegetables to imitation sauces of various kinds. There was a wide array of dehydrated foods that could be reconstituted with water, and bottles of things like pancake syrup that were made by chemical processes and would stay good for decades. It would feed them, but it was a depressing sight just the same. He opened the chest freezers and found nothing new. They were down to a few packages of ground meat of dubious origin. The rest were filled with bags of ice that kept the units from using too much power and served as an emergency water supply.

After checking all the caps on the liquid and gas intakes and finding them properly battened down, he turned toward the stairs. What he saw froze him in his tracks. Something had moved in the murky gloom across the cargo hold. He wasn't sure what it was. The running lights were set above the cargo area, leaving the periphery in shadow. Wes reached down to the thigh holster and flipped back the safety loop that held his blaster in place. It was an older model Hennigan semi auto adjustable power blaster pistol, with an attached flashlight on the rail. He pulled the weapon up from the holster slowly, never talking his eyes off the area where he'd seen movement. His thumb checked the power slide. It was already on stun, rather than kill, which would fire a laser powerful enough to breach the ship's hull. He couldn't afford a breach, especially not in hyperspace. Clicking on the flashlight was simple too. It was a tiny device with a powerful led. A bright beam of light appeared from the gun.

Wes kept it pointed at the ground and moved slowly between the stacks of cargo. A wily intruder might hope to use the cargo to hide behind, but Wes knew every inch of the *Jolly Rogue*. Someone or something was down in the cargo hold and he was determined to find out what it was. The possibility that one of Saide's rodents had escaped was the most likely culprit, but there was always a possibility that some desperate soul had stowed away. It was a constant threat on a starship. Criminals could get on board, kill the crew, and steal a ship. Forging ship registration wasn't that difficult, and a body jettisoned into space would never be found. As long as a thief wasn't stupid they could get away with piracy, but it was a big risk. Stowing away on board an interstellar ship was a crime that carried immediate consequences. A crew had every right to kill a stowaway with no questions asked. Some ports even had bounties for stowaways, as long as the crew could prove they weren't part of the ship's company.

Wes always wore his pistol on board. The ship was his sanctuary and the one place he felt safe in all the galaxy, but it was also a valuable vessel that some people would kill for. Wes wanted to protect his ship and his crew, which meant he couldn't afford to let his guard down.

"I'm not here to steal anything," a shaky voice came out of the darkness.

It stopped Wes cold. He was approaching quietly, but still in between two stacks of magnesium. Knowing there might be an intruder on the ship, he had kept his gun pointed down. He didn't want the beam of light giving away his approach. The edge of the cargo area was where he kept extra supplies. It was dark there where the red overhead lighting didn't reach, but not so dark that Wes couldn't see if someone were lurking. The shadows against the bulkhead were all familiar. A box filled with ratchet straps, the bundle of cargo netting, a row of three hydraulic dollies, and the cubbies with their space suits, nothing was out of place. And yet someone knew he was there, knew he was searching for them.

"Please, I just needed to get away from Helix Prime," the voice said.

Wes raised his pistol and let the light play over the gloomy supply area. There was still no sign of the stowaway.

"Alright then," Wes said. "Show yourself. And move slowly. Keep your hands where I can see them if you know what's good for you."

"I'm not armed," the voice said.

A head appeared. Blonde hair, light skin, a teenager. He stood up from the far side of the cargo netting. He didn't look dirty or disheveled. There was no weapon visible, not even a knife, but that didn't mean he wasn't armed. He held his hands up and Wes could see they were trembling.

"You alone?"

"Yes sir," the stowaway said.

"One lie and I'll toss you right out the airlock," Wes threatened. "Are you alone?"

"Yes," the boy insisted.

"How'd you get aboard?"

"The umbilical."

Wes wanted to curse. He had warned Saide that leaving the hatch open would make it possible for stowaways but the Hyborian didn't like having to leave the Bridge between shipments of provisions. Maybe a actual stowaway would convince him.

"Okay, kid you sit down right there on that cargo net. Keep your hands on your knees," Wes told him. "And don't move. This pistol is set to stun and I won't hesitate to use it. You try anything stupid and I'll make sure you'll never wake up again."

The boy moved slowly around the net and sat down. At least he could follow directions, Wes thought. But fearing for one's life made a person tend to do what they were told.

CHAPTER 11

Colt was shaking with fear. He had fallen asleep and woken up when the man with the gun closed the chest freezer. The lid had fallen with a thump. At first Colt had forgotten where he was and it took him a few moments to get his bearings. He tried to roll into the gap between the mound of cargo netting and the bulkhead, but he had been too late. The man with the gun had seen him. His sudden suspicion had been like an emergency siren to Colt. He could feel the emotions of fear, and anger pulsing from the man.

This is the last thing we need, Colt couldn't help but hear the man's thoughts, *some dumb kid.*

"I'm not dumb," Colt said.

"What?"

The beam of light was blinding and Colt didn't move. He knew the gun was pointed at him.

"I'm not dumb," Colt repeated.

"Who said you were?"

"You did," Colt said.

Holy smokes, this kid is a Reader!

"Please don't shoot me," Colt said again, as the man with the gun's fear hit him almost like a physical blow.

"Are you reading my mind?" the man growled angrily.

"No," Colt said. "But your thoughts are loud. I'm sorry. I'm trying to control it."

"So that's why you stowed away on my ship," the man said. "You were running from the GA."

"I don't know how they found out about me," Colt said. "They have my mother."

The man gave a long, low whistle, then said, "I wouldn't want to be in her shoes."

Colt felt the tears brimming in his eyes. He didn't know what to do. And he couldn't help but fear that his mother was being hurt. It was making him crazy and he felt helpless. Even if the man with the gun didn't shoot him, Colt was in real trouble. No money, no connections, perhaps running away was foolish. It might have been better to turn himself in. At least his mother wouldn't still be in danger.

"Are you crying?" the man with the gun asked.

Colt was too afraid to even wipe the tears that were rolling down his cheeks. He nodded.

"What a load of Sluggarian dung," the man snarled. "Get up. Walk toward the stairs. No sudden movements. You do what I tell you and I won't kill you kid."

"Y-yes sir," Colt stammered.

He had never had his life threatened before. He had heard people threaten others on television and in the movies, but not real life. His mother didn't hold back when he needed disciplined, but he never feared for his life. But he was so terrified of the man with the gun his knees would hardly hold him up.

"Can I hold onto the arm rail, please?" Colt asked.

"Whatever," the man with the gun said.

Colt felt a little better holding the railing. He moved up the stairs, toward the well-lit main deck of the ship.

"Keep going," the man said. "All the way up."

Colt obeyed. There wasn't much to see on the main deck. There were several cabins but the doors were all closed. The open space around the staircase wasn't decorated, but it looked clean just the same. Minimalistic his mother would have said. A corridor led to another part of the ship. Music was playing from that section, *...they say that breaking up is hard to do, now I know, I know that it's true.* Colt couldn't believe what was happening. He felt like he was in the middle of a dream that was too surreal to be a nightmare. *...don't say that this is the end, instead of breaking up I wish that we were making up again.*

Colt certainly hoped that he wasn't facing the end of his life. All he needed was a little understanding, but the man with the gun didn't seem open to listening to Colt's problem. He had let it slip that he was a Reader and the man with the gun didn't seem to think that was a good thing.

... have every agent in the galaxy looking for us. This is just my luck. Why can't things ever go smoothly? Is that too much to ask. God! The damn Reader is probably swimming in my head right now. What the hell have I gotten us into this time.

Colt raised his his mental defenses. He didn't think that listening to the man's thoughts would curry him any favor with the man. They reached the top of the stairs and stepped up onto the upper deck. It was a big space with a domed roof. Colt saw bundles of wires and air ducks criss-crossing the ceiling which was several meters above the upper deck. Two rooms were directly across from him, just past a large group of comfortable looking furniture. Sofas and lounge chairs were spaced around a large, ornate carpet. One of the rooms was open, and Colt saw shelves with what appeared to be old fashioned books printed on real paper. The spines were creased and ragged, and he was still being held at gun point, but he felt a glimmer of hope that he might be able to see the books.

"Sit down," the man ordered.

Colt moved toward a sofa with faux leather upholstery that was cracked like thin ice that was about to break. He sat down slowly and put his hands on his knees again without being told.

"Are those books real?" Colt asked.

The man with the gun sat on the arm of the sofa opposite from Colt. The gun was still pointed at Colt's chest. The man's eyes narrowed.

"Forget about the books kid," he said as he used his free hand to click a little metal button on the collar of his jacket. "We've got a stowaway. I want Saide to do a full search of the cargo hold. Di, you might want to join me up here in the lounge."

"Roger that," a woman's voice sounded from the tiny speaker in the man's collar.

It wasn't a high fidelity speaker and yet Colt could hear the excitement in her voice. A few seconds later there were boots clanging on the metal stairs.

"How'd they get in?" another voice with a strange, lilting accent asked.

"The umbilical," Wes said. "I told you it was a liability."

"I told Zora to batten it all down," the voice replied.

"And she did," a woman at the top of the stairs said.

"It was all locked down," Wes said. "He must have gotten in before that. Now go search every inch of the cargo space. I don't want any more surprises."

"Roger that, captain," the lilting voice said.

The woman wasn't tall or beautiful, but she was muscular and looked strong enough to bend a metal support beam. Her smile was friendly enough, and Colt could see how friendly she looked at him, with curiosity rather than hostility. Another girl appeared, the same skinny girl Colt had seen in the cargo hold. She came up the stairs silently and lingered by them without saying a word.

"Tell me what you're doing on my boat," the man with the gun said.

"Hiding," Colt admitted. "The GA was looking for me. My mother told me run so I did."

"How old are you?" the woman asked.

"Sixteen," Colt replied.

"Why is the GA after you?" she asked.

"Because he's a Reader," the man said.

The woman reacted as if she had been slapped. A hardness came to her eyes.

"He knew what I was thinking," the man with the gun said. "The smart thing might be to get rid of him before he can do any real damage."

Colt felt himself shaking. He couldn't stop it. He wasn't cold, but still trembled. The desire to put his hands in his pockets was incredibly strong, but he forced himself not to move.

"What level?" the woman asked.

Colt shrugged.

"Don't try to play us, kid," the man with the gun snapped. "We're not fooling around here. You want to live, you tell us everything."

"I don't know," Colt admitted. "I just discovered the ability a few days ago. I still don't know how the GA agents found out."

"I don't buy it," the man said.

"Well, I've never heard of an agent that young," the woman said. "They would have had to have picked him up when he was little and I heard most Readers don't develop the skill until they're in their teens."

"Doesn't mean he couldn't have bloomed early," the man said.

"I promise," Colt said, gripping his knees as tightly as he could, "I'm not lying. I just woke up one night and thought I was going insane. I'm still trying to control it."

"Tell me about the woman," the gunman said. "Did she send you?"

"The woman?" Colt asked. "I don't—"

"We haven't got time for your lies, kid," the man snarled. "Evon, did she send you? Or DaVoor?"

"No," Colt replied. "I don't even know them. I was running. Four agents came to my mother's apartment looking for me. I told them they had the wrong place and then I ran, but they already had my mom. I saw her surrounded by agents. She told me to run, to leave the space port. So I went to the docking arm and your ship was the first one that I could get into."

"I'm going to kill Saide," the man said.

"Oh, stop," the woman replied. "Look at him. He's telling the truth."

"Now you're reading minds?" the man asked.

"No, but I know when someone is lying. He's just a terrified kid, Wes. Cut him some slack. Put your pistol away."

The man glanced at the gun, then stared daggers at Colt, but he shoved the gun back into it's holster. Colt breathed a sigh of relief. He still didn't feel safe, but he wasn't worried that he was going to be killed without warning anymore.

"I'd turn him in but knowing the GA they wouldn't be happy that I did something they failed to do," the man said. "We don't need them taking a hard look at us. What do you think?

The Windsor cartel? They'll pay for a reader. He's got to be a level two at least, maybe higher."

"The Windsor cartel is worse than the GA," the woman said. "You can't do that to him."

"Well I'm not going to just pretend that he didn't sneak on board my ship. He's breathing our air, taking up space, and you'll probably want to feed him."

"You know we're going to feed him," the woman said.

"So he owes us. You got money, kid?"

Colt thought about the forty universal credits in his pocket. It was barely enough for one meal.

"I little," he admitted.

"What can you do?" the woman asked.

"I don't really know," Colt admitted. "I can hear thoughts and feel emotions."

"You can hear my thoughts?" she asked, sounding skeptical.

"I try to keep my mind shielded. I don't want to hear anyone's thoughts."

"But you can? Prove it," she challenged him. "Tell me what I'm thinking right now."

Colt focused on the woman. Hearing her thoughts wasn't difficult, but it was difficult not opening himself up to every mind on the ship. Fortunately, they were away from anyone else, and Colt could feel his mind connect to the woman's.

Spaghetti, garlic bread, and chocolate pudding.

"You were thinking about food," Colt said.

"Lucky guess. This kid's a con artist."

"Spaghetti, garlic bread, and chocolate pudding," he said calmly. "That's what you were thinking."

Her eyes narrowed. *How much can this kid do,* she thought. *He could be useful on Kellar Nine.*

"What's on Kellar Nine?" Colt asked.

"This is getting out of hand," the man with the gun snapped. "He'll know everything about us by the time we reach port."

"Can you find someone?" the woman asked, completely ignoring her captain. "You know, pick a person out of a crowd, or lead us to someone we're looking for?"

"I don't know," Colt said. "I just... I just discovered I could do this. I don't know much about it. And I didn't mean to upset you, but I had to get off the space port in Helix Prime. They were coming for me."

"And they'll still be looking for you," the man said. "When they don't find you on the space station, they'll check the flight plans for every ship that left there. It won't take them long to figure out you were with us."

"But how? There were hundreds of ships at the port," Colt pointed out.

"We're off the grid," the woman said. "We're independent. No flight log, nothing, we're ghosts."

"Don't tell him that," the man said.

"You were the one who said he would read our minds and know everything about us. There's no sense in keeping secrets," she argued. "I think we may have just gotten lucky."

"What in the world are you talking about?" the man said.

"There's a reason the GA wants all the Readers. The cartels too, it's because they're valuable. Having one on our side would be a major advantage."

"He's probably a spy," Wes said.

"Why would anyone waste a Reader on us?" the woman asked. "Face it, we're small potatoes. I think the kid's story is legit. He's running, we were leaving, he got on board and hid."

"It's too big a risk," Wes said. "If word gets out that he's a Reader, will have every criminal and the GA looking for us. That's not my idea of a good business strategy."

"He's hiding," the woman said. "As long as he stays on board the ship he won't be found. And he might be able to help us. I mean, of all the people who could stowaway on the ship, at least it was someone with real skills."

Colt didn't really know what to think of them talking about him as if he were a tool to be used however they saw fit. But he could see the value in hiding on the ship for a while. He had always planned to sign on with a ship if possible. His dream had been to have a ship of his own and explore the galaxy. A freight ship could get work in any system. And if he kept his talents under control there was no reason why he couldn't go unnoticed, probably for a really long time. And at the very worst if he could earn some money, and make some connections before the GA agents caught up to him he might be able to evade them again.

"I'll do anything," he said.

The man looked at him as if he was surprised Colt was still there.

"I'll scrub floors, wash dishes, anything," Colt went on. "And I promise I won't let my guard down. I won't listen to anyone's thoughts."

"See there," the woman said. "It doesn't take a Reader to know what you're thinking."

"Very funny," the man replied.

"Let him stay, it might be good for Zora," the woman went on. "Call it a trial period. If he doesn't work out you can always shove him out the airlock later."

"I just might do that," the man said, looking straight at Colt.

"Yes sir," Colt replied. "I can work hard. I won't complain."

"You better not. I can't believe I'm even considering this."

"It's the right thing," the woman insisted. "Besides, if he can help us find the girl, that would be everything you wanted."

The mention of a girl made Colt look past the two adults

toward the girl. She was still by the stairs, hardly moving. Colt couldn't tell if she was even breathing and he never saw her blink. But her eyes were big, inviting. He wished he could talk to her rather than the captain.

"We'll put him in the empty cabin, but I'm locking it down," the man said. "He doesn't leave unless I give him permission."

"You are a bit of a pessimist," the woman said, before turning to Colt. "Welcome to the *Jolly Rogue*."

CHAPTER 12

"This is it," the captain, who had identified himself as Wes, said.

He was showing Colt the empty cabin. It wasn't exactly empty, it had some old furniture and boxes just inside the door. Beyond that was a bunk, and in the rear of the cabin was a tiny bathroom.

"For now, just stay in here," Wes said. "You should be able to find a blanket or two. Have you had anything to eat?"

"No, not for a while," Colt said.

"I'll bring something down. If you try to get out I'll know it. The cabins have electric locks that are connected to the ship's life support systems."

"I won't try anything," Colt replied.

"Doesn't mean you won't do anything," the captain replied. "Just remember, one slip up and you're gone, and I mean permanently. We understand each other?"

"Yes sir," Colt said.

The door slid shut and he was alone again. Not that being

interrogated made him feel safe or less lonely, but it was a distraction. He walked through the stacks of junk into the cabin. The bed was a slab of metal but it had a thick foam mattress. There was enough space for a desk, and while there was nothing on the wall the wiring for a display screen and connection to the ship's computer were there.

The captain had insisted he turn out his pockets, but the woman, her name was Diana, said that a strip search was going too far. He was thankful for that. After setting on the bed for a while, Colt went to the boxes. Some had old clothes inside, another some mechanical parts he didn't recognize. Finally, after moving some things around, he found a box with sheets, blankets, and a couple of pillows. He pulled them out and gave them a sniff. They were musty, but clean. He made the bed and put pillow cases on the pillows. He was tired, although he wasn't sure why. The nap on the cargo nets had almost cost him his life, but shouldn't have left him sleepy.

It was the grief over his lost life, he decided. Just thinking of his mother left him weepy and hurt deep down in a way he'd never experienced before. His father had left when he was too little to remember him. His mother had been his whole world and knowing that he had abandoned her was too terrible to think about.

Instead he pulled an old plastic chair from the pile of furniture. Many of the items were broken, but the chair was in working order. It had a heavy base and flat metal slats that rose up from the front toward the rear of the seat which made the chair springy. He could rock in it and was surprised at how comfortable it was.

There wasn't a desk, but he found an old tray table that he unfolded and set up. The door swished open and Wes brought in a sandwich on a plate.

"Sorry about the ship bread," he said. "It's standard space fare, with protein and vitamins. You can live on it but it tastes like cardboard. That's real peanut butter though, and some grape jelly. Looks like you stay busy, that's good. Eat, sleep, we'll talk tomorrow."

Wes left before Colt could do more than thank him. He sat in the plastic chair with the plate of food on the tray table. The bread was bland, but Colt didn't care. He was hungry and ate the entire sandwich. There was a glass of watery milk to wash it down, and some pudding in a disposable cup. Colt ate it all, then took off his jacket and shoes and got into the bed. He turned the lights in the cabin off, but left the bathroom light on. As he lay on the strange mattress the tears came again. He cried and cried, the reality that would probably never see his mother again was like a mortal wound. Part of him was dying, and he couldn't help but weep.

He fell asleep crying and didn't wake up until the door opened. He had no idea how much time had passed, it felt substantial, but not enough. He rubbed his eyes.

"Time to get up," Wes told him. "We need to talk. Meet me in the library."

Colt got up and pulled on his jacket and shoes. He looked at himself in the mirror and ran his fingers through his hair, trying to make it lie down, but it refused. His mouth was foul and he rinsed it with water from the sink. Then left his room. There was no one in sight. The main deck was empty, and no music played from the corridor that Colt guessed led to the bridge. He started up the stairs. They were made from old fashioned iron that had been painted black and had an intricate design below the hand rail and along the pole in the center.

He reached the upper deck and went straight to the room with the books. The truth was, he was a little excited about the library. He had only seen a few old fashioned paper books and he hoped that Wes might let him look at one. There were three separate shelves in the room. One on each wall except for the wall opposite the doorway where there was a large, round window. Outside all Colt could see was black.

"We're still in hyperspace," Wes said. "Nothing to see."

Colt turned to the shelves. There were a lot of books. Most were hard to read, the printing on the spines were faded and most had wrinkles or creases running down them. Wes was sitting in a comfortable looking chair. It had a view of the window and table between it and the matching chair.

"Have a seat," he said. "I think Di may have been on to something."

"She was?" Wes asked.

"You've got skills. Maybe you could be useful."

"Sure," Colt said. "I'll do anything."

"Everyone on board this ship has responsibilities. What can you do besides read minds?"

"I don't know. I cook a little. I clean. I worked at a pizza restaurant washing dishes," Colt said.

"Ever work on ships?"

"No," colt admitted. "I was still in school."

"Well, there's always work for a deck hand on a ship," Wes said. "This is a Hyborian class two freighter. She's built for a crew of six. Fortunately for you, we've been running her with five for a while now. We'll see what you can do with a little on the job training, but I'm more interested right in what you can do with your mind."

Colt felt a stab of fear. What if he couldn't do what they wanted him to do? Or what if doing it got him in trouble. He was too afraid to bring up these objections, but they weighed on his mind.

"You can read our thoughts," Wes said.

"But I'm not," Colt insisted.

"Good, that's good. You should know that breaking into a person's mind is a violation of their privacy. What do you know about Readers?"

"Not much," Colt said. "I've heard about them. Seen a few in movies, but that's not real. When my talent showed up it was awful until I got it under control. My mother told me not to look into anything related to Readers, that the Government Authority might have programs that identify people trying to find out about them."

"That's true. The damn GA doesn't care about anyone's privacy. They are looking and listening all the time. It's good to be cautious."

"I read about them," Colt said. "Not Readers, but the GA agents. A woman wrote a book about the clandestine service. They were tracking down a reader. She called him an L-2."

"That's level two, they rank readers according to what they can do," Wes said. "An L-2 can hear another person's thoughts. They can also communicate with people simply by thought."

"I can do that," Colt said nodding. "I spoke to my mother with my mind when the agents had her."

"I thought that might have been the case. I want to do a few tests and just see what you can do. Is that alright?"

Colt was surprised. He hadn't expected such a turn around in the captain's opinion about him. He seemed friendly and relaxed, but Colt was still nervous. He couldn't say why, but he was afraid that he was being tricked. It was tempting to open himself up and hear what Wes was really thinking, but he had promised he wouldn't do that.

"Okay."

"Good, try to say something to me with your mind," Wes prompted.

Like this? Colt asked, after he had connected his mind to Wes'. It was a simple task, not really any different that looking at a person. All he had to do was concentrate on Wes, and think his question.

"Oh, that's strange," Wes said. "You did that quick."

It's easy, Colt told him.

"Alright, you're definitely an L-2. Let's see if you can actually read a person's mind. An L-3 can go in past what a person is thinking and learn things about them. Discover their secrets. A powerful L-3 can read a person's mind without them ever knowing it. So I want you to try and discover how old I am."

"Are you sure?"

"Yeah, go for it. Just don't scramble anything while you're digging around in there," Wes joked.

Despite his jovial manner, Colt picked up the anxiety that Wes was feeling.

"Can I do that?" Colt asked.

"Maybe, but not if you don't try," Wes said. "I've done some research of my own. Just try to learn my age."

Colt opened his mind to Wes again and was immediately aware that the captain was thinking of a poem. *Gaily bedight, a gallant knight, in sunshine and in shadow, had journeyed long, singing a song, in search of Eldorado...*

Colt pushed past deeper. It felt to him as if he were leaning over a precipice and suddenly he had fallen. He moved deep into Wes' mind, almost like it was a pool of water. He swam through memories. It was overwhelming at first, but then he remembered his mission. How old was Wes? He dove down in search of the answer. It seemed to appear before him, a glowing number - 42. When Colt thought of returning from his deep dive into Wes' mind, he did immediately and was suddenly aware of the captain's thoughts again.

... And as his strength, failed him at length, He met a pilgrim shadow. "Shadow," said he, "where can it be, this land of Eldorado?"

"Forty-two," Colt said. "You're forty-two years old."

Wes gave him an appraising glance that was stern, yet also surprised. Colt was tempted to read his mind again, to know what the captain was thinking of him, but he held back.

"That's right," Wes said. "You did that quickly."

"It was strange," Colt admitted. "It was like I was swimming in your mind. But all I had to do was think of what I was looking for and it came to me."

"Interesting," Wes said. "Let's try another. I want you to see if you can find out what I want you to do without me telling you."

"Okay," Colt said. He didn't like being on the spot, but so far the tests were easy enough that he didn't feel too put upon.

He dove into the captain's mind again. *Over the mountains of the moon...* Colt could hear the captain's thoughts as if he speaking out loud, but he ignored them and sank deep into his mind, wondering what Wes wanted him to do. A book appeared, it was thin and a dirty brown color, but Colt knew exactly where it was.

He left the captain's mind, stood up and walked over to the bookcase beside the door. He saw the thin little book just as he had seen it in Wes' mind. He pulled it out of from between two other books. The writing on the cover had faded, but the imprint was still readable. *The poems of Edgar Allen Poe.* Colt carried it to Wes and gave him the book.

"That's astounding," Wes said with a grin.

Colt wasn't sure what to say except for, "Does that make me a level three?"

"Absolutely, and a pretty strong one at that," Wes said. "A lot of people have trouble doing these things, at least that's what I've read. I think maybe you're an L-4, or maybe even an L-5. Sit down, let's see what else you can do."

CHAPTER 13

The kid wasn't fooling around. His face was pinched in concentration and Wes could feel the hair on the back of his neck standing out as the cards began to float up into the air in front of him. The test had been a good idea. Colt O'Connor was at least a level four Reader. Wes didn't trust the kid. It was like having a crate full of universal credits suddenly appear on his ship. There had to be a catch and Wes was waiting for someone, somewhere, to lower the boom.

The cards rose up one at a time until there were six slowly moving in a circle in thin air. It was an astounding trick, and one that Wes believed the boy had never done before. Colt was sweating, the look on his face was of intense effort.

"Okay, Colt, you can drop them," Wes said.

The cards fell to the table and the kid slumped in his seat. He looked exhausted.

"Was that as hard as it looked?"

"Like holding my breath," Colt replied. "Or holding up something really heavy."

"I'd say that caps your abilities then," Wes replied. "You're an L4."

"Are there more?" Colt asked. "More levels?"

"Just one," Wes said.

It was the one that no one liked to talk about. Knowing that there were people in the galaxy who could read your mind was disturbing enough, but the L5's were really scary. And Wes had to admit he was glad that the kid wasn't one.

"What can they do?" Colt asked.

"L5's can take control of people," Wes admitted. He had started the conversation and he didn't want the kid tearing his library apart trying to find the answers to his questions just because Wes wouldn't give them to him. "Most can only control some part of a person, but it's scary stuff. Others, if the rumors are true, can control another person completely."

"Do you know why?" Colt asked.

There was an eagerness to his questions that made Wes think the kid was truly hungry for answers. It really did seem as if he had just discovered his ability and knew nothing about it.

"There are a lot of reasons why someone would take control of another person," Wes said. "But there aren't any good reasons."

Colt shook his head. "No, I mean, why can some people do this?"

He waved at the cards and then pointed to his head.

"I don't know," Wes admitted. "They were studied early on, but nothing definitive was identified as why some people are Readers. Most of those studies were classified and the GA isn't known for sharing their work. The entire subject is basically off limits these days. Readers can't be studied because they are sequestered by the government or held as slaves by the organized crime."

"What?" Colt asked in surprise.

"Think about it," Wes said. "A person who can read minds would be invaluable to people who have no qualms about breaking the law, or conning people out of their money. The galaxy isn't a safe place, kid. Better get used to the fact that you drew the short straw. Everyone will want you but for all the wrong reasons."

Colt looked frightened. His eyes watered, but he didn't cry. Wes knew he was trying not to let his weakness show, and it made Wes think if the kid were acting he was a master of the craft.

"What do you want to do?" Wes asked him.

"I don't know," Colt replied, his voice shaking with the emotions he was struggling to control.

"We're going to Jurgen Downs," Wes said. He felt bad for the kid, even if he had stowed away on Wes' ship which was a cardinal sin in Wes' opinion. Giving Colt something else to think about would help him move past the emotions he was feeling. "Have you heard of it?"

"No," Colt said.

"It's a Dyson ring," Wes explained. "I'm guessing you learned about those in school?"

"Yeah," Colt said, his voice sounding stronger. "It's a structure meant to capture the energy of a star."

"That's right," Wes said. "Jurgen Downs is one of hundreds of cities on the ring. It's a rogue star, so no system name. The ring was initially constructed by a tycoon named Dennis Jurgen. His energy company was bought and rebought over the years. Energy is the station's main export, but the cities on the ring are major trade points. If you want to leave the *Jolly Rouge* when we reach Jurgen Downs, I'm sure there would be plenty of opportunities for you."

"If?" Colt asked. "Is staying on board a possibility?"

Wes couldn't deny the fact that he didn't trust the kid. During his years running the GA blockade, he had learned that his skepticism about people was a useful tool. And coincidences were rarely what they seemed. Yet over the past twenty-four hours, he had been approached by a stranger who knew more about him and his crew than he was comfortable with. And a kid with phenomenal powers just happened to stowaway on his ship. The two events could be isolated, with no connection, but the odds were much higher that Colt was part of Evon's mission to find Celeste Pierre. It made him nervous. Wes abhorred human trafficking, and yet the temptation to sell Colt to the highest bidder was strong. The kid was an L-4, he might be worth a million universal credits to the right people. Wes didn't make that kind of scratch... ever. And it would be pure profit. He could make all the upgrades to the ship he wanted with a million credits, but Colt was growing on him. The kid seemed sincere and desperate. Not to mention the fact that there was good that could be made from having a Reader on board. If they were careful, no one had to know about Colt's abilities.

"I'll introduce you to the rest of the crew," Wes said. "This is my ship and I run things, but I won't bring on a crew member unless everyone agrees. And I'm not promising that I'll keep you even if they do. You have to pull your weight."

"I will," Colt said. "Whatever you need, I'll do it."

"What if I need you to read someone's mind?" Wes asked, testing the waters just a bit. He needed to know if the kid would be useful after all.

Colt didn't seem comfortable with the question. "I'll do whatever I can," he said after thinking about it. "I just..."

"Just what?"

"I just don't really have much experience with it," Colt said.

"You read my mind," Wes pointed out.

"Yeah," he replied. "I'll do it, if that's what you want."

"We'll see," Wes said, not convinced. "Come with me. Everyone should be on the Bridge."

CHAPTER 14

Colt followed Captain Wes down the stairs to the main deck. He felt a little shaky, and his stomach was starting to growl. He hoped that Wes didn't hear it. They went past the cabins and down the corridor that lead to the Bridge. It was an oval shaped room with large display screens that filled the far wall. The ship was still in hyperspace and the screens were black although some had ship information in glowing letters. There were five seats at a long cabinet with computer consoles built into them just inside the Bridge. Beyond the five station the floor dropped down almost a meter and there were two seats side by side closer to the huge displays.

"Heads up everyone," Wes said. "This is Colt O'Connor."

"Nice to meet..." a man with a wispy beard said. He looked as if he were struggling to say more and finally spit out, "you!" as if it were a curse word.

"That's Stu, our navigator," Wes said. "You've already met Di. She's the ship's engineer."

"Hello again," the woman said kindly.

"And you remember Zora," Wes went on.

Colt gave a little wave but the girl just stared at him and made no response in reply to his wave. Colt had hoped that someone closer to his own age would be friendly, but Zora seemed indifferent.

"And our pilot is Ilk Saide," Wes said. "He's Hyborian."

"Hello," Colt said.

The red skinned alien smiled, revealing pointed teeth that looked frightening.

"Welcome aboard the *Jolly Rogue*," Saide said in a strange accent.

Colt had seen Hyborians and a host of other alien species on television. And there had been no shortage of them on the space port where he grew up, but he had never had a conversation with one. He felt self conscious because he could feel the alien's amusement at revealing his pointed teeth to Colt.

The mental barriers Colt kept in place to block the sounds of other peoples thoughts also worked to deflect their emotions, but Saide's feelings somehow bypassed Colt's defenses.

"We've got one seat left," Wes said, pointing to the end of the console next to Zora. "We'll be coming out of hyperspace soon. Why don't you just sit down and watch until we make the transition."

Colt moved down to the end of the console. He saw that Zora had stiffened and was making a point not to look at him as he walked past her. Next to Zora was Di, then Wes, and Stu sat on the far end of the console and had more space at his station than the others. Colt sat in the empty chair. It was a big, plush chair, with built in safety features. The chair was comfortable and could swivel. The console where he sat had a touch screen surface and showed the ship's communication systems which were essentially a series of radio transmission channels, including the crew's com-links.

After the quick inspection of the space he was occupying Colt turned to look at Wes who was asking questions.

"How long until we reach Jurgen Downs?" the captain inquired.

"T-t-two hours," Stu wrestled with the answer, his jaw working to produce the words, "to reach the... station. Transition is in forty-seven... seconds."

"Excellent," Wes said. "How's the ship, Di?"

"Purring like a kitten," the engineer said. "All systems green. We can top off the fuel at Jurgen Downs, but we don't have to. Your call."

"We'll be picking up a load of Merconium," Wes said. "And until we get through the blockade and make a sale, we won't have any spare credits. Let's make this trip quick."

"Transition countdown," Saide said. "Ten, nine..."

"Anything I should know?" Colt whispered to Zora. "About the transition?"

She ignored him.

"... two, one," the pilot finished.

On the big screens lights appeared. In the distance was a pale star the size of Colt's fist. He could just make out the dark ring around it. There were other ships in the distance too, all kinds and sizes, moving toward the Dyson Ring or away from it, lit by running lights and the pale glow from the white dwarf star.

"Radar is on line," Di announced.

"I'll contact flight control," Wes said. "And get us in line for docking."

"We're clear to maneuver," Di said. "No vessels in our immediate vicinity."

"Continuing ahead at full sub-light speed," Saide added.

"We're in the queue," Wes said, his fingers taping rapidly on the touchscreen at his console. "Flight control is sending guidance now."

"Got it," Saide said a few seconds later, as a golden line appeared on the display.

The guidance marker ran straight toward the star until it was close to the Dyson Ring and then it rose up, turned to the left, and angled back down.

"I just sent word to our contact. Hopefully he'll have our goods waiting when we arrive," Wes said. "Alright, are we all good?"

The others nodded. Colt didn't have anything to add and just continued to watch. Wes turned toward him, as did Di and Stu. Zora slipped out of her chair and moved into the hallway without a word. Colt thought she was leaving but she stopped once she was in the hallway as far as she could get and still see him. Saide, busy flying the ship, stayed facing the display screens.

"Ever been on a ship before?" Di asked Colt.

"No ma'am," he replied. "I've never left the space port before."

"Well this is it," Wes said. "The Bridge is where the action is. Although space flight is rarely exciting."

"Each of us has oversight of a different system on the ship," Di said. "You're at the communication console. I'm at engineering. Zora sits at the radar spot, and Stu is navigation."

"I crunch the... numbers," Stu said.

Wes moved over to Stu and put his hand on the young man's shoulder. "Stu is the reason we can work off grid," Wes explained. "Most ships have a computer half the size of this room to compute the trajectory of a hyperspace jump. Stu can do it in his head."

Stu was nodding as he began to rock in his chair. He looked all around the Bridge, but never directly at Colt.

"We all have our special skills," Di said. "I keep the ship running. Zora is my apprentice."

"Saide pilots the ship by connecting the controls to his neural clusters," Wes explained. And for the first time since entering the Bridge Colt noticed that some of the ropy hair braids from Saide's head were actually cables that connected to ports around the pilot's seat. "We don't need a copilot with Saide flying us."

"What can... you do?" Stu asked, the last two words tumbling out almost like a bark.

"Show him," Wes said.

Colt wasn't sure how he could show Stu that he was a Reader. He thought about levitating something. Until Wes had suggested it the idea had never occurred to Colt, and doing it took all his strength and concentration. But it was an amazing and fun trick that he was anxious to try again. But there was nothing on the Bridge that wasn't connected to something important. Instead, Colt lowered his mental defenses and tried to connect with Stu. Making the connection was simple enough, but the result was shocking.

A blast of sound hit Colt like a punch in the mouth, and he tumbled sideways out of his chair. In the split second he had connected with Stu's mind, the lights had seemed to intensify to the point of painfulness. He saw everything in the room with such clarity it was mind boggling. The sensory overload was more than Colt could take. He slammed his defenses down hard just before he hit the deck, and laid there with his eyes closed, not even trying to move. It reminded him of the old fashioned rockets that were used to launch satellites into space. A person couldn't be anywhere near them when the rockets ignited. The blast of heat, smoke, and debris that went billowing around the rockets was massive. That was what Stu's brain felt like, a rocket at take-off.

"Are you okay?" Di asked.

Colt opened his eyelids a sliver. She was bent over him, a worried expression on her face. Colt saw Wes peering down at him from behind her. They both looked concerned.

"I'm okay," Colt said.

"He was in my... head," Stu said with a chuckle. "I felt... him."

"What happened?" Wes asked.

"It was too much," Colt said, getting up off the deck. "His mind was like a rocket taking off."

"Most people on the autism scale can't handle a lot of sensory data," Diana said.

"Stu's got a powerful brain," Wes nodded. "I guess that wasn't such a good suggestion."

"He's a... Reader!" Stu exclaimed.

"We're taking on criminals now?" Saide asked without turning from the ship's display screens.

"I'm not a criminal," Colt said.

"The kid isn't in trouble with the law," Wes said. "Not exactly."

"Readers have to turn themselves in to the GA," Saide went on. "Everyone knows that."

"And everyone knows what happens to them," Di added.

"What the GA doesn't know won't hurt them," Wes said. "Besides, they don't get to say that a person has no rights just because they're different."

Colt got the sudden impression that the way to get Wes on his side was to point out that the GA wouldn't approve. Even with his mental barriers up Colt could feel the captain's animosity toward the Galactic Authority.

"It's dangerous," Saide said. "They find him, we could all get pinched."

"He's got no place else to go," Di said. "Do you, Colt?"

"No," he admitted. "But I don't want to get anyone in trouble."

"Nobody's in trouble," Wes said. "Not unless we're foolish. But like I said, everyone on this ship pulls their weight. You want to stay on board, you'll have to take over docking duties. That's overseeing the resupply, getting provisions on board and stowed away, keeping the cargo deck swept clean and squared away."

"Don't forget to have him pump the bilge," Saide said. "It has to be emptied once a month, or the sewage starts to stink."

"Zora and I can teach you," Di said encouragingly.

"Everyone who doesn't cook cleans," Wes went on. "And this isn't your ma'ma's house. You keep your cabin clean and neat."

"I can do that," Colt said, feeling a surge of hope.

"Plus, I want you to learn all there is to know about the communications systems," Wes added. "It might be possible that you can use your abilities even over the radio."

"That could be handy if we're in an unfriendly port," Di said.

"My thoughts exactly. But we don't take anyone on without a full vote," Wes continued. "And this is temporary. You try us out, we try you, if it works that's great, if it doesn't? No hard feelings right?"

"Okay," Colt said, nodding his agreement.

"It's hard work," Wes said. "This isn't a luxury yacht. You have to load and unload with the rest of us. There'll be some liberty in port if there's time, but not every stop. And there'll be a share of the profits."

"When there are profits," Saide said, and Colt felt the wave of amusement from the Hyborian again.

"If anyone's a no, speak now," Wes said. "Otherwise the kid is sticking around. At least until we finish the job on Kellar Nine."

Colt tensed, waiting for someone to speak against him. But the Bridge was silent. He could feel the tension from Saide, but the alien didn't speak. When Colt glanced at Zora she was staring at him, but then slipped away down the hall.

"And with that, you're a member of the crew," Wes said with a sigh. "Let's get something to eat kid. We might not get another chance for a while."

Colt followed Wes back up to the top deck. They ate processed pastries and drank protein shakes. When they went back down to the deck they were less than thirty minutes from the station.

"What's our ETA?" Wes asked, dropping into his seat with a sigh.

"We're twenty-seven minutes from docking maneuvers," Saide said.

"There are nine other ships ahead of us," Di added. "It should work out just about perfect."

"That's the way I like things," Wes said. "Almost perfect is just fine with me. Colt, put on the communications headset and see what chatter you can pick up. And do a network search. We should be in range to log in. I want to know what's going on at Jurgen Downs."

Colt looked at his console. There was no headset, and no compartments. It was essentially one big touch screen. He leaned over and looked at the side of the long counter. At either end was a set of stairs that led down to the pilot seats. Hanging on a hook at the side he saw a head set with one ear cuff and a mic that could be folded down over his mouth. It was bit old fashioned, but serviceable. He picked it up and put it on. There was a button on his touch screen that said COMMS MENU. He tapped that and a list of commands appeared, including one for audio. He tapped it and then the icon that looked like his headset. Another of the buttons said BRIDGE and another was listed TRANSMIT. He had been worried that learning the communications system would be difficult, but it seemed to be self explanatory.

The voices over the headset were mostly other ships trying to contact flight control. Colt listened and on the screen of his console brought up a window to the Jurgen Downs information network. The Dyson Ring was a huge installation with dozens of cities. Colt scanned the headlines of a news site, but it was mostly just stories of the installation's record energy sales. Most of the inhabitants held shares of the energy station's profits. The small dwarf star wasn't nearly as bright as a regular system star, but the Dyson Ring was so efficient that the installation was producing dozens of the high output batteries that could run the average household on most worlds for a year on a single charge every hour.

"Find anything interesting, kid?" Wes asked.

Colt had been so engrossed in his task that he hadn't noticed the captain approach.

"No sir," Colt replied.

"This station is more of a trading post and fuel depot than anything else," Wes said. "The bank has been a target a few times, but that's mostly cyber crimes. The GA has a presence here of course, and a few of the larger cartels have wise guys looking for angles, but we shouldn't have problems."

"He's all business," Di said with a wink. "And a bit of a worrier."

"I worry so that you don't have to," Wes said. "Although the ship could probably stand from you worrying a bit more."

"The ship is in perfect condition," Di insisted. "Things are made to wear out over time. And when they do, we replace them. It's as simple as that."

"As long as we can find the parts," Wes grumbled.

"We're next in line," Di announced.

"Moving into position," Saide said. "Ready for docking maneuvers."

"Any word from our contact?"

"Not yet," Wes said. "Take us in and we'll send him another message."

Colt watched in fascination as the ship got closer and closer to the Dyson ring. It was a mammoth installation, with fast moving transport cars racing between the cities on the outside of the ring. The cities were easy to spot because they were built larger than the ring, so ever thousand kilometers or so another city swelled out like a jewel on a tiny wedding band. The cities were built on the outside of the ring too, and rotated around the ring so that the inhabitants had hours of direct sunlight and hours when they faced away from the sun and were in shadow. The spaceport in Helix Prime was large and Colt had always thought that it was technologically advanced, but he realized it was just a city in a bubble. There was nothing exotic or fancy about it. The Dyson Ring called Jurgen Downs was much more advanced, and with an energy surplus, they could do things that other space stations could only imagine.

"It's not exactly a tourist attraction," Wes said. "But it's something, eh kid?"

"It's amazing," Colt replied, as the ship rotated around and docked with the rear hatch to the port.

On the *Jolly Rogue's* display screens Colt could see hundreds of star ships, the light from the little star illuminating their hulls so that it looked like they were glowing bright against the back drop of deep space. For the first time since leaving his mother, and hiding on the *Jolly Rogue* to escape the GA agents, Colt felt a thrill of genuine excitement. He regretted what he had lost, but he was doing what he had always imagined. He was seeing the galaxy, and in his brief experience, it was breathtaking.

CHAPTER 15

"Still no word," Wes announced. "I'll go pay the harbor master. Hopefully we won't be here long."

"Long enough to order in I hope," Di said. "Zora and I are hungry for something other than pasta."

"Fine, but meet them at the airlock," Wes said. "I don't want anyone else on board this ship. Come on, kid, you can see the port. We won't have time for anything else."

Colt jumped at the chance. He was wearing wrinkled clothes and felt unprepared, but he was going to walk on a space station that wasn't his home. It would be his first real visit to another place and he was excited to see what the exotic port looked like.

They went down to the cargo bay and cycled through the airlock. While they waited for the airlock to pressurize Wes handed Colt a little device.

"Take that," Wes said.

"What is it?" Colt asked, looking at the little silver button.

"Com-link," Wes told him. "Snap it on your collar. Just tap it to activate, but remember anyone close by can hear it."

"Yes sir," Colt replied.

"And while we're at this, consider it a test," Wes said. "You can tell me what the harbor master is thinking when we get back to the ship. It might be useful when we meet our contact."

Colt nodded, but felt a little guilty. He knew that reading peoples minds wasn't right. A person's thoughts were private. But he had told Wes that he would do whatever it took to stay on the ship. And as soon as the airlock opened, he forgot all about his misgivings.

Unlike Helix Prime, the port arm on Jurgen Downs was part of the larger station. Colt could see massive buildings that were built of chrome and glass. There was neon lights and huge screens that filled the sides of skyscrapers with video playing on them. It was like being in a movie and yet they were in a simple port with dozens of other ships. Colt followed Wes, but part of him wanted to go and explore. For the first time since discovering his gift the temptation to use it for ill entered his mind. He was a Reader, and that meant he could swim in another person's mind. In the movies, Readers were usually con men, or cyber thieves, using their psych abilities to steal from other people. Wes wanted to explore the bright, colorful space station, but to do that he would need money. If he used his abilities there was no limit to what he might be able to do. Wes had tested him, and Colt was a level four Reader. The station was so tempting. As they approached the harbor master's office, which was nothing more than a small hut with windows where a man took payment for ships that docked in the port, it occurred to Colt that he was seeing just one of dozens of cities on the Dyson Ring. It felt like a host of wonders to his young mind. A place of glitz and excitement where anything was possible.

"Eighty credits for half a day," the harbor master said as they approached. "One twenty for a full day. Do you need rates for an extended stay?"

"No," Wes said.

Colt remembered his assignment and opened himself up to the man. He was immediately hit with a twinge of guilt and shame. ... *do it all the time, I'm no different. And this dumb spacer doesn't know the difference. It's just a little lie. I'm not hurting anyone...*

Colt found the thoughts and feelings of guilt odd. The man was ripping them off, and yet it was clear he didn't want to. Colt pushed harder into the man's mind, looking for the answer. It wasn't hard to find. A memory played in Colt's mind, as if he were watching a video screen of the Harbor Master's memories. He saw a small man with a smile that didn't look normal. He approached the Harbor Master in the booth and held out a PA with video of a little girl being walked to school by her mother. The girl had pig tails and a pink backpack. She walked with a limp, and held her mother's hand.

"You ready to play ball," the smiling man had asked.

"You bastard," the Harbor Master snarled. "If you touch them I'll—"

"What? What will you do?" the man waited for an answer, but it was clear the Harbor Master was bluffing. "That's what I thought. Sweet young thing like that deserves better than a pot o'pork like you. Now you pay us what you owe, or we'll get our credits from them. Fifteen K a week with the vid. You got that? Every week, like clockwork. Fifteen K."

"Colt, let's go," Wes said.

Colt wrenched himself away from the Harbor Master's mind. It was jarring. All the emotions the Harbor Master had felt, guilt, fear, a deep, horrid sense of desperation, it was clinging to Colt like a bad dream.

"Sorry," Colt whispered.

"You can't lose yourself like that," Wes said. "You were standing there like an android whose battery just went out. What happened."

They were nearly back to the ship.

"He was ripping you off," Colt said.

"Nothing new there," Wes said. "Most government workers are paid peanuts. Harbor Master is a highly sought after job because it's so easy to skim. It's just part of this life, nothing to get in a tangle over."

"No," Colt said. "It just made me curious. So I looked a little deeper. He's in trouble."

"Let me guess," Wes said. "He owes someone money?"

"Yes, a lot of money," Colt said. "How did you know that?"

"Doesn't take a mind reader to pick up on the cues," Wes said. "He's wearing a gold watch, expensive clothes, the kind of stuff a Harbor Master can't afford. Probably gambles."

"Someone threatened his family," Colt said.

"Yeah? That's too bad. No one should have to pay for someone else's sins, you know?"

Colt did know and couldn't help but think of his mother. Was she paying for his sins at that very moment? Was she suffering because he had run away? He didn't know, and couldn't know unless he went back home. And if he did that he would be caught by the GA agents and they would lock him away to either serve as their slave or to test like a rat in a laboratory. He tried to tell himself that his mother had made a sacrifice for him and he should honor it. For all he knew she was back at home after answering their questions. But for some reason, he couldn't really believe it.

CHAPTER 16

"How was the kid?" Di asked.

"Okay," Wes said skeptically. "Saide is showing him the ropes down in the cargo bay."

They were sitting together on the bridge, waiting for their contact to message them about the shipment of Merconium they were supposed to be picking up.

"Did he use his powers?"

"He did, but he didn't tell me anything I didn't already know," Wes explained. "The Harbor Master overcharged us."

"What's new?"

"Exactly," Wes said. "I don't think he's lying about his age."

"But you think he's lying about something?" she asked skeptically.

"I think the chances are better than even that he isn't telling us everything," Wes said. "But if he's pretending to have just found his powers, he's extremely convincing."

"Why would the GA send a Reader after us?" Di asked. "Yeah, we run the blockade, but so do a hundred other ships.

The GA doesn't even care. We're within their so called 'margin of error.' They wouldn't waste a Reader on us."

"Someone sent us to find the PM's daughter on Kellar Nine," Wes said. "They knew who we were, what we had on board, and where we were going. The only way that happens is if they were watching us."

"But we don't even know who the 'they' you're talking about is," Di pointed out.

"But that's strange," Wes insisted. "Not beyond the scope of the GA, or even the Freight Hauler's Guild. Hell, for all we know it might be one of the big cartels. They keep Readers too."

"But why?" Di asked. "If they know so much about us, why do they need to send a Reader to us as well?"

"Maybe he's their link," Wes said. "The more I think about it, the more a cartel makes sense. I mean, if Celeste Pierre really is alive and they got their hands on her..."

He let the thought trail off. It wasn't a pleasant thought. The criminals had more power than the GA in some systems. Handing over the Prime Minister's daughter to a criminal organization would compromise the government. Perhaps they already had leverage on the PM's replacement and needed a reason to move their asset into power. Or maybe they simply wanted to cash in on a powerful man's misfortune. Either way, if they really had a lead on Celeste's whereabouts, they might also have a person onboard the ship. Most successful criminals found ways to keep their hands clean and let other people do their dirty work.

"No, not even the most famous missing person in the galaxy is worth as much as a Reader," Di argued. "They would never give Colt up once they had their hands on him."

"Who says they're giving him up? It's an assignment," Wes

said. "And he'll be right back in their hands once it's all said and done."

"Or maybe he really is just a scared kid who doesn't want to be a GA stooge. That's not so hard to believe."

"It's possible," Wes said. "I'd love to believe it, and the kid is convincing I'll give him that, but I can't put all our lives at risk just because he's likable. I mean, even if he's legit, the kid's a danger to himself and anyone around him. He zoned out reading the Harbor Master's mind. I had to shake him out of it. If he does that ever time he's reading people there's no way we keep it secret. And once that cat's out of the bag we'll have everyone in the galaxy after us."

"It might not be good for business," Di admitted. "Our contacts are shaky under the best of circumstances."

"Exactly," Wes agreed. "If they find out we've got a Reader on our crew they'll think we've been playing them. There would be no way to convince them otherwise."

"But we can't just turn the kid loose," Diane said. "He'll get picked up by the GA within hours."

"Maybe we could find a place where he could blend in," Wes said. "An Alliance world maybe, with people that wouldn't take advantage of him until he's ready to be on his own."

"You mean people like us?"

Wes realized instantly what she had done. He was in a corner with no safe way to turn. If he said they weren't a good place for Colt, it would prove that he only really cared about himself and what he deemed best for the *Jolly Rouge*. Of course, if he agreed with her, the decision would be made. And while Wes felt there was a chance that everything the kid had told them was true, he just couldn't believe it.

"I think there are better options than on our ship," Wes said. "He would be happier on a planet with fresh air and space to move around. No teenager wants to be cooped up on a freighter all the time."

"That's his decision to make," Di said. "Zora likes it here well enough."

"Does she?" Wes asked, still holding on to the argument. "She hasn't spoken a word that I've heard since we brought her on board three years ago."

"She needed time to heal," Diana said. "But she talks plenty when she feels safe."

"I don't make her feel safe?"

"You remind her too much of her past," Di said. "She's working through it. But the ship has given her the safe space she needs. Pretty soon she'll bloom into an incredible young woman and you'll be glad you were there to see it."

"Alright, I'll take your word for it," Wes said. "But Colt stays on a short leash. If you're wrong about him..."

"If I'm wrong we're already in serious trouble," she said. "We have nothing left to lose."

"Unless we give him a few credits and send him on his way now," Wes said.

He didn't really want to do it. Deep inside he liked Colt, but hard experience had taught him never to trust anyone. The kid was likable, but that didn't mean he needed to be part of their crew, even if he could help them in ways that Wes could only imagine.

"If he's an agent he's already gotten everything he needs from our minds and he'll want to go," Di said. "I say we leave it up to him."

A beep on Wes' console ended the conversation. He turned to the embedded screen in his section of the command console. A message had just come through. The sender was an anonymous series of numbers and letters that gave no indication who had sent it. There was no signature either, just the message.

Go to the 66 club, one hour. We'll be watching.

"Looks like our guy is ready to meet," Wes said, doing a quick search of the network for the 66 Club.

"We should bring Colt," Di said. "He could be useful."

"Okay, but you're responsible for the kid. I don't want to do anything that would spook this guy. Without his Merconium we won't even break even on this run."

"I got it," she replied. "I have a feeling this could be a good thing."

"If you say so," Wes said.

He felt torn. He didn't mind Colt tagging along under normal circumstances, but it wasn't just the kid's abilities that made Wes nervous about the meet. Colt was inexperienced, and they didn't really know him. What if Colt said something that upset their contact? Wes didn't even know how the kid felt about the GA and the Alliance. Young people were sometimes ideal- istic and the GA fostered an image of goodness that hid their sadistic side. If Colt said something, even in passing, that the contact took for pro-government sentiments, he might bolt and they would be left holding the bag. They had twelve thousand credits tied up in their cargo of magnesium. And they had already spent another seven in fuel and supplies. With the Merconium, which Wes was planning to pay three thousand credits for, they could double their investment on Kellar Nine. Without it, they would be lucky to get their twelve grand back, and there was no margin for error. If they lost their seed money there would be nothing left to get another cargo. They would have to spend what little they had to keep the ship running and hire themselves out to the shady types who took none of the risks and kept all the rewards. And once a crew signed on to work for the cartels there was no leaving. They would be trapped, no better than slaves, forced into perpetual servitude and only earning a sliver of the profits.

After downloading the directions to the establishment where he had been instructed to meet their contact to his PA, Wes stood up.

"It's not very close," he told Di. "We should go."

"I'll get the kid, you get the credits," she said with smile. "This is going to be fun."

Wes couldn't help but smile. Her enthusiasm was contagious and while he tended to be a worrier, Di's carefree spirit helped balance him. He would get the credits, as well as his peace-maker, a forearm blaster that could be hidden under the sleeve of his jacket. It had sensor controls on tiny adhesive pads. One one on his pinky, one on his middle finger, and the activator went on his thumb. When he touched his pinky and thumb together the barrel extended over his hand, protruding from the sleeve in a fraction of a second. Once deployed, all Wes had to do was touch his thumb and middle finger together to fire the weapon. Most space ports had laws against carrying firearms, but what the authorities didn't know was fine by Wes. And it wouldn't hurt that his contact had no clue they would be armed either. It was just an added layer of protection, insurance for those working just outside the protection of the law. And Wes was being honest, that's where he felt the most comfortable. He trusted himself more than any group of paid peacekeepers, espe-cially the GA agents.

CHAPTER 17

"Before we go, I have an offer to make," Wes said.

Colt, his mind spinning with all he'd learned about the cargo bay, looked up. Part of him felt like the captain was respecting him enough to make choices about his future. But the other part felt put on the spot again and made him feel shaky. Zora was on the stairs on the far side of the cargo bay. She was always watching and he felt drawn to her. There was something about the girl, so different, so mysterious. He wanted to know what she was thinking, but he wouldn't dare enter her mind. That would be an unforgivable breech of trust and he wasn't the type of person who could live with deception.

"I've got a hundred and fifty credits," Wes said, holding out a universal credit chip. "We've been talking and if you feel that you might be better off on your own, you could take this and go."

"You mean leave the ship?" Colt asked.

"We can part ways, if that's what you want," Wes said. "I don't want you staying because you feel like you have no other options."

"Do you want me to leave?" Colt asked.

"No," Di said. She was leaning against the door of the airlock watching him. "You have a place on this ship as part of her crew, but it has to be your choice."

"You decide," Wes said, still holding out the credit chip.

The temptation to stay and explore the Dyson Ring was strong, but Colt knew if he took the credits and ventured out on his own, he would have to resort to crime. He didn't have identification. There would be no way to get a job or even a place to live without breaking the law. His new abilities made that possible, but it wasn't want he wanted. Colt liked the *Jolly Rogue* and he liked the crew. Saide had spent nearly a hour showing all about the resupply and provisioning process. He had his own cabin, which was almost as big as the apartment he'd grown up in. Not to mention the library. Colt wanted to explore it, to examine every title, perhaps even read them all. And there was Zora. He couldn't explain it, but he knew he couldn't leave.

"I want to stay," Colt told Wes and Diana. "I want to be part of the crew. That's my choice."

"Told you," Di said with a grin.

"Good," Wes said, although he didn't seem pleased as he stuffed the credit chip back into his pocket. "Let's go. Keep your eyes open and your mouth shut, kid. Watch and learn, you got it?"

"Yes sir," Colt said.

He followed the captain and the engineer into the airlock. It was obvious at a glance that they were comfortable with each other. He had on a brown leather jacket over a plain shirt, and she wore a tunic over tight, stretchy pants. Her boots came up to her knees and Colt noticed that something was tucked into the back of the wide belt that cinched her tunic around her narrow waist. He looked closer and saw that it was a blade of some type.

His own clothes were second hand, and wrinkled. He didn't have a spare outfit and hoped that he might get the chance to pick something up before long.

They left the ship and the docking section, moving through the city which was built on a grid. Many of the buildings were multiple stories high. Traffic on the street was light, mostly people walking. They passed some auto taxies, and crossed through a park with a fountain. There were stores and entertainment venues, restaurants, coffee kiosks, and street vendors. It was so different from what he was used to that Colt couldn't help but gawk a little.

"Not bad for a GA station," Wes said.

"It's amazing," Colt replied.

"Jurgen Downs is okay, but I prefer a real world to a space station," Di said. "Have you ever been on a world, Colt?"

"No ma'am," he replied.

"Just wait," she went on. "You haven't seen anything yet."

Colt couldn't imagine anything more amazing than the Dyson Ring. Just knowing there were many more cities on the ring made him want to explore them all. He felt a sense of excitement just looking through the windows of the shops, and smelling the food being cooked by the vendors.

"Here it is," Wes said. "Club 66."

They went into a building and down a flight of stairs. The ceiling of the club was low, and the entire place was dark. There were neon lights around the mirrored shelves that were filled with bottles of ardent spirits. The club was full of small round tables with stools. On each table was a small light with an opaque shade that directed all the light down onto the surface of the table and did nothing to illuminate the space above.

"I'll get us drinks," Wes said. "You two find a table."

Di led the way, and Colt followed. They sat down in a dark

corner and Di leaned close to him. She tapped the side of her head and said in a low voice only he could hear. "Listen to me."

For a moment Colt didn't know what she meant. She wasn't talking, how could he listen if she wasn't saying anything? And then the truth dawn on him. He could listen to her even if she wasn't talking. He felt guilty opening his mind up to her, but he did it anyway, hoping that he had understood her.

... eyes open and use your gift to find out what people in this club are thinking. No one knows you or what you can do. Can you even hear me?

I hear you, Colt said.

Di twitched. It was as if she had been caught off guard by his voice in her head.

Listen to the people, he replied mentally, pushing his thoughts to her so that she heard him. *I got that. What am I listening for?*

Anyone focused on us, she replied. *Anything you think we should know.*

Got it, Colt said, just as Wes returned to the table. He had three glasses of bubbly liquid. One had two straws and he set it down in front of Colt.

"Drink up, kid," the captain said. "That's Cuba Libre sans rum."

"Any signs of our contact?" Di asked.

"I wouldn't know," Wes said. "We've never met. He'll have to approach us."

Colt sipped his drink. It was a bit sour from the lime juice. Normally he enjoyed cola, but his mind was busy scanning the other patrons in the bar.

... she will never know if I don't tell her... a heavy set man at the bar was thinking. *Who am I kidding. She'll know. She always knows.* A wave of shame rolled from the man. Colt didn't want

to know what he had done to feel so bad about. The big man threw back a shot of something strong, trying to assuage his guilt. Two women huddled at table close to the door and spoke in quiet tones about helping a friend who was in some kind of trouble. A couple in the opposite corner were cops, partners in fact, who had crossed the line between co-workers and lovers.

The couple in the corner are cops, Colt pushed the thought to both Wes and Di. *But they're hiding out here.*

Hiding from what? Wes thought.

Other cops, Colt explained. *They're having an affair.*

Good to know, Di thought.

"Keep an eye on them," Wes told Di.

She nodded and took a drink of her own cocktail. There was no one else in the club. The bartender was busy thinking about a screenplay he was working on in his spare time as he washed glasses and set them on a rack to dry.

"How long are waiting?" Di asked.

"Long enough to finish our drinks," Wes said. "Saide has the ship locked down, but he's keeping an eye out for anyone nosing around."

"I have a platter of freshly baked bagels that will be delivered at the ship in an hour," Di said. "Along with real cream cheese and some fruit."

"How much did that cost?" Wes asked.

"Fifty credits," Di replied, taking another sip of her drink. "You know rum makes me melancholy."

"How'd you pay?"

"The dummy account," she said. "But it will be worth it."

"You can bake on the ship you know," he insisted.

"It's not the same," she replied. "And you know it. Be nice and I'll share with you."

They continued their conversation but Colt was distracted

by a new presence in the room. No one had come in, but he felt a wave of suspicion and heard a calculating presence in his mind: *Three? They needed three people to make a deal? And one's a kid. I don't like it.*

He's here, Colt pushed the thought to Wes and Di. They continued talking and sipping their drinks.

Where? Wes thought.

Colt wasn't sure. He couldn't see the person, but the strong waves of suspicion were coming from across the room. It was dark and Colt couldn't be sure, but he thought that perhaps there was an alcove or hallway on the far side in the darkness. The person was lingering there, knowing he was invisible to the people in the bar.

It's not worth it, the suspicious person thought, still watching from the darkness. *DaVoor should pick better people. I'm not sticking my neck out for a measly three grand. If they're legit they'll know what to do. Three people, damn it, that's too many people.*

He's nervous, Colt relayed the information. *He doesn't like that that there are three of us.*

I'll wait outside, Di said. *Can you keep me in the loop, Colt?*

I think so.

She stood up. "I want to do a little window shopping. Do you have any credits?"

"You need credits to look?"

"I like to be prepared," she said, flashing him a smile while Wes pulled out the chip with the hundred and fifty credits. The same chip he had offered to Colt. She took it, and made a show of slipping it into her back pocket while she bent over and kissed Wes on the cheek.

Is he buying it? she wondered as she began to walk away from the table where Wes and Colt said.

Colt could feel a sense of relief from the hidden man. *I think so,* Colt thought, pushing the words from his mind to Di's.

The man watched her, then turned back to Wes and Colt. His suspicions were laced with fear as he started forward. Colt continued to watch the door, keeping an eye on the cops, who were huddled together, sipping drinks and making plans to sneak away together for a long weekend.

He's coming, Colt warned Wes.

Got it. Stay cool, kid. This guy's jumpy but we aren't doing anything wrong. Just making a buy. It's all legit.

Colt could tell Wes believed that, but from the fear radiating off the man approaching their table Colt didn't think that was the case.

"You Wes," the man said.

"I am," the captain replied. "This is my nephew, Eli."

Who cares, the man thought as he sat down where Di had been a few moments before.

"Buy you a drink?" Wes asked.

"No, this is my place," the man said. "Let's just settle our business and you can move along."

"Okay," Wes said. "You have the Merconium?"

"It's in a storage unit at the dock," the man said. *And you ain't getting it until I get my money.*

"You want to show us?"

"No," the man said. Colt didn't have to read his mind to know he was afraid.

Ask him where he got it, Colt pushed the thought to Wes.

"Well, how is this going to work then?" Wes asked.

"You pay me, I'll give you the key and the storage number," the man said.

"DaVoor said you're stuff was legit," Wes asked. "Where'd you get it."

"In a trade," the man replied, but Colt could feel the deception. It was almost as if his voice had gone up an octave and a wave of fear came crashing out from the man.

He's lying. He's really scared.

"How do I know you didn't steal it?" Wes asked. "There could be law enforcement waiting to pick up whoever opens that unit."

"No," the man said.

His mind was swirling. His fear and worries were like popcorn in his brain.

"Look," Wes said. "I don't know you and you don't know me. So let's do this right. I'll give you the money. You bring the cargo to my ship."

"That's not how this works?"

How desperate is he? Wes wondered.

Colt feel the man's fear that the deal was falling apart. But he was afraid of getting the cargo. He didn't know if someone was watching the storage building, but he had his suspicions. He was also terrified of not getting the money.

Very, Colt replied. *But he won't budge on the storage unit. He's afraid it's being watched.*

"You tell me how it works then," Wes said. "Because I've got deadlines to meet. I can't play games all day."

"You think this is a game?" the man snapped. *If they don't take the Merconium and it get's found by the authorities they'll trace it back to me. I have to get rid of it.*

He just wants the cargo moved, Colt thought, pushing it to Wes' mind. *He doesn't want to get caught with it.*

"I think you're in trouble and you're hoping I can get you out of it," Wes said.

"Is that what DaVoor told you?"

Another wave of fear and suspicion crashed into Colt from

the man. Wes shook his head and made a placating gesture with his hand.

"Calm down. Let's work this out," he said, then followed that with a thought. *Send Di back to the docks to check out the storage units.*

Colt found her with his mind. It was surprising to feel her familiar thought patterns even though she wasn't all that close. She was lingering a few stores down the street, looking at a water desalination kit that was on sale in a hardware shop.

Diane, Colt thought, *Wes wants you to go back to the docks and look for storage units. There might be people watching them.*

I hear you, Colt. I'm on my way, Diana replied.

She's going, Colt informed Wes.

"You pay me," the nervous man was saying. "I give you the key. We never have to see each other again."

"No, it doesn't work like that," Wes said. "I can't take that kind of risk. How about I show you the money and you give my nephew the key. He can go check out the storage unit and report back to me. If everything is on the up and up, I'll pay you."

A kid? the nervous man was thinking. *Dear God, what if he gets picked up. At least he doesn't know my name.* "Fine. Show me the credits."

Wes reached into the inside pocket of his jacket and pulled out three universal credit chips, each showed three thousand credits on their small, digital screen.

"Three grand, untraceable," Wes asked. He set the chips down on the table, but kept his hand close to them. "We're running a clean job here taking medical supplies across the blockade. That's all, no funny business. DaVoor vouched for you. That's good enough for me, but I need the Merconium."

"It's there," the man said, and this time he wasn't lying.

I can get it, Colt urged the captain. *Even if it's being watched. I know I can.*

"Okay," Wes said, speaking both to the nervous man and to Colt. "As an act of good faith I'll trust you. But I'm only paying two grand if I'm taking all the risk."

We pushed two of the credit chips across the table. Colt scanned the room. Nothing had changed. No one was paying them any attention.

"This is robbery," the nervous man said as he scooped up the credits. "I want three. It's worth three."

But Colt could feel the man's relief. All he wanted was to move the Merconium, to get it off the space station where it could never be traced back to him.

He'll cave, Colt warned Wes. *He's just posturing.*

I can see that, Wes replied. *Good work.*

"I'm offering two," Wes said. "Take it or leave it."

The man looked around nervously, licked his lips, then pulled a key card from his pocket. "Unit twenty-two."

He dropped the key on the table and left. Colt thought he was going too fast, but no one noticed. The people in the club were too focused on themselves.

"Well that was different," Wes said. "Let's go see what we just bought."

CHAPTER 18

Wes and Colt caught up with Diana who had made a pass by the storage units. They were sitting at an outdoor cafe, sipping coffee. Colt found it bitter, but with enough sugar and cream it was tolerable.

"I didn't see anyone," Di said.

"Doesn't mean there aren't people watching," Wes said. "That guy was a flake and maybe just paranoid, but he has me worried."

"DaVoor said he was skittish," Di pointed out. "It's not that far from skittish to paranoid."

"We have to know," Wes said. "We can't pull the cargo out of there just to get pinched by the authorities."

"I can do it," Colt said. He had brought his mental barriers up part way. He was only picking up the people close by. "Let me try. If I get caught, the rest of you can leave."

Maybe that's just what he wants, Wes said, as suspicion radiated from him like heat from a fire.

"No one is getting caught," Di said. "There's no one

watching a load of Merconium. Even if it's stolen it's not worth much. They don't use it in narcotics, or synthetics. It's small potatoes. No one is throwing up a sting operation for a pallet of Merconium."

"Okay," Wes relented as he slid the key card for the storage unit across the table. "Give him the credit chip. If it gets hot kid, you get out of there. But don't come straight back to the ship. Meet us two cities over, the manufacturing section, where they build the batteries. You got that?"

"Got it," Colt replied, taking the credit chip and the key card, putting them both into his pocket. "I should be able to communicate with you both from the unit."

"Use the com-link," Di said. "Never rely on anything that might get you into trouble." *You don't want people to know or even suspect that you're a Reader.*

Colt nodded. He felt like Di cared. Wes did too, but he was still a long way from trusting Colt. The young Reader could only hope that getting the load of Merconium might change the captain's mind about him.

"Do a walk past the unit," Wes said in a low voice. "Stay cool, no matter what you feel or hear. Go down to that ice cream vender and get a treat. Then walk back. If you feel good about it, open up the storage unit. We'll be watching. Use your com-link and tell me everything. We've got your back."

"Okay," Colt said.

He got up and started down the street. The city was turning away from the sun and the shadows were growing long. He opened up his mind and let the noise of the city in. At first it was a roar, like a thousand televisions being turned on at once, all on different channels. But he forced himself to concentrate. He filtered the sounds and emotions, searching for anything that might be suspicion or surveillance related. There was nothing.

The people all around the dock and the storage units were focused on their business.

When he reached the end of the block he bought a small cup of frozen ice cream pellets. The vendor gave his frozen treat a stir with a ladle which produced a sonic wave that broke the pellets apart so that they were easy to scoop up with the little plastic spoon he included in the cup of frozen goodness. Colt ate the ice cream as he wandered back toward the storage locker. There was still no sign that anyone was watching the unit.

He pulled the card from his pocket and swiped it across the lock. The mechanism beeped and the door opened slightly. Colt had to bend down, grab the handle and raise the door. Inside the unit was a pallet of boxes wrapped in clear plastic. The boxes said MEDICAL GRADE MERCONIUM. Colt tapped his com-link.

"This is Colt," he said, feeling self conscious.

"We hear you, kid," came Wes' reassuring voice, although it was small and sounded as if he were talking from a thousand kilometers away.

"It's here," Colt told them. "There's even a dolly to move the pallet."

"That's good. Now take your time," Wes told him. "Di is headed to the ship. She'll be ready to receive it, but don't rush. Look around. Use your head. Make sure it's safe before you pull that load out."

"Yes sir," Colt replied.

It felt like over kill, as if he were being too cautious, but Colt walked around the pallet. There was nothing else in the storage unit. The floor was concrete, the metal walls were bare. There were no shelves, and nothing else in the unit, just the pallet on a fabricated base that was made out of recycled plastic. Colt touched the handle of the dolly when the signal went out. It was an electronic pulse and Colt had no idea how he'd noticed it, but he could feel the tracking device sending it's intermittent signal.

"There's a problem," Colt said, before deciding he didn't want to reveal what he knew over the com-link that could be hacked. Someone was keeping tabs on the Merconium and they might be monitoring the radio waves too.

There's a tracking device, Colt thought, pushing the alert to Wes and then to Diana. He couldn't send it to them at the same time, they were to far apart.

You sure? Wes asked.

Positive.

Leave, Wes ordered. *Lock the unit and meet me at the ship.*

Colt did as directed, moving slowly despite the urge to rush. He felt like someone was watching him, someone he couldn't see. It disturbed him and he was shocked to realize how much he had come to depend on the advantage that his psychic ability gave him. He closed down the storage unit door, his back tingling. He wondered if someone was behind him even though he couldn't sense anyone. Still, the urge to whirl around and look was so strong it made him feel weak. His legs were trembling and so were his hands as he swiped the key card to re-engage the lock. Finally he could turn around. There was no one there. No assassin, no government agent waiting to arrest him, his path to the *Jolly Rogue* was clear.

Slow and steady he told himself. *Just breathe.* Perhaps there was another Reader snooping inside his head. If so, he wasn't fooling anyone. But all he could do was return to the ship and hope that he hadn't ruined everything for his new friends. It was hard not to hurry. He told himself to act casual, there was no reason to believe anyone was watching, and yet he felt so self conscious. When he finally reached the ship, the airlock was open and waiting for him. He stepped on board, finally feeling safe as the airlock cycled. When the door opened, Di and Saide were waiting for him.

"You're sure there was a tracking device?" Di asked.

Colt nodded. "Positive."

"How can you know if you didn't see it?" Saide asked, his dark eyes reflecting the lights from around the large cargo bay.

"I heard it," Colt said. "As soon as I touched the dolly."

"Do you always hear electronic signals?" Di asked.

"I don't know," Colt admitted. "I've been trying so hard to keep everything out that I never noticed."

"Where is the captain?" Saide asked.

"He's watching the unit to see if the tracking device is drawing someone," Di said. "We'll wait here. Colt, keep searching for anything that might tip us off as to who is searching for us. Saide, let's go back to the bridge and watch the ship's video feed. It's possible someone might come poking around."

The Hyborian gave Colt a sidelong glance and with his mental barriers down Colt felt the wave of suspicion. Saide didn't think that Colt was betraying the crew, he thought Colt was lying about the tracking device. It wasn't the smartest plan if Colt wanted to engender trust with the crew, but that didn't stop Saide from suspecting Colt of lying.

A quick scan of the immediate vicinity around the ship revealed nothing. The closest person to the ship was the Harbor Master, still in his booth trying to devise a way out of the trouble he had landed in. Colt felt bad for him, but there was nothing he could do, and he had issues of his own to deal with. An hour later, Wes returned to the ship. Di and Saide came down to the cargo bay. Colt caught sight of Zora lingering on the stairs. She wanted to be in on the conversation without actually taking part.

"Well?" Di asked.

"Nothing. Didn't see another person between the docks and

the storage unit," Wes said. "I think whoever put that tracking device on the Merconium wants to keep tabs on the ship. They want us to get that cargo."

"Are you certain there is really a tracking device?" Saide said. "The kid could be mistaken."

Colt wanted to argue that he wasn't mistaken. But decided to keep his mouth closed. Speaking up, even to defend himself, would only drive a wedge between himself and Saide.

"There's only one way to find out," Wes said. "We're going back."

"Why not just leave?" Di said.

"We need the money, you know that," Wes replied.

"We'll find a way to make things work. We always do."

"No, I have a plan," Wes said. "Besides, taking a look at the device might give us a clue as to who is behind it."

"It's too much of a risk," Di said.

"We won't be risking anything to take a look at the tracking device," Wes said. "You watch for the authorities. Saide, ready the ship for immediate departure. If the coast is clear we're bringing it back on board. I want to get moving immediately."

"Watch yourself," Di said. "Two grand isn't worth dying for."

"I'll be careful," Wes said. "Besides, I'll have Colt to watch my back. Let's go kid."

They went back. There was no one on the street which by that point was lit with street lamps that hung from ornate poles and gave the city a dazzling effect that was completely different from the way it looked in the day time. Fear nagged at Colt and he could feel worry radiating from Wes. At the door to the storage unit Wes told Colt to keep watch.

"All frequencies," Wes concluded. "You get me?"

"Yes sir," Colt said.

He was leaning against the wall between the unit doors, trying to look bored. There was no one in sight in either direction. A few of the ships in the docking bay had lights on, but Colt couldn't sense anyone in the vessels. More than half of the port was empty anyway.

The door rumbled up after Wes unlocked it and they went inside. To Colt's surprise, Wes flicked on the overhead light, then shut the door again.

"Can you still sense the tracking device?" Wes asked.

Colt nodded. The captain pulled a small flashlight from his pocket and began looking around. "I don't see it," he said. "Must be somewhere in the pallet." He got down on his hands and knees and looked into the end of the pallet, where the loading forks were inserted. The dolly had loading forks and took up all the space on the opposite end of the pallet, but there was a little space on the end where Wes was looking.

He gave a low pitched whistle.

"What?" Colt asked.

"Question," Wes said, looking up at him. "Can you send a picture with your mind?"

CHAPTER 19

"I don't know," Colt admitted. "I've never tried."

"Well, get down here and take a look at this thing. I'm not sure I can detach it here. But I want you to send a picture of it to Di. We can take it off in the ship, but only if it will still work. I don't want whoever put it on the pallet to know we're on to them."

Colt got down on his hands and knees and looked inside the pallet. The tracking device was a small, round device that was stuck to the side of the outer pallet support. There were no lights or wires. Colt fixed the image in his mind and pushed it toward Di, unsure if she would see what he was seeing or not.

Whoa, that's strange, Di thought.

Colt heard her as if she were in the storage unit with them.

"I think she got it," Colt said.

"What's she think? Can we remove it?" Wes asked.

Di, can we remove a tracking device like this one? Colt asked.

Yes, it looks like it was built into the pallet but that type is made to be self contained.

Colt gave the captain a thumbs up.

"Alright, let's move. We see trouble, you run. We'll meet at the rendezvous."

"Yes sir," Colt said.

"Raise the door," Wes ordered. "Close and lock it behind us. We don't need to leave any obvious clue that we're in a hurry to leave."

"Got it," Colt said.

As Wes took hold on the dolly handle, Colt slid open the door. It rattled upward in its track. There was no one outside. Colt had scanned the area with his mind and shouldn't have been surprised, but he still half expected a small army with guns drawn to be waiting on them. The street was quiet and Wes didn't hesitate. He started pulling the heavy load. The dolly did the work. He had to steer it across the street to the dock. Colt yanked down the door and then scanned the key card. The lock cycled with an electronic *chunk!* sound. Then Colt followed, walking quickly but not running. He didn't want to look frightened, even though his heart was pounding in his chest and his legs were trembling.

"Almost there," Wes said.

Colt gave one last look backward. There was still no one following them. The only person he could sense with his mind was the Harbor Master who was watching a television show on his PA. It was quiet, almost peaceful, and as Wes maneuvered the load of Merconium into the airlock, Colt felt himself beginning to calm down. He started to feel as if everything really would be okay.

"There's not enough room for both of us," Wes said. "I'll go first."

Without waiting for Colt to reply, the captain stepped into the airlock and shut the door. At first Colt didn't realize what had happened. He saw the airlock close, but his mind wouldn't accept it. And then, with nothing else to do, he turned around and looked out past the dock, toward where the coffee shop was located. A man was sitting down with a cup of coffee. The ship beside Colt was humming, the sound growing louder as the quad engines were fed power. A light began to flash indicating an imminent departure.

Are they leaving me? Colt wondered, fear turning his insides into a quivering mass. He thought he would be sick. And the door opened. Colt felt like he couldn't move, but Wes grabbed him and tugged him inside. Just before the airlock closed, he saw the man at the coffee shop looking toward them.

"We're in," Wes said into his com-link. "Let's go."

"There's a man out there," Colt said. His voice sounded strange and his mouth was bone dry.

"Where?" Wes asked.

"The coffee shop," Colt said. "He just sat down, but he was looking this way."

"Did you get anything from him?" Wes asked.

The ship was pulling out of the dock, the clamps releasing, the magnetic seals around the airlock and loading ramp which they hadn't opened, popped off the hull. Colt reached out for the man and found him. But while he could sense the individual, he couldn't read his mind.

"No," Colt said. "I think he's blocking me."

Wes cursed, but Colt knew he wasn't mad at him. When the captain started for the stairs Colt followed. Without turning Wes shouted to Colt.

"Get that pallet cinched down," Wes ordered. "We lose that Merconium and we'll be out of business."

"Yes sir," Colt said turning back to the pallet.

The cargo bay floor had built in nodes for hooking the cargo netting. As the ship pulled away from the Jurgens Down space station, Colt found cargo straps and ratchet devices. He hooked in one side of the straps to the floor, then pulled the bright yellow straps over the load of Merconium. The ratchet straps hooked into the floor on the far side of the pallet, and Colt fed the straps into the mechanism. He cranked the handle on the ratchet back and forth until the straps pulled taut. A net went over the load next and was hooked down in front and back, as well as on both sides. There was no need to tighten the net, it was just there as a precaution to keep the cargo from spilling out everywhere in the event of a disaster.

Colt double checked his work, and was about to head up to the Bridge, when he heard someone behind him. Without really thinking about it he had raised his mental barriers once he went into the ship. He didn't want to hear what his crew mates were thinking. In fact, he just felt a strange sense of revolving emotions. Fear was the most dominate. Having been left out of the airlock Colt was certain he didn't want to be left behind. Perhaps he had forged a bond with the ship and it's crew in the void left by his mother when Colt had fled from his home space port. He couldn't begin to understand why he felt like he did about the *Jolly Rogue* but he knew he didn't want to be abandoned. Fear was followed by doubts. Had he missed something, some important clue that would reveal the danger they were in, or who was tracking them. Colt couldn't help but fear they were following him. It was the GA's clandestine service, just like the book he had read a sample of before the agents had buzzed the intercom at his apartment door. After fear came intense curiosity. Had the man at the coffee shop been a Reader? There was no way to know. Colt knew almost nothing about the power he possessed. And finally, he felt relieved. They were safe, leaving Jurgen Downs for outer space, and yet that relief was quickly overshadowed by fear again. He was so wrapped up in his own thoughts and emotions he didn't notice Zora approaching until he turned around and saw her standing a few paces away.

"Can you read my thoughts," she asked in a quiet voice. There was nothing small or weak about it, just quiet. Colt felt an electric jolt of excitement shoot through him. He couldn't keep from smiling even though he feared that he looked foolish.

"I never would," Colt promised.

Zora nodded, then stepped away, between two tall stacks of magnesium. She wasn't moving toward the stairs, and Colt was tempted to follow her, but his feet felt heavy and he didn't want to seem desperate. He managed to step to the gap between the stacks of cargo, but Zora was gone. She was like a ghost when she wanted to be. Still, she had spoken to him, and he felt like he was walking on air as he headed for the stairs.

CHAPTER 20

"We all secure down there?" Wes asked when Colt appeared on deck.

"Yes sir," the kid replied.

Wes knew he would go down and check the kid's work. Colt had a lot of enthusiasm and almost no experience. He needed time, and Wes would give it to him, but he feared that Colt wasn't in it for the long haul. "Outstanding. Stu, how long until our first jump is ready?"

There was no reply from the navigator, who was sitting at his console and staring at the computer screen. Their on board computer could do the advanced mathematics needed to calculate a hyperspace jump, but it wasn't built for that kind of high level computing. It was an operational system that regulated the quad engines and thrusters, ran radar, communications, and life support. Tasking the system with calculating a hyperspace jump took the other systems off line until it could finish, and the machine took twice as long as Stu, who not only did the math in his head, he had memorized much of the galaxy's published trade routes. He could get them just about anywhere, including off the beaten path to avoid the blockade when they needed to make a run across to the Alliance of Free Worlds space.

Still, there was no rushing him. Once he began the advanced computations for a jump, he wouldn't do anything else until he was finished.

"Don't rush him," Di chided from her seat.

"Fine, but I want to make an unscheduled stop," Wes said.

"Where?" Saide asked.

"Maker's Point," Wes said.

"You know how to get a lady's attention," Di said. "You are talking my language. What are we looking for? I saw a desalinator back at Jurgen Downs. I think I could build one with the right parts."

"We're dropping off, not picking up," Wes said.

"Are we trading?" Saide said.

Wes knew that Saide meant dealing Colt to someone. It wasn't unthinkable when a person considered how much a level four reader was worth on the free market. Wes couldn't exactly blame Ilk Saide. The Hyborians had completely different ethics than most humans. They were pure capitalists. Little things like ethics were of no concern to a Hyborian. Saide wanted two things in life. First, he wanted to fly, and not just any ship. He wanted to pilot a Hyborian vessel. It was a point of pride for Saide that he was the *Jolly Rogue's* pilot. Second, he wanted money. How they earned it was of little concern to Saide. He wasn't willing to do something that would mark him as a criminal for the rest of his days, but he had no qualms about running the blockade. And while piloting the *Jolly Rogue* didn't earn him the kind of paydays he wished for, Ilk Saide would sacrifice his second desire to ensure the first.

"No," Di said flatly. "I'll have no part in that."

Wes glanced at Colt who was watching the display screens. He seemed completely unaware that they were talking about him. Wes was once again struck by how believable Colt was as the naive teenager. The kid had no clue that he was worth hundreds of thousands of credits to the right people. Not that Wes would sell him. In his mind, that was dirty money and he wanted no part of trafficking human beings.

"We aren't trading," Wes said. "But we are going to move that tracking device."

"Why not just throw it out the airlock and be done with it?" Saide said.

"Because if we do that whoever put it there will know that we're on to them," Wes said.

"You want to put it on another ship," Di said.

"That's right, just a little mis-direction. We'll stop long enough to get rid of the tracker and then we'll continue our run."

"Fine, but we've got to make it convincing," Di said. "Zora and I just need two hours."

"If she's getting off ship, so am I," Saide said. "I need provisions."

Wes tried not to shudder at the thought. He like meat as much as the next guy, but preferred his butchered humanely and cooked. Saide ate his rodents while they were still alive.

"No problem," Wes said. "Colt and Stu can look after the ship."

"Speaking of provisions," Di said, getting to her feet. "My bagels are upstairs. You're all welcome to try one, but don't waste them. Colt?"

"Sure," he said.

"Wait a second, did you run the pre-jump diagnostics?" Wes asked.

"What do I look like, rookie?" Di said. "Of course I ran them. This ship is a well oiled machine, green across the board."

"What about fuel?"

"We have plenty. Stop worrying," Di said. "You should come up and have a bagel with me."

"I'll see to our first jump," Wes said. "But thank you."

"Suit yourself."

Wes watched Di and Colt leave the Bridge. He felt a twinge of jealousy. They would be enjoying delicious baked goods while he worried on the Bridge, but that was a captain's job. His crew trusted him, and he refused to let them down. Besides, even if he were upstairs eating he wouldn't be able to relax. Not until he knew who was tracking him and why. Was it the same people who had commissioned him to find Celeste Pierre? He couldn't say. A tiny part of him worried that Colt secretly worked for the same group and that he was there to do some terrible deed that would silence them forever once the missing girl was found. He felt a slight burning sensation in his stomach. It wasn't hunger, but more of a stress related ailment. There were too many possibilities and it didn't help that Colt was so powerful. It was possible that the kid could turn their minds into jelly before Wes even knew what was happening. That kind of thing made it impossible to let his guard down, even if having it up wouldn't save him.

The truth was, Wes didn't think Colt was a plant. He wanted to believe the kid, and Colt was certainly convincing. Yet the odds against him were just too high to ignore. Anyone with the power that Colt possessed couldn't possibly just wander onto his ship. It was like winning the galactic lottery, still possible but not probable. And Wes wasn't sure it was a fortunate circumstance. The longer Wes was part of the crew the more they would think of him as family. Once that happened, there would be no getting rid of Colt O'Connor. But once the word got out about the kid's abilities, and word always got out, there was no such thing as a secret anymore, the GA and every criminal they crossed paths with would be trying to get their hands on him. And no one on that list would hesitate to murder Wes, his entire crew, and/or destroy the *Jolly Rogue*. That thought made his stomach burn again.

"Trajectory calculated and transition... prepared," Stu announced suddenly.

"Where are we going?" Wes asked.

"First jump is to the Achillies... Cluster," Stu said, wrestling with the words.

"I need us to swing over to Maker's Point," Wes said. "Can we do that?"

"T-t-twelve... hours," Stu stuttered. "That's how much l-longer it will... take."

"Okay, we can manage that," Wes said, thinking about what DeVoors had told him. They had three days to reach Kellar Nine and move their product. It was just enough to make the detour to Maker's Point. As long as they didn't have any other trouble along the way. The pain in his stomach returned and Wes grimaced. Who was he fooling, trouble was their middle name.

CHAPTER 21

"Have you ever had a bagel?" Di asked.

"Sure," Colt replied. "A time or two."

"These are the best," Di went on. "Blueberry, sweet onion, poppyseed, pumpernickel, and everything bagels. And we have fresh cream cheese too, not the over processed paste you usually get, but made fresh and hand delivered. There's fresh fruit too, strawberries and blueberries. You're going to love it."

Colt enjoyed fresh food whenever he could get it, but he had grown up on a space station with no animals. When meat or produce was brought up, it was usually frozen, dehydrated, or canned. And in most cases it was cheeper to buy processed food ingredients, such as protein and carbohydrates in powder or wafer form that could be mixed with flavor crystals to taste similar to freshly prepared food. In reality it was a poor imitation, but served the purpose of fueling the body. Colt had worked in a pizza restaurant as a dishwasher. The pizza crust had been baked using powdered eggs, and milk, which gave the pizza a bland taste. The toppings were either protein imitations or rehydrated. The cheese was made from powder too, but like most things it was passable once it had all gone through the oven.

Di cut through the first bagel and gave half to Colt. She slathered hers with cream cheese and then added the fresh blueberries. Colt followed her example and was just about to taste the bagel when Zora appeared. She reminded him of a cat. Zora came up from below, stopped long enough to survey what was happening in the galley, then moved through into the engineering space.

"She doesn't talk much at first," Di said after swallowing a bite. "But she'll warm up to you. Give her time."

"Sure," Colt said. He had been thinking that it was strange how Zora rarely ever spoke. And for a moment he wondered if Di could read his mind.

"Try the bagel," she said with a grin.

He took a bite. The bagel was soft, but substantial at the same time. There was a yeasty flavor to it, and the cream cheese was light and tangy. Di had been right, he enjoyed the bagel very much. They sat quietly, enjoying the freshly baked treats for a few moments.

"How old are you?" Di finally asked.

"Sixteen," Colt said.

"I think Zora is about your age."

"Are you her mother?"

"Me?" Di asked with a giggle. "Oh, no, I never had kids and don't plan to. Not that I don't like them, but I've been around radiation most of my life. Not enough to hurt me, but enough keep me from having kids."

"What happened to her parents?" Colt asked.

"Di pressed her lips together as she considered her answer. "They aren't here," she said. "There's a story there, but it's not mine to tell. Suffice it to say that we took her aboard a few years ago. Wes has a soft spot for hard luck cases. But I guess you know that."

"He doesn't really trust me."

"Captain Wesley Hanzor doesn't trust anyone. He's old school, a jack of all trades master of none. He got this ship running though. Bought her cheap when most folks just saw a hunk of space junk. Then he found a crew. I've been with him since the beginning. We flew charters for a while, even hauled bio-waste, whatever it took to keep flying and make improvements. But he's on your side, kid, never doubt it. Even if it's only to stick it to the GA."

"He said the ship is off the grid?" Colt asked. "What does that mean?"

"You know there are two big organizations that try to manage space travel. The GA is one, they've got their giant nose in everyone's business. Do you know what the other is?"

"The Space Transport Union?"

"Bingo. Sounds like your education on Helix Prime wasn't a complete waste," she said with a smile. "The space union is essentially a huge monopoly. They control the hyperspace network. Most ships have a special computer, bought at three times what it's worth, just to connect to the Hyp-Net since they run it on their own operating system. It was started to stablize space travel, back when there were different ways to break the speed of light barrier. They lobbied for one consistent FTL drive and a single source of coordinating interstellar flight."

"You're talking about hyperspace drive engines," Colt said.

"Exactly. They convinced the GA to essentially outlaw every other type of faster than light travel. And since they built the Hyp-Net, they have complete control of it. For access, they require a ship to be registered with their union, including yearly dues. They put tracking software on their nav computers, ostensibly to keep track of the ships and avoid accidents. But it wasn't long until they were working with the GA to keep up with who was where and why. Anyone who didn't like the way the STU did things were banned from the major space ports, or charged double the docking fees. Fuel and work was harder to get, not to mention the need for a dedicated navigation computer which is expensive. Wes won't join the STU, and he is firmly against the Galactic Authority's need to control everyone. So we run supplies from the GA side of space to the Alliance of Free Worlds."

"You're blockade runners," Colt said with enthusiasm.

"Bet your boots we are," Di said. "And there aren't many of us left. To get past the blockade you have to operate outside the dedicated trade routes, which wouldn't be a big deal except that the STU and GA have now classified the space maps around Alliance space. Most people have to jump blind, which is incredibly dangerous. The GA even has interdictor ships that can pull a vessel out of hyperspace. Lucky for us, Stu had dozens of routes into Alliance space memorized. He's a genius and another of Wes' hard luck cases."

"How does he do it?" Colt asked.

"No one knows. Some people on the autism scale have no abilities. Others, like Stu, struggle with simple tasks like talking, but have savant capabilities. Stu is a human computing machine, but the GA wanted to put him in a home despite his incredible abilities. Wes rescued him and put him to work."

"That's pretty cool," Colt said, imagining the captain rescuing Stewart from a heinous Galactic Authority facility.

"If you're honest," Di said, "and don't mind working hard, you'll be fine here. You want to see the engineering space? It's where the magic happens."

"Sure," Colt said, secretly thinking what he really wanted was to see Zora again.

The engineering space was impressive, even though there was a lot that Colt didn't understand. The *Jolly Rogue* had four engines mounted on rotating arms that could turn a full three hundred and sixty degrees and allowed the ship to fly both in space and in atmosphere.

"She burns a lot of fuel in atmo," Di pointed out. "And this is the hyperdrive."

To Colt, it looked like an old industrial washing machine, not too different than the one in his basement back home.

"We just put a new power converter on her," Di said. "She needs a complete overhaul, but that takes time and we're still looking for a few more parts. Maybe we'll get lucky at Maker's Point."

Colt saw the system that combined hydrogen and oxygen to make water that was pure enough to drink, but it was unreliable and needed repairs. The ship also had a waste water system that recycled their water supply which could then be used in the ship's human waste system.

"Everything is recyclable," Di said. "The key to space travel is learning how to use things over and over again. When the water is too contaminated to use anymore, it gets split in the reactor back into hydrogen and oxygen."

Colt did his best to seem interested. He had learned about chemical reactions and their uses in space travel when he was in school. Seeing it in action was fascinating, and yet his mind kept wandering back to the girl in the corner. Zora sat on a stool by a work bench nibbling on a bagel which she was pulling apart one pinch at a time. She seemed happy enough, and completely oblivious to Colt or Diana. He thought Zora was captivating and had trouble not stealing glances at her.

It wasn't long before Wes appeared in the doorway that separated the engineering section from the galley. "Mind if I get a bagel?"

"Sure," Diana replied. "I'll give you a hand."

She followed him out of engineering and Colt was alone with Zora. He tried to be calm as he approached her and moved slowly. The last thing he wanted was to weird her out. Girls he had known back on the space port at Helix Prime often treated him as if he were a complete idiot. Ignoring him was the standard operating procedure, especially for the pretty girls who hung out in groups and intimidated any boy who tried to approach them.

When Zora didn't look up from her bagel Colt wasn't surprised. He wanted to talk to her, but he also wanted to respect her silence. Di had told him she would warm up to him, but he doubted that. Still, it was enough just to be close to her. And then to his surprise he heard her humming. It was soft, so soft at first that he thought he was hearing things, or that some strange signal was getting through his mental barriers. But then he realized it was Zora, humming the tune of a song he didn't recognize. He leaned against the workbench and looked at the tools and component parts, but really he was just listening to Zora. She raised her hand and deftly smoothed her dark hair behind her ear, and Colt saw that she had on tiny ear buds. She was listening to something and humming along. Maybe that was why she wasn't talking, he surmised, and why she hadn't fled the engineering bay. She didn't even know he was there.

Before he knew it Wes was at the doorway again, a half eaten bagel in his hand. "Colt, let's check your work down stairs."

He ducked back out and Colt stood up, wishing he had more time with Zora. They hadn't spoken but he liked listening to her hum. For the first time she notice he was there. Her hand went up and tapped the ear bud, pausing her music. There was just the slightest flush to her face and Colt guessed she was a little embarrassed that he had heard her humming.

"I'm leaving," he said. "Sorry."

She didn't reply, but the look on her face wasn't unkind. He imagined that she wanted him to stay just as much he did. It was a pleasant thought and it gave him comfort, even if he was just imaging things.

CHAPTER 22

They reached Maker's Point nearly twenty-four hours after leaving Jurgen Downs. Stu had calculated two jumps from the Trindell system, which consisted of two tiny planets too close to the system star to be inhabited. Maker's Point was an old space station. It had started as a scientific outpost, and was later expanded to be a trading port, but as the routes through space shifted, Maker's Point was left abandoned. For decades salvage operators had used the old space port to tear the derelict spacecraft they acquired apart. Eventually the space between the station and the system star became a ring of space junk, or a vast interstellar junk yard. And the station became a haven for people looking for salvage parts. Dealers who collected second-hand tech also took up residence in the station. It was a mecca for those who preferred to build things themselves or repair old technology rather than buy new.

The crew of the *Jolly Rouge* had just under twenty-four hours to deliver their load of magnesium and merconium. Running the blockade forced them off the trade routes and through empty space. The first jump would last eighteen hours. The second would take ten hours, and leave them a couple of hours outside of Kellar Nine. With that timeline in mind, Wes had no intention of dilly-dallying in Maker's Point. He had promised Di two hours and given her the last of their petty credits, a little over twelve hundred credits after saving a thousand on the merconium in Jurgen Downs. Wes reminded himself to thank Colt when he got back to the ship, but his first priority was to move the tracking device.

Di had taken nearly two hours to remove it from the pallet of merconium. She couldn't tell if it was still activated, but Colt swore that it was. Wes still wasn't certain the boy wasn't playing them. He'd never heard of a Reader who could sense electronic impulses, and tracking devices were built to be low frequency. The one he carried sent a compressed signal every sixty seconds. The communications equipment on board the *Jolly Rouge* couldn't even pick it up and they were looking for it. If the entire thing was a hoax meant to endear Colt to the crew it was working.

Stu was indifferent, but the navigator was busy showing off his collection of music CDs when Wes disembarked. Diana was taken with him. Wes attributed her affection for the kid to her maternal instincts and the fact that she knew it got under his skin. Saide still had his doubts and wasn't ashamed of his desire to sell Colt to the highest bidder. Even Zora had come around, tolerating Colt's presence. The kid followed her like a lost puppy every chance he got. Wes tried to keep him busy, but the kid was a terrific worker. The cargo area was ship shape, and his cabin was tidy. They needed to move the junk out of it, but Colt didn't seem to mind. He did dishes without complaint, and hadn't argued when Wes informed he needed to stay on board while they were docked at Maker's Point.

He walked down the docking arm corridor. Maker's point was built like a giant wagon wheel, with docking ports standing out from the space station's hub in the center. No one lived on the station anymore, but there were dozens of ships docked at the station that never left, their owners using them as private quarters rather than space vessels. Di and Zora, having agreed to their two hour time limit, had rushed ahead, anxious to shop in the crowded market where vendors set up tables and booths to hawk their wares. Wes had different plans. He was looking for someone who had already made their purchase and was on their way out of the system. Someone with a piece of equipment where they might not notice a tracking device for a while. He reached the center hub of the station without seeing someone he could pass the tracker off to.

There were people everywhere in the center hub where the main trading floor was kept. Wes took a set of stairs up to the upper level which was open and allowed a person to look down on the trade floor. The second level was essentially a food court. Most of the offerings were repackaged meals, but it was the drinks that people came for. Space was an excellent place to brew spirits of all kinds and there were several distinguished distilleries housed on the station. Wes found his favorite, a company called Two Fisted Black Eyed Mary. They sold bottles of sour mash bourbon. He picked one up, after ordering a tumbler with two fingers of the ardent spirit. One sip left his tongue tingling and his throat burning. The first drink wasn't pleasant until the liquor hit his stomach and began to relax him. With his taste buds numb from the first sip, the following drinks went down easy. But Wes paced himself. More than one tumbler would begin to impair his decision making and he needed a clear head.

The waitress, a young woman with low waisted pants and a

shirt that was too short, exposing her midriff with an exotic looking belly button ring and a colorful tattoo on her back, brought him a glass of water to chase his bourbon. He gave her a hundred credit chip from his personal finances. It didn't leave much for a tip, but he wasn't a high maintenance customer. He was halfway finished with his drink when he spotted the perfect mark. A pair of spacers pushing a refrigeration unit from the trade floor on a furniture dolly. It was a big piece of equipment and Wes knew the pair. They flew an older Huntington Retriever salvage ship.

Wes threw back the rest of the bourbon, setting his throat and stomach on fire. The pain he'd felt the day before had subsided, but reappeared when the large gulp of bourbon hit his stomach. He stood up, took a few swallows of water, then set the cup on the table. The waitress nodded at him, and Wes hurried for the stairs. By the time he reached the main level, the two spacers with the refrigeration unit had entered a docking corridor. Wes followed. He didn't have to move faster than a brisk walk to catch the pair, who were encumbered with the large piece of equipment.

"Andre, Persephone?" Wes said. "What is that monstrosity?"

The spacers, a man and woman, stopped walking. The woman looked slightly annoyed, but she wasn't pushing the refrigeration unit. The man looked relieved to have an excuse to stop pushing the heavy piece of machinery.

"Wes Hanzor, you scoundrel. It's been a long time," Andre said.

"Too long," Wes replied. "I have to keep moving just to earn enough for fuel and air."

"Tell me about it," Andre said.

"Whatever you're selling, we aren't interested," Persephone said. "And we have to keep moving. We're on a schedule."

"Let me help," Wes said. "I'm docked on this arm."

It was a lie, and he hoped that they wouldn't call him on it. Persephone was a stern woman, and trusted people even less than Wes did. But Andre looked relieved. He stepped to one side of the refrigeration unit to give Wes space. The captain of the *Jolly Rogue* put one hand on the back of the machine and palmed the tracking device before raising his other hand to the corner of the refrigeration unit.

"Alright," Andre said. "Thanks for the help."

"Any time," Wes said, before whispering, "she still busting your chops?"

"Keeps me honest," Andre said with a chuckle.

The unit they were pushing was heavy and cumbersome. Persephone was walking ahead of them, sometimes guiding them if they needed to move around something in the corridor. There was no shortage of supplies piled up by airlocks, and more than a few destitute spacers passed out on the deck. Wes slipped the tracking device into a crevice behind the heat exchange. The small disk was held in place by a magnet. When they reached the salvage ship Wes offered to help them get the unit inside, but Persephone refused.

"No one goes on our ship," she said. "Never."

"It's nothing personal," Andre said. "You know how it is. We have to watch out for stowaways and pirates."

"I completely understand. My back will probably thank you tomorrow," Wes said jovially.

"And mind will be killing me," Andre said. "It's good to see you. Touch base when you're out this way again, we'll have a drink."

He pointed at the bottle of bourbon Wes had sticking out of his jacket pocket. Persephone rolled her eyes, which only made Wes grin. "You bet," he told Andre.

To complete the ruse he had to continue strolling up the wrong docking arm. He went all the way to the end before turning back. There was no doubt that Persephone would be watching for him. If she saw him coming back, even if he had a believable excuse, she would suspect something was up. The last thing Wes wanted was for the spacers to find the tracking device. He hadn't come twelve hours out of his way for nothing. Fortunately, but the time he turned around Andre had the refrigeration unit inside their ship and Persephone had closed down the airlock. Wes had no idea how a friendly guy like Andre could live with a hard nosed woman like Persephone. It made Wes thankful for Diana.

When he got back to the hub he saw Di and Zora. They had a rolling cart full of items. Most were old tech, but there were a few tools as well. Strangely enough, there were also clothes.

"What's going on here?" Wes asked as he approached.

"We're finished," Di said. "We hit the jackpot."

"Okay, I can't wait to hear about it," Wes said. "But what's with the clothes?"

"They're for Colt. We had some extra money, and there's a second hand shop. Zora picked out a few outfits, nothing too extravagant."

"I guess the kid could use a change of clothes," Wes said.

"He had to borrow one of my coveralls just so that he could wash his one outfit," Di said. "I don't mind, but you know he needs something of his own. Besides, he saved us some money on Jurgen Downs."

"I'm not complaining," Wes said.

They started for the docking corridor, Wes pushing the cart for them.

"Looks like you got what you came here for," Di said, giving the bottle of bourbon a light thump. Her nail clinked against the glass.

"I'm a man of opportunity," Wes said. "It's one of the things you find charming about me."

Di laughed and Wes thought he saw the slightest little grin at the corners of Zora's mouth. He was about to crack another joke when someone grabbed his jacket from behind and spun him around.

"Hey!" Wes said, just before a burly man drove his fist into Wes's stomach.

The air shot out of his lungs and he crumpled to his knees, gasping for air. The burly man tried to knock Di aside, but she ducked under his blow, then sprang up and jabbed him hard in the throat with her fingers bent but stiff. The burly man squawked and staggered back, but Di wasn't finished. She kicked him hard between his thick legs and he crumped to the ground. In her anger she moved to finish him with a devastating kick to his face but another man stopped her with his blaster. The shot was vibrate blue, a stun beam that caught her in the chest.

"No!" Zora screamed.

Wes looked up and recognized the man. It was Paxton Miller. His hair was so thin it laid across his bald pate in thin, greasy lines. He had a pot belly, and bowlegs. One eye was slightly crossed, and his beard was patchy, but there was no mistaking him. He stepped forward and grabbed Zora by the arm. She went rigid at his touch, a look of absolute horror on her face. Paxton didn't point the gun at her, but kept it trained on Wes. The captain was calculating his chances of getting his own weapon out and getting off a round before Paxton saw him, but the cross-eyed deviant was focused on him. So focused he didn't notice when Zora tapped the com-link on her jacket collar.

"You tried to steal my property, Hanzor," Paxton snarled.

"She's a human being," Wes said. "Her name is Zora. You should know that you pig. You named her."

"Shut it, you scumbag. One twitch of my thumb and this blaster goes from stun, to kill. You know I'll do it. Hell... I'd enjoy it."

"She doesn't want to go with you," Wes said.

"You think I give a damn what she wants?" Paxton said. "This little tramp is mine, ain't nobody gonna say..."

His voice trailed off, and his eyes took on a vacant look. Wes wasn't sure what was happening but then Saide hurried up the corridor. He had a blaster in one hand, and a traditional double ended Krigger knife in the other.

"Wes?"

"Get Di," the captain said slowly as he tapped his thumb and pinky together and stood up.

The barrel of his hidden blaster extended slightly from the sleeve of his jacket.

"This is for you," Paxton said, handing his blaster to Zora.

She took it in a trembling hand. He let go of her and she stepped away from him. It was painful to see her so frightened.

"Go!" Wes hissed at her, his chest aching from the blow the burly man had hit him with.

Wes moved over to where Saide was bent over Di. She was completely unconscious. Saide slid his knife into a sheath at his back. He still held his blaster ready, but took Di by the arm. Wes took her other arm and they lifted her up. He could feel the muscle beneath her baggy sweat shirt. Her head lolled forward and a hot sense of fury rolled through Wes. He wanted to shoot Paxton Miller, but his hidden blaster had only one setting, and it wasn't stun. If Wes killed Paxton, with fifty or sixty spacers watching, half of whom agreed with the pasty haired deviant that a child was a man's private property, he would be ostracized from the people he did business with on a regular basis.

It was so tempting to pull the trigger anyway, but Wes held himself back. And then, to his surprise, the burly man stood up. His wide back was to Wes and Saide who were moving slowly down the corridor with Di. She gave a moan just as the big man lumbered toward Paxton, who shook his head and looked around in surprise. He caught sight of Wes leaving.

"Joss, get out of the way!" Paxton shouted at the big man.

He started to point his blaster at Wes, who was raising his own weapon. But before either of them could take aim, the big man Paxton called Joss leaped on him. Wes and Saide stopped and watched in awe, as the burly man crushed Paxton to the deck, then rose up and began dropping his massive fists onto his helpless victim like an angry god meting out judgement.

Wes tapped his thumb and pinky together again, retracting his hidden blaster, and pulled Diana's arm over his shoulders. He slid his hand down to her waist and grabbed on tightly. They hurried back down the corridor.

"What just happened back there?" Saide said.

"Paxton hit us from behind," Wes said. "Sucker punched me. Stunned Diana. They were taking Zora. Where'd you come from?"

"We heard Paxton threaten you on the com-link," Saide said. "Where's Colt?"

"Still on the ship with Stu," Saide said. "I came running as soon as I heard you were in trouble."

"I appreciate it," Wes said.

"But that doesn't explain what happened?" Saide said.

"I don't know what happened," Wes said as they approached the airlock. It was already open and they shuffled through with

Diana. "But I have an idea. Get us out of here, before Paxton comes after us again."

"I don't think that's going to happen," Saide said. "That big beast was trying to kill Paxton."

Wes understood what his pilot meant. The brute named Joss had beaten Paxton mercilessly. The last thing Wes had seen of the pair was the big man's bloody fist raising up. Blood had flung from the massive fist, and Wes had experienced the man's power. It was an image that was burned into his brain.

The airlock cycled and Saide ran for the stairs, as Wes pulled Diana into the cargo bay. She was still out of it, but trying to walk as she leaned heavily on him and moaned in pain. Getting stunned was no picnic. The electrical charge spasmed every muscle and left the victim exhausted. It usually took at least half an hour for a person to come around after getting stunned. And if the victim fell, they could break a bone, or smash their face on the ground. Fortunately, Di had fallen backward. She would probably have hit her head on the metal deck plates, but she wasn't bleeding. He would have to give her a thorough examination when he had time, but he needed to get her to a safe place first. Her cabin would be best, but he wasn't sure he could get her up the stairs alone.

Zora appeared. She was pale and trembling, but came to his aid as he approached the spiral staircase. She didn't speak and Wes could see that she had been crying.

"We're leaving," Wes said as they started up the stairs. "I'm sorry."

They continued up in silence. Wes' body ached from the punch, and his stomach was on fire. It felt like there was a blowtorch inside him. He groaned in pain, and Di moaned. Zora took a shuttering breath and Wes knew she was on the verge of breaking down in tears again. He didn't blame her. They had rescued the young girl from a life of bondage and abuse at the hands of her sick father. He couldn't say for certain, but he imagined her biggest fear was being captured by him again. It infuriated Wes that he had almost let it happen. Zora was closest to Di, but Wes cared for her like a little sister. Protecting her was paramount, but he had let his guard down. And the truth was, he hadn't thought of her deviant father as a real threat. It had almost cost him dearly.

"You stay with her," Wes gasped as they got Di to her cabin and laid her on the bed. "I'll be right back."

Zora didn't respond, but she sat beside Di and held her hand. Wes left them there and rushed down the hallway to the Bridge. Stu was rocking in his chair, the way he did when he was nervous. Saide was in the pilot's seat, and one glance at the huge display screens showed him they were already leaving the dock.

Wes turned to where Colt was sitting. He was slumped in his chair, his eyes closed. The kid's skin was pale and his lips were blue. His hair was wet with sweat and clung to his forehead. Wes moved over to him.

"Colt," Wes said, "are you okay?"

"Saved... you!" Stu said, nearly choking on the words.

"He sure did," Wes agreed, but from the looks of things the effort had cost him.

Wes knew that some Readers grew stronger over time. And from what he'd seen happen on the space station with Paxton Miller and his strong man Joss, it was clear that Colt was not just an L4, he had moved on to L5 and controlling people with his mind.

CHAPTER 23

"Come on kid, wake up," Wes said, but his voice sounded strange and far away.

Colt opened his eyes slightly and saw the captain's face. He was bending down and looking at Colt closely.

"I'm okay," Colt mumbled.

"Alright, stay right here," Wes said. "You did good."

Wes squeezed Colt's shoulder and then hurried away. Colt tried to remember what had happened. He had heard the man threatening Wes on the com-link. Saide had rushed off the ship, and Colt had opened his mental defenses. It had only taken a moment to find Wes. In his rush to help, Colt had touched Zora's mind, but it was blank with an overwhelming fear. And then he had touched the mind of Paxton Miller. The memory of it was sickening. He felt like his stomach might revolt and he thrust the memory away, but not before the images flashed in his mind. They were memories of his daughter, but they were ghastly. Colt understood why Zora was cautious, and why Wes had rescued her in the first place.

He shivered with revulsion, and fatigue. After the shock he had pushed his will onto the man, if he could truly be called a man. He was a monster, and all that Colt could think was that he couldn't let him hurt Zora ever again. What happened after that was hazy. It had taken all Colt's concentration and strength. He felt as if he had run, not just jogged, but run at a full sprint until he dropped from total exhaustion. Moving was difficult. His mouth was so dry his tongue felt swollen. It was hard to open his eyes more than just a crack.

Wes returned with a bottle of electrolytes in a fruity drink. He helped Colt take a sip. The drink was cold and sweet. It revived him and he felt immediately better, but also desperate for more. He reached out with shaking hands and took the bottle.

"Slow," Wes said. "Just sip it. You drink it too fast and you might be sick."

"Okay," Colt replied.

"When you're up to it," Wes said, "go to your cabin. If you're too shaky I'll be back to help you."

Colt nodded and Wes stood up straight.

"How far are we from our first jump?" the captain asked.

"Twenty-three hundred kilometers," Saide said. "We'll transition is forty-seven minutes."

"How long will we be in hyperspace?"

"Eighteen... hours," Stu managed to say.

"That's right, okay. Good. We all need some rest. Saide, you've got the first watch. I'll relieve you in a couple of hours. Stu, can you watch Colt? Maybe help him to his cabin."

"Sh-sh-sure," Stu said.

"Okay, the Bridge is yours Saide," Wes said.

"I've got this, Cap. No problem," Saide replied.

Wes gave Colt one last look. Colt raised the bottle he was

drinking from. "I'm fine," he croaked. Wes nodded and hurried out.

Colt didn't move. He sat in his chair and sipped the fruity beverage until they made the jump to hyperspace. Once he finished the drink he felt like he had enough strength to get to his feet. It was difficult, his legs were shaky and weak. He leaned against the console, then pushed off it and lurched toward the corridor that led from the Bridge back to their cabins. Stu joined him. He had trouble communicating, and didn't like to be touched, but he grabbed Colt's arm and marched him down the corridor, humming the tune to one of his old songs. With his free hand Colt steadied himself against the bulkhead of the corridor. The metal was cold and Colt was suddenly aware that only a few inches of hull separated him from the void of space. It was a sobering realization.

Stu helped Colt to his cabin. They passed through the stacks of junk and to the bed. Colt didn't bother getting undressed. He just dropped down on the bed, his body yearning for sleep. He leaned over and let his head fall into the pillow. The musty smell of the pillow case was welcome to him. He felt safe in the *Jolly Rogue* and it was a good feeling. Stu unlaced his boots and took them off. Then he draped a blanket over Colt and left, turning out the light.

The bathroom door was cracked open, the light inside spilled out in a soft glow. Colt lay on his side, surprised that sleep didn't immediately over take him. His body was still coming back from the strain of pushing his mind and will into Paxton and then the big man named Joss. Colt didn't want to think about it. He didn't want to feel the hate and sadistic desire of Zora's father, but it was impossible not to. Laying in the darkness of his cabin, it felt like Paxton's evil heart might swallow him alive.

He was surprised when the door to his cabin opened, but not frightened. It closed and Colt couldn't see who was in his room. Someone was approaching his bed, a shadow in the darkness. so quiet that he wondered if perhaps he was asleep. She didn't say anything at first, just sat on the edge of his bed. Colt didn't speak either, but he summoned what little strength he had left and scooted back, making room for her. Zora lay down, her back to him. Colt lifted the blanket and she pushed herself into him. He draped the blanket over her, and put his arm on hers. Zora was trembling with fear, he could feel it coming off her in waves, even with his mental barriers up. They lay there together for a few minutes, neither speaking. Colt felt himself relaxing. She was the good thing he had discovered even though his life had become chaos. And she anchored him in the darkness. The evil he feared seemed powerless when she appeared in his room.

"Thank you," she whispered after a while. "Thank you for saving me."

Colt wasn't sure how to respond, but Zora took his hand and pulled his arm around her shoulder. She held his hands in both of hers, and they fell asleep together.

CHAPTER 24

Wes was in a chair beside Di's bed. His whole body hurt, and his gut was on fire. But it was his mind that was hurting him the most. He couldn't help but wonder if Colt had lied to him, if he had pretended not to be as strong as he was just to set the crew at ease. A level five Reader was ultra rare, and it seemed impossible that Colt's story was true. Yet the kid was so earnest that Wes was baffled. Was he an enemy agent, a plant to spy on them, or just a confused kid who had stumbled onto their ship out of desperation?

"What happened?" Di said. "This hangover is killing me."

"You got shot with a stun blaster," Wes said. "You fell and hit your head."

"Lucky me," Di said.

"It is lucky," Wes said. "You could have been killed."

"That might have been better. I feel like the ship just ran me down. Everything hurts."

"Did you hear me?" Wes asked, his voice shaking.

He and Di were lovers, but they were casual about their feelings. Shipboard romance was a cliche, but almost impossible when people were cooped up on a ship together. Still, they tried their best to keep things professional when they weren't together in the privacy of their cabins. The last thing either of them wanted was to make the rest of the crew uncomfortable.

"I heard you," she said softly. "I'm sorry. Now tell me what happened. Did you kill him?"

"Paxton? No, I didn't. He had the jump on me."

"Dear God, tell me he didn't get Zora. I'll kill him myself, that sleazy scrap of human—"

"She's fine," Wes said. "Paxton didn't hurt her. She's safe on board with us."

"How?"

"Colt," Wes said. "The kid's an L-5 Di. He took control of Paxton so that Zora could get away. And then..."

"Then what?"

"Then he took bodily control of that big thug who hit me," Wes explained. "He turned him on Paxton and I don't know what happened, but I think he may have beaten the old man to death."

"Good," Diana replied. "It's what he deserved. In fact, that monster got off easy in my book."

"Diana, did you hear me? Colt took control of another person's body against their will."

"I heard you," she replied. "He did it for Zora. I'm not surprised. I've seen the way he looks at her."

"You're okay with this?" Wes asked, grimacing as a searing pain flared in his stomach.

"Am I okay with the newest member of our crew saving all our lives from a sadistic, twisted, madman. Let me see... YES!"

"That's not exactly the whole story," Wes said.

"There's more?"

"No, I mean, Saide showed up and we got you out of there. But what I'm trying to say is the kid is dangerous."

"More so than a thug with a blaster?" Di asked. "Face it Wes, the galaxy is a scary place. One tiny hole in our hull and we're all dead. If the hyperdrive fails, we're toast. We could say the wrong thing to the wrong person and they could pull a blaster and blow us away. That's the truth of the matter. We got jumped on Maker's Point. You were blind sided, I was stunned. Bad things happen all the time, and no matter how vigilant you are, you can't see everything coming."

"But the odds of an L-5 randomly stowing away on our ship is so vast it's borderline impossible. What if the kid is working for someone? What if he's planning to take over the ship?"

"It would have been easy to do once Paxton had murdered you, left me for dead, and taken Zora as his slave again," Di pointed out. "But he didn't do that. He saved us. Why can't you just trust him. I mean, even if he's a plant, he hasn't done anything but save us money and rescue us when we were in trouble. I'd say he's earned a spot on this crew."

"You won't be saying that if he betrays us," Wes said.

"No, but that hasn't happened. And I don't think it will. He's a kid with a super ability that is just as lost and confused as Zora was. Why can you trust Stu but not Colt?"

"I'm trying but my mind won't let go of the fear that we're being naive. You, this ship, that's all I've got in this galaxy and I'm pretty desperate to hang onto you both."

"You have more than that," Di said softly, reaching for his hand. "You have Stu, and Saide, and Zora. They all love you and respect you."

"All the more reason why I can't put them in danger," Wes said. "No one really knows what L-5's are capable of. Some think their power will drive them insane. What if he murders us unintentionally?"

"What if I make a mistake that strands us between systems?" Di countered. "What if Saide turns the wrong way and crashes the ship? We're living with risk every moment of every day."

"I can't turn it off," Wes said, rubbing his stomach and wishing the burning would stop.

"Just be with me," Di said, pulling him toward the bed where she sat up and propped her self on one arm. "Just be in this moment. We can't control everything sweetheart. The future will take care of itself."

"How can you be so sure?" he said.

"I read that somewhere. Probably in one of your dusty old books."

"I need a new book," Wes said. "One that tells what a level five Reader can really do? For all we know, he's manipulating things. Maybe we're all living a dream that he planted in our head."

She raised his hand to her lips and kissed it. "This feels real to me. He might be able to do a lot but he can't replicate the love I see in your eyes, or the way your skin smells to me. Everything is okay. Trust me."

"I do trust you," he said.

They kissed. It was soft and reassuring. Then she laid on her side and probed the back of her head with her fingers.

"I've got a goose egg here," she said. "It hurts."

"I'll bring you some pain killers and something to drink."

"Did we get the stuff we found to the ship?" Di asked as he stood up.

"Are you kidding me?" Wes asked.

"No, that was really good stuff," Di said. "You think someone will hold on to it for us?"

"I'll message the administrator, but don't get your hopes up," Wes said.

"Okay, well get me the pain killer before my stomach decides it's had enough."

"Roger that," Wes said. "Be back in a flash."

He thought about what she had said. Worrying wasn't helping him. It was giving him an ulcer and making his life crazy. The kid had saved them and from the looks of it, almost killed himself in the process. As he climbed the stairs to the galley where they kept their medicinal supplies, a new thought occurred to Wes. People had seen what happened on Maker's Point. Whether Joss beat Paxton to death or not, the big man would confess that he had no control over what happened. It wouldn't be long before a report of a powerful Reader went out. No one had seen Colt, but the crew of the *Jolly Rogue* had been involved in the incident. When people started looking for whoever had intervened they would start with Wes and his crew. Keeping Colt and his abilities a secret would soon be impossible. The pain in his stomach flared again. But not because Wes was worried about the trouble having Colt on board his ship would bring. His worry wasn't how to keep the ship and crew safe, it was how to keep Colt safe.

CHAPTER 25

After sitting with Diana for a few hours, Wes spent a shift on the bridge. Four hours later, he was relieved by Saide. He went immediately to his cabin and fell exhausted into bed. He slept nearly six hours before his com-link woke him up. It blared a warning signal loud enough to wake him up even though the com-link was still on his jacket which he had tossed haphazardly onto a chair. He sat up rubbing his eyes and felt a hot stab of pain in his gut. He needed rest and a little tranquility if he was going to get over the stomach ulcer.

A second later his door swooshed open. Only Diana had the lock override authority in the biometric mechanism, but Wes couldn't remember if he had locked his cabin door or not.

"We've got trouble," Di said from the doorway.

Wes looked at her, and was happy to see that she seemed back to her usual self. Only the perpetual smile that normal graced her attractive face was gone. Her mouth was pressed into a hard line, and there were wrinkles on her forehead between her eyes.

"The hyperdrive?" Wes asked, his heart pounding in his chest as he pulled on his boots.

"Worse," Di said. "We got yanked out of FTL by a GA Interdictor ship. They're hailing us."

"What?" Wes asked. "That's not right. Stu took us off the trade route."

He jumped up, grabbed his jacket and followed Di down the hallway to the Bridge. Stu was sitting at his console rocking back and forth. He was humming too, another obvious sign that he was afraid. The GA had laws about running the blockade, and while their claims of authority over interstellar space were dubious at best, they were big enough to enforce them.

"Can we get clear?" Wes asked. "Make another jump?"

"They're already hailing us," Saide said. "They will have registered our ship. If we run now, we'll be wanted in every Galactic Authority port we stop at."

"Why the hell are they here?" Wes asked.

He was looking at the view screens that covered the far wall of the Bridge. There were more than one GA ship. They were unmistakable in their gleaming white, high gloss paint with maroon lettering on the side. Wes could see the interdictor ship, two small corsairs, and a battle ship.

"Where are we?" Wes asked.

"Just outside the Freemont..." Stu struggled to say, his head turning as he wrestled with the last word, "system."

"Freemont?" Di said. "It's uninhabited. Not even a space station."

"That we know of," Wes said. "Stu, have we gone this way before?"

"Not in a... while," he said.

"There's only two reasons they're here," Wes said.

"It's obvious why they're here," Saide snarled, the cables

running to his neural clusters falling away as he jumped to his feet from the pilot's seat. "That damn kid betrayed us."

"What?" Diana asked as Saide raced around the Bridge console.

The Hyborian could be scary. They were predators and Saide was lean but muscular. He moved with swift purpose, bolting past Wes and down the corridor.

"Where's he going?" Diana asked.

She and Wes both ran after their pilot. Wes knew where he was going and hoped deep in his heart that Saide was wrong. The pilot was fast. He was at Colt's door and punched in the access code before Wes and Di could stop him. They hadn't bothered to change the access code on Colt's cabin yet. They all still had things stored in what had been the spare cabin, and while Di was convinced that Colt should stay, Wes hadn't fully believed that the kid would stick around. The door slide open and Saide bolted inside, with Wes and Di right behind him.

"Wait!" Wes shouted.

Colt woke up startled just before Saide grabbed him.

"You betrayed us!" the Hyborian snarled, his pointed teeth flashing dangerously close to Colt's face.

"What?" Colt bellowed.

"Saide, we don't know that," Wes said grabbing the pilot's sinewy arm. He could feel the muscles under the Hyborian's coat as taut as steel cables.

"Let him go," Diana pleaded.

"How else would they know where we were?" Saide said.

"Take a breath," Wes said, acutely aware of the terror in Colt's eyes. "The kid didn't know what our course was. Stu calculated it and put it in the computer himself. The kid didn't have access to it, and saving our bacon on Maker's Point took all of his strength. You saw him after."

"It's all an act," the Hyborian snarled. "Let me rip his throat out before his GA scumbag friends take the ship."

"What? No!" Colt said, trying to push Saide away but failing.

"They're here for another reason," Wes insisted. "They wouldn't send four ships to capture us. Think about it."

"Then maybe they're just here for him," Saide said, shoving Colt backward.

The kid fell back on the bed and pushed himself to the bulkhead as far from Saide as he could get. Wes saw him looking around almost frantically as if he were looking for something to fight with, but there was nothing close by. The kid had nothing but the clothes on his back. Yet Wes was thankful Colt hadn't used his psychic ability to defend himself. In his panic he might have turned all their brains to mush.

"Maybe they lost him and they've been searching for him," Saide theorized. "We should hand him over to them."

"That's the last thing we should do," Di replied.

"They aren't here for him either," Wes said. "A battle group like that is either preparing an assault, or guarding a hidden installation."

"What are the odds that we would just stumble upon them?" Saide said.

"Astronomical," Wes agreed. "And we would have gone right past them if not for the interdictor, which tells me they were expecting the possibility that ships might be passing this way. They don't want unexpected visitors showing up. It's an invasion."

"That's..." Di said, "a little thin. Where would they be invading?"

Everyone looked at each other. Colt was still frightened. He looked like a cornered animal and Wes took a step back.

"Let's get back to the Bridge," he ordered. "All of us, you too Colt. We'll answer their hail and find out what they want."

Wes turned and led the way back out of Colt's room. He never saw Zora peeking out of the tiny crack in the door to the bathroom. As he walked back down the corridor Di moved close behind him and spoke in a quiet voice.

"You know we have a way to know exactly what they're doing," she said.

"Saide doesn't trust him," Wes said.

"Saide doesn't trust him, or you don't?" Di asked. "There's no way he gave us up. He wouldn't do that."

"I don't think he did, either," Wes said. "But I can't deny that it's possible. And we're right on the razor's edge here. We make a wrong move and we could end up on a penal colony."

"We have a powerful resource here, don't waste it," she warned him.

Wes moved to his console and sat down. He could see the hailing signal on his display, and the plot showed the four GA vessels. Fortunately, none of them had changed course. They weren't coming after him.

"What's on radar?" Wes asked.

"One battleship, two corsairs, one interdictor..." Di paused, leaning over her console, "and it looks like a squad of fighters."

"We can't outrun fighters," Saide said as he settled back into the pilot's seat.

They were like a fly caught in a spider's web. The interdictor projected a gravity well into space, they were like flying black holes. Fortunately, the interdictor wasn't powerful enough to crush them with gravity, but they couldn't make a hyperspace jump until they were clear of the gravity field. And while they might be able to outrun the bigger GA ships, they couldn't escape before the war ships could fire on them. The battle ship probably already had targeting data on the *Jolly Rogue*. If they tried to run they would be blasted into space dust. And then there were the fighters. Wes' ship was fast, but not fast enough to outpace fighters.

"What's going on?" Colt said from the doorway of the Bridge.

Zora moved past him and slipped into her seat without a word. Wes turned and looked at Colt O'Connor. He wanted so badly to trust the kid? But he feared he was putting the lives of the people he cared about on the line.

"Sit down, Colt," Wes said. "We've been pulled out of hyperspace by a GA task force. Let's find out what they want."

Wes pressed the icon for the communication system and took a deep breath. A voice boomed out over the Bridge speakers.

"Unidentified vessel, this is GA taskforce Epsilon. Transmit your identification, manifest, and destination. Over."

"They don't know who we are," Di said. "They weren't looking for us."

Wes felt a glimmer of hope. He pressed a button that sent the ship's transponder code.

"Taskforce Epsilon, this is the *Jolly Rogue*. We're an independent ship with a load of medicinal supplies. Magnesium and Merconium, over."

"Stu," Di said calmly, what's close to this system."

"That's GA affilated," Wes added.

The navigator responded instantly. "The Warder... system," he managed to say. "Warder C is a mining... planet."

"What is your destination, *Jolly Rogue*? Over," the stern voice asked.

"Warder C, in the Warder system. Over," Wes replied. He knew that the GA officials could check with the nearby world.

But that would take time and he hoped they wouldn't want to do that. "Colt, can you reach them?"

"You mean, mentally?" the kid asked.

"Yeah, can you discern their intentions?" Wes asked.

Before Colt could answer the stern voice from the GA ship came through the Bridge speakers. "*Jolly Rogue,* turn to course two-seven-niner and prepare to be boarded for contraband inspection. Over."

Saide turned in his pilot seat, looking over his shoulder to Wes. "That's it. Once they're on board we're finished."

Wes made up his mind in a heartbeat. No one was taking his ship from him. Not the GA, not space pirates, nobody. He turned toward Colt.

"Respond," he told the young Reader. "Use your mind and convince them not to board us."

"I don't know if—" Colt began.

But Wes cut him off. "You can. Convince them to let us go. Stu, get us a jump configured."

"Aye, aye... captain," Stu said.

Wes never took his eyes off Colt.

"You said you'd do anything to be part of the crew," Wes urged. "This is the one thing you can do that no one else can. You convince them to let us go. Otherwise I'm running, and we'll end up vaporized by the laser cannons on that battle ship. But better that than hand over the *Jolly Rogue* to those GA bastards."

Colt glanced at Zora, then back at Wes. He nodded and picked up the communications headset and put it on. He adjusted the mic then pressed the transmit button on his console. Wes felt a stabbing pain in his stomach, and his chest felt tight. He was putting all his hopes on the shoulders of a sixteen year old, untested Reader. And if Colt failed, they were all dead.

CHAPTER 26

Colt cleared his throat. He'd seen enough movies about space ships to know the basics of radio communications. But he had no idea if he could reach someone that were over a hundred kilometers away. He didn't even know which ship the person in charge was on.

"The fighters are turning this way," Di said. She was studying the radar at her console.

Colt glanced once more at Zora. Her big eyes were on him, and he knew he couldn't let her down. He lowered his mental defenses and reached out toward the GA ships. He could feel the men and women on the ships, but they were far away, their mental voices and emotions mingling into a kind of distance noise.

"Say again, Taskforce Epsilon," Colt said, his voice trembling a bit. He did his best to stay calm and sound like an adult. "Your message is breaking up. Please repeat, over."

He closed his eyes, forcing his mind out toward the GA ships. What happened next was something Colt had never experienced or anticipated. It was like he was flying. He could feel the seat he was in, and the headphones on his ears, yet it felt like he was zooming toward the GA ships. Their mental voice grew louder, more distinct. He could feel their emotions, mostly boredom, resentment, and surges of ambition. And there was something else, something completely different. It was a kind of bright, hot, loud, presence. In some ways it reminded Colt of touching Stu's mind. The thoughts and feelings were powerful, yet constrained. Colt couldn't read the thoughts. It was like hearing muffled voices from the next room. Something was blocking him.

Before he could probe further, the voice over the Bridge speakers, and his headphones took his full attention. Colt was able to pick out of the crowd of voices on the GA ships as well.

"*Jolly Rogue*, come to heading two-seven-niner and prepared to be boarded for contraband inspection."

"Taskforce Epsilon," Colt replied, feeling a little more confident as he pushed his will at the person giving the orders. "Contraband Inspection isn't nesessary. We are a trade vessel of no interest to the GA."

There was a pause and Colt could feel the confusion of the communications officer. He searched the minds of the people near the person he had found who was giving them orders. Someone in command. *I want that ship captured or destroyed! Epsilon Station and the work being done with the Readers there is too important to be compromised.*

Colt felt stab of excitement. The taskforce wasn't looking for them, Di had been right about that. They were guarding a secret GA installation. He pushed his will into the commander's mind. *The* Jolly Rogue *is of no consequence. Let her go.*

"*Jolly Rogue*," the communications officer began. "You will—"

Never mind, Colt heard the commander say. *They're of no importance. Let them go.*

"Correction," the communication officer said in a slightly confused voice. "Turn to heading three-one-seven and leave this sector. Taskforce Epsilon out."

Colt felt a thrill of victory. He had influced the minds of people far away, and saved the *Jolly Rogue*. He was pulling back, leaving the task force. The flying sensation just started to come over him again when he heard another voice. It rose above the white noise of the ships crews. Colt felt the unmistakeable power in the voice. *Well, hello there. Where'd you come from?*

Colt jerked back, his whole body going stiff with fear. He raised his mental barriers and his eyes popped open.

"Good work, kid," Wes told him. "Saide."

"I'm already going," the Hyborian declared.

"Stu, do we have a trajectory ready?"

"Imputing the vectors now... c-ca-captain," Stu replied.

Colt heard his crew mates, but all he could think about was the voice. It seemed to echo in his mind. Someone with great power had noticed Colt and the young Reader didn't think it was a good thing.

"Colt? Are you okay?" Di asked.

He shook his head. "He saw me," Colt said.

"Who?" Wes asked.

"That task force is guarding a secret installation. I didn't see it, so I'm not sure where it is, but the commander said it was too important to be discovered."

"The GA has secret bases all over," Wes said. "The whole government is rotten to the core."

"No," Colt said. "They're working with Readers there, and I, I heard one of them."

"You heard another reader?" Di asked. There was a look of concern on her face.

"He saw me," Colt went on. "They will know about me now."

"Wonderful," Wes said. "Di."

"I'm checking," she replied. "They haven't mov— wait, the fighters are moving to intercept."

"Damn, I knew it couldn't be that easy," Wes complained. "Stu, how far to the jump point?"

"Eigh-eight... minutes," Stu replied.

"Saide, maximum speed to the jump point," Wes said.

"We can't outrun those fighters," Saide replied. "They're twice as fast and more agile. And the targeting systems on their ships can take out our engines and leave us dead in space."

"They better not," Di said angrily.

Wes moved over beside Colt, who was still shaken from the encounter. It wasn't just being caught that bothered him. It was the sound of the voice, and the sheer power of it. Whoever had spoken to him was not just strong mentally, but there had been a note of demented joy in the speaker. Whoever it was had felt a surge of twisted happiness at having discovered him. And Colt felt like a defenseless rabbit that had been discovered by a hungry wolf.

Wes bent down and put a hand on Colt's shoulder. "The pilots in those fighters. Can you distract them?"

Colt had to shake off the sense of fear and dread he felt. He managed to nod, but he felt shaky and weak. His hands gripped the arms of his console chair as he sent his mind out toward the fighters, who were halfway between the *Jolly Rogue* and the task force of GA ships.

... moving into range in thirty seconds... one of the fighter pilots said. Colt had to filter out the technical information the

pilot's mind was absorbing from the ship's instrument panel. ... *weapons hot. Prepare to take out the runner's quad engines.*

There were six fighter ships. Each with a single pilot. Colt could hear them communicating and knew they were powering up their laser targeting systems. Unsure what else to do, Colt imagined a huge dreadnaught class battle cruiser. It was something he had seen in a movie, a huge war ship popping out of hyperspace right over the *Jolly Roger.*

Abort, abort, abort! one the pilot's shouted. *Evasive actions! Pull back to protect the task force!*

Colt imagined flashes of laser light streaking around the ships and the pilots responded. Through their minds he could hear their flight controllers questioning them, and Di's announcement that the fighters had turned around, but he kept the illusion up.

Can't you see that battleship? one the pilots snapped in reply to her flight controller's questions. *It's right behind us.*

Shooting at us, another pilot declared.

Delta flight, there are no other ships in the sector. Check your instruments, the flight controller declared.

He's right, the scope is clear, one of the pilots shouted.

It must have some kind of cloaking technology. We all saw it.

That thing is right on our six. We can't shake it.

Colt felt the fear of the pilots, who were zig-zagging in their ships desperate to escape the illusion he had pushed into their minds. The plan was working until he felt an outside force pressing him out of the pilots' heads.

"Someone's fighting me," Colt said.

"Just a few more minutes kid," Wes replied. "We're almost clear."

It is an illusion, the bemused voice spoke into the minds of the fighter pilots. *Turn around and bring us that ship.*

They must have a reader, the flight commander declared. *Don't believe anything your instrument panel doesn't show you.*

Roger that, damn mind swimmers, another pilot said.

That ship looked so real, a third pointed out.

Colt couldn't fool them all, but he could still see into their minds. It was a simple matter to focus on the commander and see what he saw. The pilot was focused on his control panel, not willing to trust his eyes. *We'll be in maximum range in sixty seconds,* the commander declared. *Another thirty to zero in on their engines.*

Delta Flight, disable the ship only. We want the crew brought in alive, over.

Roger that flight control, the commander said. *Almost there.*

Colt saw a handle labeled emergency. He took control of the pilot, forcing his will on the man and made him reach for the handle. There was shove, a mental push that nearly shook Colt loose, but he managed to make the pilot jerk the ejection handle before he lost contact. A second later he was lurking at the edges of another pilot's mind.

What the... Captain Jenner just ejected! the fighter pilot shouted. The fear in the man was pungent, like a bad odor in a confined space.

Delta Flight, do not—

Colt didn't hesitate. He took control of the next pilot and repeated the ejection process. Once again he felt the resistance of the Reader somewhere in the task force trying to push him back.

Delta three just ejected, flight control. Permission to fire at maximum range, another pilot asked. Colt saw the man glance over at another ship that was flying right beside him. He could feel the pilot's anger and animosity. The pilot wanted to obliterate the *Jolly Rogue* and Colt couldn't let that happen. He pushed into the man's mind and forced the control stick to the side. At the same instant that the pilot's ship flipped straight into his comrade's vessel, causing a catastrophic collision, Colt felt a stab of pain. It felt like someone had driven a spike into his head. He screamed, and felt himself falling out of his chair, just before his mind went blank.

CHAPTER 27

Wes had stepped back to his console and brought up the countdown that showed how long it would take them to reach the jump point. They only needed a minute more to make good on their escape when Colt screamed. He turned and saw the kid falling. Zora caught him and kept his head from smashing into the metal deck plates.

"Two of the ships just collided!" Di announced, pointing at the view screens, one of which had the ship's rear cameras pulled up. On the video feed Wes saw two of the vessel spinning out of control and venting gas.

"Is he okay?" Wes asked.

"I don't know," Zora said, her voice sounded small, but strong.

Wes realized he couldn't worry about Colt at that moment. As a captain, his first priority was the ship. Even though in reality Wes cared for every member on his ship, and the new kid was growing on him, he had to ensure they got away.

"That still leaves two," Saide said.

"Evasive actions," Wes said. "Don't give them an easy target."

Wes pressed the icon to raise the *Jolly Rogue's* deflector screens. It pulled a third of the ships power and he hated to see the countdown reverse directions and start climbing, but without full power to their engines the *Jolly Rogue* simply wasn't as fast.

Saide pulled the ship to their left, then dipped down. Flashes of laser light shot past them and out into space.

"They're at maximum range," Di said. "And closing."

"Saide, don't make it easy," Wes said, wishing his ship had the capability to fire back.

The *Jolly Rogue* could have been rigged with hidden guns. Most criminals had hidden weapons they could deploy in a pinch, but Wes had never crossed that line. Unregistered weapons on a freighter was grounds for immediate impound-ment of said ship, confiscation of all goods, a minimum sentence of ten years in a class three penal colony for the crew, and a hundred thousand credit fine for the owner. The point was having the weapons hidden so that they weren't discovered by some nosy wrench spinner or harbor master, but that was a chance Wes didn't want to take. He only hoped the descision to play by the rules didn't cost them everything.

The ship rocked hard as a series of laser blasts ricocheted off the *Jolly Rogue's* deflector screens. The count down was at thirty seconds.

"Another hit like that and we'll lose the shields," Di said. "We're burning through fuel fast. We just past half of capacity."

"Almost there," Saide said, as more laser fire flashed by.

"Fifteen seconds," Wes announced.

All they could do was wait and hope. Saide bobbed and weaved, but at the seven second mark the ship was rocked again. A red light appeared on Wes' console, and an alarm sounded.

"Shields are out," Di announced. "We're dangerously close to a power overload."

"Hold on," Wes shouted.

More laser blasts shot by them. Wes knew the fighters were gaining on them. He felt like the fire in his stomach was burning him up from the inside out. Gripping the console he stared at the approaching fighters on the rear view camera feeds, willing them to give up. Then suddenly everything disappeared as Wes felt the sudden lurch of the ship jumping into hyperspace. The screens went black. There was nothing to see outside the vessel as it hurdled through space faster than the speed of light, and at the same time several more alarm sounds chimed.

"The reactor's overheating," Di said, before racing away from the Bridge.

"Make sure he's okay," Wes shouted at Zora as he turned and followed Di.

A fusion reactor meltdown could go two ways. It was built to maintain pressure on the hydrogen gas the fueled the ship, making it burn like a tiny sun. The reactor absorbed the heat and converted the energy into electricity. If it was pushed too hard, the reactor could get out of balance and the hydrogen fuel could either burn out, like a candle flame snuffed between wet fingers, or it could explode, rip the ship apart and kill the entire crew.

"We've got to bleed off the pressure and heat," Di shouted as they bounded up the spiral staircase to the upper deck. "You can't just go from full burn to nothing. The heat will melt down the fusion reactor's energy converters."

"Tell me what to do," Wes told her.

"Get to the port valve. It has to be opened by hand," Di said. "On my count, pull the lever all the way down until she clicks. We'll be dumping fuel, so only hold it open for a count of one and then close it."

"Got it," Wes said.

He didn't really understand, but he knew where the port valve was located. Running to it, he gripped the handle and looked at Di.

"Now!" she shouted.

Wes pulled down on the handle. It was stiff and didn't want to budge, but he yanked harder until it slid down and clicked. There was a keening sound, and the ship began to vibrate. Wes feared the entire vessel was going to break apart, and he shoved the lever back up. It clicked into place and the vibrating stopped.

Di dashed over to the reactor and opened the tiny window that showed the interior of the contained fusion chamber. Light appeared on her face and she visibly exhaled in relief.

"Are we okay?" Wes asked.

"We didn't lose the reactor," Di said. She moved to her console, a replicate of the one on the Bridge where she monitored the ship's systems. "We're down to a quarter of our fuel supplies. We need to get somewhere quick."

"But we can fly?" Wes insisted.

"For now," Di said. "I'll need to do a visual check on everything. We might have lost a gasket or blew a hose somewhere. We put her through a lot of stress."

"At least we're alive," Wes said. "Do what you need to do. I'll send Zora to you as soon as I check on Colt."

Di nodded and pulled out the tool belt she kept in the engineering bay. He loved to see her with the sleeves of her coveralls rolled up, the tool belt hanging around her hips, and a bit of grease on her face. She never looked more beautiful or more alive than when she was in the middle of a project. But there wasn't time for him to admire his chief engineer, not when the newest member of their crew had been hurt saving them from the Galactic Authority. Wes hurried back down to the main deck and through the corridor that connected the *Jolly Rogue's* Bridge to the main body of the ship.

Colt was sitting up. He looked pale, and there was sweat on his forehead. His lips had the same bluish tint they had after saving Wes and Zora on Maker's Point.

"How are you feeling?" Wes asked him.

"Like someone stabbed me in the brain," Colt said.

"Are you going to be sick?" Wes asked.

"I don't think so."

"Good, let's get him upstairs Zora," Wes said.

He took hold of Colt's free arm and heaved the young Reader up. Colt was unsteady, but they took it slow.

"Stu, where are we headed?" Wes asked as they headed for the corridor off the Bridge.

"N-n-no-nowhere, dead... space."

"And from there?"

"We sh-sh-should be able to jump to Kellar... Nine."

"Good, because we're almost out of fuel and we're completely out of money," Wes said. "If anything changes, let me know. I'll be upstairs with Colt."

"Hey," Saide said, standing up from the pilot's seat and looking back at Wes and Colt. "Good job kid."

"That's about as close to an apology as you'll get from a Hyborian," Wes said, as they shuffled off down the corridor.

The stairs were a challenge, but Colt made it up with Wes on one side and Zora helping from behind. They moved him to the table where they ate meals. Colt dropped onto the bench and leaned onto the table top with both elbows.

"Di needs your help," Wes told Zora.

She slipped into the engineering section without a word. Wes was a little surprised that she was helping Colt. Under different circumstances he might have given their friendship a little more scrutiny, but he had other worries occupying his mind.

"Here, drink this," Wes said as he shook up a protein drink. "You should eat something too. How about a bowl of oatmeal?"

"Sure," Colt replied.

Wes took a minute to heat the artificially flavored oats. He set the steaming bowl in front of Colt then sat down across from him.

"So, tell me what you learned," Wes said.

"I learned not to use my gift when there's another Reader around," Colt said, rubbing his temples.

"I meant about the GA space station," Wes said. "Any idea what it was?"

"Can't say for certain, but the commander giving orders on the battle ship was serious about keeping it a secret," Colt explained. "He said the work they were doing with Readers was too important."

"So it was a Reader installation," Wes said. "I wish we knew if it was the training station or something else."

"Why?" Colt asked. "You planning to bust in and free the captives?"

"No," Wes said. "Although I'm sure they deserve to be freed, getting away from GA would just make them vulnerable to the cartels."

"There's no place to escape it is there?" Colt asked. "No matter where I go someone is going to be looking for me."

"That's true. And now that they know you're on our ship, they'll be looking for us," Wes said. "It changes things."

"I never meant to get you into trouble," Colt said, before spooning some oatmeal into his mouth.

"Kid, you just saved our bacon for the second time," Wes said. "Some things are outside a person's control. But knowing about that installation is going to help other blockade runners. And the info about the Reader installation will be valuable to the right people. But I need you to consider something."

"What's that?"

"First, I think it's best if you stay with us. People will be looking, but at least we know that. And having you on the ship will give us an edge over the people trying to get their hands on you. Even the GA."

"But they'll get me eventually," Colt said in a dejected tone.

"Maybe, maybe not," Wes said. "I had considered finding a place that might be safe, where you could pretend to be normal. But I don't think those places exist. Second, we need to be careful how you use your abilities."

"What do you mean?"

"I mean you're taxing yourself too hard," Wes said. "It couldn't be helped, and I believe in time your strength will grow. But I don't want you pushing yourself, not if we can help it. You have a gift, but we need to be smart about how you use it. Taking control of a person is an L-5 skill. From what I've read that kind of psychic power is extraordinarily rare. There may be no limit to what you can do. But that doesn't mean you can do whatever comes into your head. Let's be smart, exercise your skills, stay hidden, and let your power do what it can do. Nothing is worth you hurting yourself for."

"But I can't put you all in danger," Colt said. "If I stay, the GA will never stop hunting you. And they have who knows how many powerful Readers on their side?"

"They'll be looking for us anyway," Wes said. "That's what I meant when I said you should stay with us. Leaving only puts us in more danger. We need you."

"You need me?" Colt asks.

"That's right. We're safer with you than without you. And

we're going to find a way out of this mess we've found ourselves in. That's my superpower. So let me do my thing, and you do yours."

"Okay," Colt said, a look of relief crossing his face.

"Good, that's settled. Now tell me what happened. Why'd you pass out."

"I was attacked," Colt explained. "When I interfered with the first two pilots I felt the other Reader pushing me away. The third time, something broke through my defenses and plowed straight through my brain."

"How long was he in there?" Wes asked.

"I don't know. It felt like something was stabbed into my head and I passed out."

"So he might no nothing, or he might know everything you know."

"I guess," Colt said.

"That's alright. As long as we know that they know, we can plan for it. We'll assume they know everything. That will give us an edge."

"Wes, you got a minute?" Di asked, sticking her head out of the door to the engineering bay.

"You good?" Wes asked Colt.

"Yeah, thanks," Colt replied.

"On my way," Wes replied to Di.

The demands on a captain's time never ceased. But Wes knew he wouldn't have it any other way.

CHAPTER 28

Hussain was angry. The most powerful Reader he had encountered in well over a decade was gone. Not that it was surprising. A Reader of such power could easily turn the tide in a skirmish. The GA's fighter pilots were no match for his discovery, even with Hussain trying to protect them.

"Sir, we logged their trajectory. Should we send out searchers?" the task force commander asked.

"That won't be necessary," Hussain said. "Send an alert over the network for the ship though. I want to know where they show up."

"It's most likely Alliance space, sir," the commander said.

He was a competent man who had risen to the rank of Admiral through hard work and good fortune. But hunting down Readers was Hussain's job and he didn't need the GA navy telling him how to do it. If Hussain had been on the bridge things would have ended differently. But everyone needed rest. The sudden presence of the powerful Reader had woken him from a sound sleep. After scrambling to keep his new discovery from slipping away, Hussain was left to plot his next move. And if Hussain knew anything, it was that a Reader with such power could not be allowed to fall into the wrong hands.

Hussain was an L-3, with more experience in the GA's clandestine service than any Reader alive. Adaptation was the key to his success and longevity. To many of his brethren, especially the L4's & L5's as rare as they were, couldn't come to terms with a life of servitude. They felt themselves enslaved. But everyone was enslaved to something. Freedom, in Hussain's opinion, was merely an illusion. All one needed to do was to change their perspective. It was true that Hussain worked for the GA who set the goals he would pursue and how his service was best spent, and yet Hussain had learned that his place within the clandestine service also gave him a great deal of authority. Case in point being the Naval Admiral who was doing what Hussain told him. Once a Reader could see the power they could wield within the system, they had no more issues with servitude.

"Of course," Hussain said. "I know a blockade runner when I see one. But like every runner, they will return to civilized space and when they do we shall be ready for them."

"Very good, sir," the Admiral said.

Hussain had no official rank, no standing within the GA navy. He was a ghost who didn't legally exist, but who could command admirals in charge of entire battle groups. Known to most merely as the Hunter, they stepped aside when they saw him approaching and made a point to ensure he had whatever he needed. His team consisted of two L2 Readers and a Fringian special operator. They had just returned to the Farm, the secret GA space station where the off books Reader program was carried out. His team preferred to stay with the task force rather than on the Farm. Most Readers had traumatic memories from their time there, where many of the GA processors had a sadistic bent. Hussain had been beaten and abused during his time there, both by older residents and many of the processors. But he had risen above the trauma of his past and many of the processors who had tormented him had met unfortunate ends.

It was important to rest, especially for readers. One of the dangers of using his powers was the debilitating weakness that often followed. Hussain and his companions didn't waste their time swimming in the minds of the people around them. They kept strong barriers in place and only used their powers when they were on the hunt. But they all needed time off and Hussain's new quarry would have to wait. He would use his down time to prepare and when the *Jolly Rogue* popped up on the Galactic network, Hussain and his team would be ready.

"Prepare your reports and alert the high command that we have a new target. I will contact the brass after I've rested," Hussain said.

"Yes sir," the Admiral said. "We shall see to it that you are not interrupted again."

Hussain nodded and walked away. The Command Center of the battleship *Watchman* was a busy, crowded place. And Hussain did not enjoy being there. He preferred his own ship, which was docked in a special hanger reserved solely for teams led by Readers in the clandestine service. It was a Sterling V series space yacht that was modified with Hassal engines and a full weapons suite. The crew was made up of three androids who saw to Hussain's every need and ensured that any targets they acquired stayed safely sedated until they reached the Farm.

He made his way down to the hanger, a spacious area with only one ship inside. With only a few ships to service, most of the hanger's periphery had been converted to luxury and enter-tainment areas. They could rest in the hanger for a week without getting bored or restless. Hussain went to his ship and used the bio access to unlock the ship. It read his DNA, facial structure, and voice to unlock the ship. Once aboard he went to his suite of rooms. Working for the GA had benefits. The Sterling yacht was spacious and comfortable. Hussain passed through his private salon and went into his cabin. It was a large room with a private entertainment console, a large bed, polished wood paneling, and gold accents on the hardware. His bathroom had marble tile and a spacious shower. There was also a small hidden compartment, just big enough for Hussain to stand and utilize the encrypted communication unit with a direct line to the head of the GA's clandestine services - director Emmitt Turkov. Hussain was one of the few people with access to the director, but that access arose from a mutual trust and dedication to the idea that the clandestine service was the most important division within the Galactic Authority. Emmitt Turkov had a foundational belief that power was to be wielded by the strong, not the petty elected officials, or the heads of bloated departments that had long passed their usefulness. Hussain shared that belief, and understood that the more powerful the clandestine service became, the more feared he would become.

Direct messaging was a bit of a misnomer. Hussain would send a message directly to director Turkov, and it would be launched from the yacht utilizing a hyperdrive equipped message buoy that would travel directly to the system where the director was at the fastest speed possible. But that still required hours of travel time, sometimes days depending on where Hussain was transmitting from. And even more time for a reply. Hussain would therefore send his message and then rest as he waited for the reply.

"Director, I have encountered a rogue target. The interdictor ship pulled a vessel from hyperspace. One of the crew was I believe an L5, although I did not have the time to confirm that status. We did our best to apprehend this new subject, but were not prepared for the amount of power we faced. We did however map the vessel the target was traveling in. Admiral Phillips has prepared a high alert status on the ship, a Hyborian freighter, and we will be ready when it docks again in GA space. I believe this could be the Reader we have been hoping to find. Know that I will be pursuing this target personally, and will update you when we know more."

Hussain ended the message, typed in his security code, and did the usual biometric encryption process before launching the communication pod. It shot from the ship like a missile, maneuvered through the task force and made for open space. His officially duties completed, Hussain retired to his bedroom. Sleep was slow in coming as he imagined what he would do if he wielded the power of an L_5. The idea amused him. He was a powerful Reader who could swim through a person's mind and learn their most closely guarded secrets. But the power to take control of another person's body was almost too intoxicating to contemplate. If Hussain were an L_5, no one in the galaxy would be safe from his power. And perhaps bringing this new target under his control was the next best thing to wielding such heady power himself.

CHAPTER 29

Colt ate and drank and slept again. When he woke up the ship had just come out of hyperspace. His clothes were clean and folded on the chair next to his bed, but Zora was nowhere to be seen. He had hoped to speak with her after she had crawled into bed with him, but there hadn't been a chance. Using his power to bend other men to his will was difficult work and extremely taxing. And the *Jolly Rogue* had been pushed to her limit in their flight from the GA ships. Zora was kept busy helping Diana with repairs. So Colt got up, washed, and pulled on his clothes, then joined the rest of the crew in the Bridge.

He saw Kellar Nine, which seemed tiny next to the massive gas giant it was in orbit around, on the Bridge display screens as he walked up the passageway to the Bridge. He stopped and stared at the tiny moon for several minutes, just absorbing what he was seeing. Not a space station, no a man made structure, but a world hospitable to life. It was a rarity in the galaxy, even though there were tens of thousands of star systems with planets.

A world, be it a moon or a planet, that could host life was a treasure.

"Hey kid," Wes said, when Colt finally entered the Bridge, "how you feeling?"

"Better," Colt admitted. "Sorry I've been out so long."

"Just nine hours," Di said. "I never heard of a teenage boy who wouldn't spend at least that much time in the rack if they could."

Zora didn't look at him, but the edges of her mouth were angled up. It was the closest thing to a smile he had ever seen on her.

"Thanks for washing my clothes," he said softly.

Her head bobbed in slight nod, and the smile grew a little more pronounced.

"You sure we're in good enough shape to go into atmo?" Wes asked Di. "I just heard back from my contact and he's ready to take the cargo."

"We'll be fine," Di said. "We lost a few hoses and belts but we had replacements. Engine three needs a rebuild, but she'll hold together."

"Rebuilds, overhauls, when do you think we'll have time do make such lengthy repairs?" Wes asked.

"Who can say," Di replied. "Things always work out. Stop worrying."

"How long until we reach orbit?" Wes asked.

"S-si-sixty eight... minutes," Stu said, barking the last word.

"Alright, we should have approval to enter Kellar Nine airspace by then," Wes said. "Saide, keep me posted."

"Aye, captain."

"Colt, come with me. We have a job to discuss," Wes said.

He headed out of the bridge without waiting for a reply. Colt was willing to do any job on the ship. He felt as if luck had led him to the perfect crew, they even had a cabin for him. And yet he was still tired. He felt stretched thin and hoped the job that Colt had for him wasn't strenuous. They went down the corridor to the open space near the stairwell. Wes led the way around the stairs and went into his own cabin. Colt had never been in the captain's private berth. It was larger than his own, and decorated in a masculine style. He had several comfortable looking overstuffed chairs. They weren't real leather, but they looked like old, well worn leather and the faux brass studs at the seams were polished bright. There was also a desk area with computer access, and a large wardrobe. The captain's bed was much larger than the one in Colt's cabin, and neatly made. There were paintings on the walls, mostly of animals, and a collection of souvenirs from the various worlds Wes had visited in his lifetime.

As Colt looked around he realized the cabin was exactly the way he would have imagined it to be. Growing up with only his mother in a pod sized apartment on Helix Prime's spaceport, there had been no room or money for furniture or decorations. All of Colt's belongings could have fit a single duffle bag. And since leaving his home he had even less. Looking around the captain's cabin he realized that he wanted a similar style in his own room.

"This is amazing," Colt said, as Wes settled into one of the comfortable chairs.

"Glad you like it," Wes said. "Have a seat. We need to talk."

"Okay," Colt replied, sitting down in one of the push chairs across from his captain.

"Let me explain how this usually works," Wes said. "We're going into Kellar Nine with a full cargo load, and we should make around three times what we spent on it in Galactic space."

Colt nodded. He understood how commerce worked.

"Of that money, we'll invest a third into the ship. That goes to resupplies and repairs as needed, depending on what's available and what we can afford," Wes continued. "A third is reinvested in something we can turn a profit on. That can be anything from essential resources like the magnesium we're bringing in now, to passengers. We need to get something on this side of the blockade that people will pay for on the other side. In most instances that cargo isn't illegal. Crossing the blockade is illegal, but if we don't get caught no one really cares. The GA is just making a show of it, keeping the Alliance worlds from doing business as usual in the hopes that they'll cave and join the GA. You with me?"

Colt nodded.

"Good," Wes said. "Now the final third is profit, we split that evenly between the crew. That's how I've always operated. Occasionally we have side jobs that can potential earn us more while taking less time and less resources, but we follow the rule of threes no matter the job."

Colt nodded. He liked the equality of the idea, and was excited at the prospect of earning money for himself. Growing up, anything he earned he turned over to his mother or used for practical needs. Now that he was on his own, whatever he earned he could spend however he saw fit. And while on the *Jolly Rogue* he wouldn't have to spend money on food or rent. Although, looking around the captain's personal cabin, he could see that he had a lot of personal needs still, like clothes, furniture for his cabin, perhaps even a blaster for protection.

"Oddly enough, around the same time you were sneaking aboard, I was offered a side job," Wes said. "And now that you're a full member of this crew I want to tell you about it and see if perhaps we can find a way to get it done."

"Okay," Colt said. It seemed odd that the captain would

want to talk with him privately about a job. And he felt more than a little nervous about it.

"A woman named Evon talked to me," Wes said. "Have you ever met her?"

"No," Colt replied. "I don't think so."

"Alright, well, have you ever heard of Celeste Pierre?"

Colt thought about the name. It sounded familiar, but he couldn't place it. "I don't think so."

"She was, or is I suppose, Prime Minister Guy Louis Pierre's daughter," Wes explained. "She was kidnapped when she was just a little girl, but that may have been before your time. It was a big story. Her father was a rising political star back then, and wealthy. But there was never a ransom demand. She just disappeared. Her father was away on GA business at the time, her mother never recovered from the loss. And the story has become conspiracy theory legend."

"Wow," Colt said. "That's crazy. They never found her?"

"No," Wes went on. "Most people believe she was killed and buried in an unmarked grave somewhere. A missing child isn't rare and many are never found. Most people watched the story on the network feeds, but then lost interest. That was over a decade ago. Evon, the woman I told you about, contacted me because she is part of a group searching for Celeste Pierre. She said they have tracked her to Kellar Nine. This woman knew who we where, what we had on the ship, and where we were going. I don't know how, and that worries me. But she gave me this."

He pulled a black card from the inside pocket of his jacket. It was black, with gold pinstripes on it.

"Know what this?" Wes asked.

"No," Colt said, leaning forward to get a closer look.

"It's a universal pass, the kind they give to diplomats and the ultra-rich," Wes said. "With this pass we could go anywhere, dock wherever we wanted, trade with whoever had the most lucrative jobs, and no questions asked. We could get work reserved for members of the Freight Hauler's Guild without registering or paying dues. We could dock in STU ports no questions asked. It would even keep the GA off our back. But to unlock it, we have to find Celeste."

"How are we supposed to find someone on a world full of people?" Colt asked.

"That's the thing, kid. We had no way of doing it until you showed up."

Colt felt a stab of fear. The ship was depending on him, and yet he had no idea if finding a person would even be possible. He had never tried it before. He mostly kept the barriers to his mind closed. Hearing people's thoughts and feeling their emotions was not pleasant. Sure he could get someone's secrets, but he had to swim through their mind to do it. And it left him feeling strange, partly guilt, but also something else. Like he was a peeping tom trying to see something he wasn't supposed to. It was the sort of thing a perverse person would do, and he didn't like that.

"Me?" Colt asked. "How am I supposed to find someone?"

"Well, the truth is, if Celeste is alive she might not remember her former life, but the people around her would. She's probably going by a different name. So we look for people who are hiding something."

"I'll help," Colt said. "You know that, but I don't know if it's possible."

"Look, Kellar Nine is a manufacturing world," Wes said. "It's got a thick atmosphere, and a lot of geothermic activity. The Alliance of Free Worlds took advantage of all that free energy and set up shop. There are only three cities of any size, and most of the population works in the processing facilities there. My guess is that if the people who kidnapped Celeste have her down there, they won't be mingling with the locals. They're either in the business side of one of those three cities, or somewhere in the undeveloped part of the world hiding out. You might be able to find them from a distance."

"Okay," Colt said, feeling a sense of the captain's expectation that he hoped he could live up to. "I'll try."

"That's all we're asking. The plan, for now, is to spend some time on Kellar Nine. We'll drop our load of magnesium and merconium, replenish our fuel, reprovision the ship, and take a little time for R&R. You can spend some of your pay on new clothes," Wes said. "Explore the city a bit. But while you're down there, keep your senses open. If we're lucky, we'll run across her or someone who knows her."

"And if we do?" Colt asked. "Are we going to kidnap her and take her to the Prime Minister?"

"No," Wes said. "Our contact wanted us to find her, or find out about her. It's possible that she was there but left already. If we can get some information they can use, they'll activate the universal pass for a year."

"But what if she's there?" Colt asked. "What if she has no memory of her past and is happy, living her life?"

"She's the daughter of the most powerful man in the galaxy," Wes said. "I can't see how finding that out wouldn't be to her benefit."

Colt couldn't argue that point. If someone had told him his father was fabulously wealthy and anxious to find him, he wouldn't turn away from that. Perhaps going to his father would have hurt his mother's feelings, but Colt could have used the money from his father to help her. And he would. The last thing Colt would ever do was forget about his mother. It made him feel sick not knowing if she was okay as it was. Yet staying away was the only hope she had. If she had contact with Colt, if she knew where he was, the GA's clandestine service agents would torture the information out of her. They may have already tried, but Colt couldn't stand thinking about that.

"Alright," Colt said. "I'll do what I can."

"Good, but don't push yourself too hard. We've seen how that leaves you. I don't want you passed out in the street down there," Wes said. "And you shouldn't go anywhere alone. Keep someone with you."

"What about Zora?" Colt asked, feeling an intense anxiety. His feelings for Zora were growing so rapidly that it scared him, and yet the thought of not being with her every chance he got made him feel sick.

"Zora's fine. But you both keep your com-links on. And watch your back. Kellar Nine isn't a hostile place, but that doesn't mean there aren't people who might hurt you. If you feel another Reader close by, you let me know immediately and get back to the ship."

"Yes sir," Colt replied.

"Alright, let's go make some credits," Wes said. "This is the fun part of the job."

CHAPTER 30

"Forty-five, that's a fair offer," Jon Zorn said. He was the buying agent for Allied Pharmaceuticals. Kit DaVoor had arranged the buy, and while Wes had no idea how or why, there was no doubt in his mind that the greedy facilitator on Helix Prime was getting a cut somewhere.

"I was thinking sixty," Wes said.

Jon Zorn frowned and shook his head, but it was all an act. Wes didn't need Colt's Reader abilities to know that the business man on Kellar Nine would go above forty-five thousand credits for the *Jolly Rogue's* supply of magnesium and merconium. They were the primary ingredient in a number of medicines, from pain relievers, to sleeping aides. And Wes had reached Kellar Nine before a larger supply ship that would have flooded the market with magnesium, which meant their cargo was worth more.

"Sixty is much too high. It cuts our margins too thin," Jon Zorn said. "I could go fifty, but that's my top offer."

"Fifty-three," Wes countered. "And you pay my docking fees for a week."

The businessman did his best to look chagrinned, but the sparkle in his eye told Wes that Jon Zorn felt he had won the negotiation. And Wes didn't mind that. In fact, he liked leaving his buyers with the feeling that they had gotten the upper hand. The truth was, Wes couldn't have gotten a third of that price in Galactic space. And a third of fifty-three thousand was seventeen thousand, six hundred, and sixty-six credits. Wes had been hoping to get forty-five thousand for his load of magnesium, but with the extra fuel they burned escaping the GA task force, and the additional repairs needed on the *Jolly Rogue* he was glad to have the extra money. Plus, they were splitting the profit six ways instead of five. His cut would be just under three grand.

Jon Zorn punched the numbers into a buyer's contract he had pulled up on his data pad. Then he turned the device around for Wes to read. Everything was legit and the contract promised to deliver the payment when the goods were picked up at the dock yard. The Alliance dealt in universal credits, which meant that Wes could spend the funds wherever they were. And with the heat from their recent encounter with GA, they would need to lay low for a while. There were still plenty of places in GA space that wouldn't report them to the government, but those types of harbors could only be had for universal credits. Wes was glad to be getting a stack of them.

He signed his name, and pressed his thumb onto the print reader which copied his thumbprint to make the contract legal. Jon Zorn did the same thing and messaged a copy of the purchase agreement to Wes' PA, which beeped when the contract came through.

"Good doing business with you," Wes said, getting up from

the table in the dock side business center. The *Jolly Rogue* was on a landing pad less than a kilometer away.

Jon Zorn looked at his watched and then nodded. "Looks like I've got time for a coffee before my next appointment. Care to join me?"

"Actually, I have some work to do. Getting through the blockade wasn't as easy as we had hoped."

"The GA is really pressing their ludicrous sanctions," Zorn said. "Stay in touch. It was a pleasure doing business with you."

"I will," Wes said, as he thought that the pleasure was all his.

Walking back to the ship was enjoyable. The gravity on Kellar Nine was a bit high for his taste, and the air seemed thick, but being outside on an actual world was always a treat. Wes loved his life on the *Jolly Rogue*, but there was no comparison to being on a real world. The sights and smells were enticing, the feeling of freedom was invigorating, and having his feet on the ground made him feel more human somehow. When he reached the ship he was met by the entire crew, even Stu was anxious to know how they did.

"Well?" Di asked as Wes passed through the open airlock.

"Fifty three," Wes said, holding up his small Personal Access device to show their copy of the purchase order.

"That's more than we hoped," Diana exclaimed.

"But how much per person?" Saide said. "There are six of us now."

"Just a hair under three thousand credits each," Wes said. "And a little extra for repairs. Plus the buyer is covering our docking fees."

"You drive a hard bargain, sir," Di said with a wink.

"We got here at the right time," Wes replied.

"When's it coming?" Saide asked.

"Tomorrow at 0800 when the workers arrive to pick up the cargo," Wes said. "Payment upon delivery, all universal credits."

"S-sw-sw-sweet," Stu said.

"I want everyone on board to help offload in the morning," Wes continued. "I'll be making the reprovisioning orders this afternoon, but you are all free for the day. Just don't get into trouble."

He looked directly at Colt, who have him a reassuring nod.

"Zora and I are going to see what we can find to fix a few minor issues," Di said. "Care to tag along Colt?"

"Sure," he said.

The kid was anxious to get off the boat and Wes couldn't blame him. He had never set foot on a real world before. Kellar Nine was actually a moon. Wes could see the huge glowing gas giant filling most of the sky. Kellar Nine had three twenty four hour phases. When the moon faced the sun and had full daylight, followed by another twenty four hour phase when they faced the planet, who's glowing swirl of gases reflected the sunlight onto the surface, which was followed by a full twenty four hours of darkness. It was an interesting world, adaptable to humans and a host of other intelligent races from various parts of the galaxy. Wes had seen mostly humans, but more than a few Feringians and Rangolians around the port.

Wes watched them leave, followed by Saide who was almost certainly on the hunt for something alive that he could eat. The captain of the ship turned to Stu who was standing by the door, looking outside. It was clear there was a war going on in his mind. He would like to leave the ship too, but he couldn't process everything going on. It overloaded his mind and put him in a catatonic state.

"Why don't we go up the Bridge and get some music going," Wes told him.

"I-I-I know just the... thing," Stu replied, hurrying back through the stacks of magnesium toward the stairs.

Wes hit the button to close the airlock and followed him. The afternoon flew by. He scheduled to have provisions delivered mid morning on the following day. Water and hydrogen would be piped into the ship's tanks, while food would be brought in crates then stored in the supply lockers and freezers. Once Wes finished his work, he began to plan for their next job. There was nothing produced on Kellar Nine that couldn't be purchased cheaper in GA space, but he had a few contacts on the Alliance worlds. He let them know the *Jolly Rogue* was available for hire. But he planned in time to search Kellar Nine for Celeste Pierre too. They would spend at least a day in each of the cities. And while Colt did his thing, Wes would log into the local networks and search for any clues he could find about the missing girl. She would be a young woman, perhaps even on her own, but he doubted it. Whoever had taken her, if Evon was right and she was still alive, wouldn't let her go. And that meant that Wes would have to tread lightly. Finding her was one thing, doing so in such a way that no one knew they had found her was the real trick.

"How's... this?" Stu asked.

They had already listened to greatest hits album by a group called Chicago. Wes thought some of the songs were good, others were too lovelorn for his taste. He put a new disk into the slot on his console and looked over at Wes.

"Have you... heard the... news? he wrestled out, followed by a chuckle.

Music began to play, a booming heart beat sound pounding out of the Bridge speakers. Wes leaned over to look at Stu's console. The display showed the name of the CD. It was called

Sports, by a group known as Huey Lewis and the News. Wes chuckled at the joke.

"Catchy," he said to Stu as he slapped him on the shoulder. "I haven't heard the news."

"Whoo!" Stu yelled, his customary vocal troubles seemed to vanish when he sang. Unfortunately, it all came out in a monotone, but that didn't stop him from singing along.

New York, New York, is everything they say, and no place that I'd rather be! Where else can you do a half a million things, all at a quarter til three!

Wes had no idea what New York was, but it sounded fun. And he imagined that if he lived in the past he might agree with the singer. But at that moment in time, he was on Kellar Nine, and the crew of the *Jolly Rogue* had a job to do.

CHAPTER 31

Colt tried not to stare with his mouth wide open, but he simply couldn't believe he was on an actual world. The air was thick and there were no walls or windows holding everything in. He had never felt wind before, but as they strolled through an open air market where used components and gear were restored and resold, he felt a warm breeze lifting his hair.

"Try not to go all touristy on us, Colt," Di said with a grin.

"Sorry," he said, but the smile simply wouldn't leave his face.

As Di leaned over a table to look at an old alternator Zora gave Wes a playful bump with her shoulder. He looked at her and his smile was contagious. She turned her head but not before he saw the corners of her mouth turn upward.

"Is that a gravity amplifier?" Di asked the person at the booth.

"Sure is, works good too," the heavyset man replied. He had a thick beard and a leather apron with small pockets where he kept dozens of small tools which he was using to clean and restore a pile of small components still in a plastic bin by his feet.

"Have you ever converted one to amplify thrust on a quad engine hybrid?" Di asked.

"Not personally, but I've heard it can be done," the man said.

Di nodded. "I'll have to look into that. I'm coming back tomorrow. Would you consider sitting that gravity amp back for me?"

"For a fine woman like you, I'd be a fool not to," he said as he picked up the shoe sized component and set it under his table.

"I'm Diana."

"Wade," the man said. "Everyone here abouts knows me. How long are you in town?"

"Just a few days," Di said. "What I really need is an engine rebuild kit for a Hyborian quad 8590."

Wade gave a low whistle. "Not much Hyborian tech around here, not since the embargo anyway. You might try Glynda over at the salvage yard. She might have something."

"Good to know," Di said. "See you tomorrow, Wade."

"Looking forward to it, sweetheart."

Colt had been too overwhelmed with Kellar Nine to really start looking for Celeste Pierre at first. But as Di talked to the mechanic Colt had opened himself up. The market was full of people, mostly engineers and mechanics. Their thoughts were on the projects they were working on, and Wade's sudden, lustful thoughts about Di made him blush.

"You okay, Colt?" Di asked.

"Yeah," Colt said, blocking Wade from his mind. "Do you know what that guy was thinking?"

"Sure," Di said. "But it's harmless. I can't control what a person thinks, but if they make it obvious the way Wade did well, I don't mind taking advantage of it. We work with what we've got, right Zora."

Zora made a sound, almost a giggle but she clamped down

on it so hard it ended up being a kind of squelch. She turned away from Colt, embarrassed. He didn't have to read her mind to know that. And while he did have her blocked, he did feel the sudden surge of embarrassment in her emotions. Being close to a person it was impossible not to feel the really strong emotions, even though Colt wanted to keep a mental barrier between them. Whatever Zora thought or felt he wanted her to have the privacy she deserved.

They walked toward the salvage yard which took up one end of the market and was surrounded by a fence. Colt could see the rusting hulls of old ships over the top. At the entrance an old woman sat at a table, reading on her PA.

"Are you Glynda?" Di asked.

"That's me, what are you looking for, hon?"

"A rebuild kit for a Hyborian quad engine 8590."

"There's no kit, but if you go in and stay to the right, you'll come across a couple of Hyborian vessels. Can't say what's left on them, but you might find what you need," Glynda said.

"We're off loading cargo in the morning, and I won't have credits until then."

Glynda handed her a strip of orange ribbon. "If you see what you need, mark it with this ribbon. What's your name?"

"Diana."

Glynda typed out the name on her spread sheet along with the color of the ribbon she had just given Diana. *What a beautiful family*, the older woman thought. Colt felt an intense longing, followed by a wave of loneliness. Glynda was already focused on the book she was reading on her PA with a look of complete detachment on her face, but Colt knew it was all a facade.

Di led the way into the salvage yard. It was a massive field full of old ships, some in pieces, many with scorch marks and crash damage. Most of the ships had parts missing, but Colt could feel the excitement coming from Di. He did his best to give his crew mates their privacy, but blocking their emotions was difficult.

"You like it here?" Colt said.

"Look around," Di replied. "What do you see?"

"Junk ships," Colt said. "Trash. I suppose there's plenty of metals that could be recycled."

"No," Di replied. "This is so much more than that. It's a wonderland of possibilities. Given enough time and the right tools you could build your own ship, Colt. Think about that. A little from this one, a component from that one, anything is possible."

Colt didn't have the skills to build things. He was more of a general labor type person. Never one to shy away from hard work, Colt would give his all to whatever he was doing, but he had no real skills. He had hoped to learn a skill once he finished school and went to work. He was bright enough, but fixing things didn't come naturally to him.

It didn't take long to find the two Hyborian ships. Their hulls were mostly intact, and they had smooth flowing shapes, instead of the harsh, blocky angles most of the other ships had. Di took her time exploring each vessel. The airlocks had to be pried open to get inside, and Zora stayed with Di, while Colt lingered just outside. He spent the time letting his mind wander through the city. There were hundreds of people, but he wasn't looking for a man, so that made his search easier. Most people were focused on mundane tasks, like what to prepare for supper or what they were planning for their time off. Colt knew he was searching for someone young, perhaps only a few years older then himself. It didn't take long to discover how to find out a person's name and age. He gave tiny prompts and most people had no hesitation to think about themselves. He wasn't intrusive, and he doubted that anyone knew he had touched their minds.

"Let's go," Di said after searching the second ship.

"Did you find anything?"

"Did we ever," Di said. "Zora will tell you all about it."

Colt looked at her and she glanced at him, before turning away. They had spent the night together, Colt's arm wrapped around her narrow shoulders, but talking wasn't a bridge they had crossed yet.

"I'm going back to the ship," Diana said. "I want the two of you to have a little fun. You both have your com-links on?"

Colt reached up and touched his collar. The little device was pinned in place. He nodded, and so did Zora.

"Do you have money?" Di asked.

"A little," Colt said.

Zora nodded again.

"Good. This isn't a shopping spree," Di explained. "Just look around. There are vendors and shops to explore. And when you get tired, come back to the ship. We've got an early start to the day tomorrow."

"Got it," Colt said, while Zora nodded again.

"Good, have fun," Di said. She left them just outside the salvage yard.

"Where to?" Colt asked Zora.

She shrugged her shoulders. She seemed small, but strong. She wore a long jacket that flared outward below her waist, and had a stiff collar. Colt wasn't sure, but he thought she was carrying a small pistol under the jacket. Her dark hair was pulled back which made her facial features stand out even more.

"I'm not going to bug you all evening," he said, as he started toward the edge of the open market. There was a row of buildings with large windows and brightly painted signs. He decided to go to them and begin exploring. "But I thought we could talk a little."

"Okay," Zora said softly.

Colt took that as a good sign. He led the way and she stayed close beside him. Beyond the market the shops were for ship parts and customizations. Nothing that interested Colt and Zora seemed unenthused. They moved on and found a vendor selling drinks. Colt spent ten credits to get them both an ice filled beverage. The walked and sipped and took in the sights. Colt knew he should be looking for Celeste, but all he really wanted to do was get to know Zora. She was beautiful, and mysterious, and yet somehow charming at the same time. He couldn't get enough of her. Occasionally he made jokes and a few times she even laughed. They looked at clothes, toys, shops that sold food and sundries. They even came across a second hand store. Inside, they found a small collection of printed books.

"Look at this one," Colt said, holding up a ragged copy of a book called *The Evolution Of The Human Mind*. "Do you think the captain has it already?"

Zora shrugged her shoulders. A sign over the books said they cost twenty credits, but Colt looked over at the clerk. He only had ten credits left in his pocket and he held up the book.

"Would you take ten universal?" he asked.

"Let me see it," the clerk said, sounding bored.

As Colt took his book to the front, Zora continued browsing.

"I don't know man, the owner loves that book," the clerk said. "I can't let it go for less than fifteen." He was frowning, trying to seem disturbed, but his mind was wide open. *A sucker born every minute. Who would pay money for a musty old book anyway? What a dweeb.*

"On second thought, I can't pay more than five," Colt said.

"Dude, I said fifteen."

"It's a worthless old book," Colt said. "You know it's just taking up space. No one has read this thing in fifty years. Five credits. Take it or leave it."

What the hell, the clerk thought. "Fine, five credits."

Colt set the credit marker down and the clerk picked it up.

"Nice doing business with you," Colt said, realizing he could make their money go farther than he thought.

Zora appeared beside him with a plastic sleeve with a CD inside. The CD had the faces of four men on it. They had long, black hair, black and white paint covered of their faces and their eyes glowed. The CD was titled *Creatures Of The Night*. Colt supposed they looked frightening, but he had seen aliens who were much scarier.

"For Stu?" Colt asked.

Zora nodded.

"That's nice," he said, genuinely impressed that she had found something for their navigator. It hadn't crossed his mind that he might do something for someone besides himself.

She paid for the CD and they left with their purchases as the planet that lit the moon began to fade. All around them lights were being turned on for Kellar Nine's long night.

"What to get something to eat?"

Zora nodded. He smiled and reached out for her hand. She looked up surprised as he took it, but she didn't pull away. Colt felt like he had somehow stumbled into the most incredible life he could have imagined. He was a member of the crew on a starship, a blockade runner. It was exciting and he was exploring a world with a beautiful girl. He couldn't imagine anything better as they set off to find something to eat.

CHAPTER 32

Colt hadn't known what would happen when they returned to the ship. He and Zora had walked for nearly three hours through the town of Brighthaven on Kellar Nine. They ate fried chicken strips for their dinner, and took in the sights before returning to the ship. Colt didn't know if Zora would come to his cabin or not. She wasn't a talkative person, but Colt could sense at times that she wanted to speak. He did his best to prompt her, and ensure that she felt safe with him, but in the end she wasn't ready. So when they returned to the ship he walked her to her cabin and she went inside while he returned to his own room.

Music was playing from the bridge, Colt heard voices from the upper deck and strange animal sounds could be heard from Saide's room. Colt didn't want to talk to anyone, or think about what Saide was going to do to the animals he had purchased. He went into his cabin and was surprised to find the boxes and old bits of furniture, and spare parts for the ship were gone. He looked at his room, recognized the bed clothes, and the small table and chair, but there seemed to be twice as much space in the little berth as before. Someone had even set up an old flat panel display on the wall and connected the ship's computer to it. It was really his room and he could fill it with whatever he wanted. Tears stung his eyes, and he felt so good that he couldn't believe how incredibly his life was changing. Stowing away on the ship had been the low point in his life. He had never been more afraid or felt more alone than that day. But not even a week had passed and he was happier than he had ever been. His mother always told him that God was watching out for them, and he could see why she believed that. Things had worked out better than he could have imagined.

Sitting on his bed, he thumbed through the book he had purchased. Books had always been an escape for Colt. The one good thing about school had been access to the online library with millions of books he could check out and read on his PA. But there was something even more special about the old paper book he had purchased. It represented something to him, not just the object, but it said something about the person that he was. He was the kind of person who valued knowledge and saw reading as a way to increase his. The edges of the pages had yellowed over time, and the cover felt loose, but there was no water damage to the book. He opened it up and started to read.

A pounding on his door woke Colt. He had fallen asleep reading. The book lay open on his chest, and Colt's neck hurt from having turned to the side while he rested.

"Time to unload and get paid!" Saide's voice said.

"On my way," Colt shouted back.

He rushed through his morning routine. Brushing his teeth and washing his face before racing down to the cargo bay. The rest of the crew, minus Stu, were already there.

"Alright, we'll move this load off the ship once the crew from Allied Pharmaceuticals gets here," Wes said. "Colt, no one comes on board. That's a standing rule. We'll bring the goods out to them. We don't let strangers on board the *Jolly Rogue*, ever. You got that?"

"Yes sir," Colt said.

"Alright, let's get paid," Wes said as he raised the control cover and pressed the button that lowered the ship's loading hatch.

Colt was watching the wide hatch slowly descend to form a ramp that would make moving cargo into and out of the hold easier. Wes waved to him.

"Start unstrapping the Magnesium," the captain ordered. "Saide and I will move the pallets out."

Colt began to flip the latches on the ratchet straps nearest the cargo hatch. Once the straps were loose, he flipped the cargo netting over the tall stacks of boxes and tossed them against the bulkheads. He would have to fold them all up later, but speed seemed to be the important thing. Di and Zora helped with the cargo straps and netting. The five of them had the entire load of magnesium and merconium offloaded in under an hour. When they finished, Wes closed the cargo hatch. The workers from Allied Pharmaceuticals had already given him a stack of credit chips. They were flat rectangles made of plastic, each one loaded with a certain amount of universal credits.

"I'll have to break up the last of these," Wes said.

He handed Colt seven cards, each with a tiny digital display that showed the amount on them. There were four one hundred credit markers, one for five hundred, and two that showed a thousand credits each. He had twenty-nine hundred credits in his hand, more money than he had ever possessed at one time. In fact, it was the equivalent of what his mother made in a month, and from that she paid their rent and bought their food. Colt couldn't believe his eyes, which once more stung with the threat of tears.

"Don't spend it all on in one place," Diana said.

"She's right kid," Wes said. "We set up the biometric lock on your cabin. I'm the only person with the override. You've got a hidden security locker up there and you should keep most of your credits in that. Walking around with a pocket full of money may sound like fun, but trust me, you don't want to do that."

"We're going to the salvage yard," Di said. "I can rent a cargo cart, but I'll need help getting the gear we're buying up to engineering."

"I'll be here," Wes said. "We've got supplies scheduled to be delivered in an hour."

"I can help too," Colt said.

"Great!" Di replied. "See you boys later."

She and Zora left the ship, followed by Saide, as Wes led Colt back up to his cabin. They went inside and Wes was headed to the bathroom when he stopped and looked at the book on Colt's small bedside table. It was built into the wall, just a floating shelf with a built in chrono that showed the ship's time. Colt had left his new book on the shelf.

"What's that?" Wes said. He picked up the book. "This isn't one of mine."

"I found it last night," Colt said. "In a resale shop."

"Any good?"

"I fell asleep reading it," Colt said.

"That boring?"

"No, actually it's really interesting. I mean, it's all conjecture, but the author believes people like me are the future of the human race."

Wes raised his eye brows. "That so?"

"I just mean that my abilities are a natural progression in the evolution of the mind," Colt said.

"That was a common idea when Readers first appeared. Before the GA began rounding them up. Here, this is your locker."

He pointed to a place on the wall in the bathroom directly opposite from the toilet. It was nearly impossible to see unless you were looking for it. Wes reached out and slid the panel to one side. Behind it was a biometric lock.

"Put your thumb on there," Wes told him. Colt did and the door popped open. "No one can open that but you and me, kid. It's a good place to stash your valuables."

The small security locker was the size of a small shoebox. Colt put in all but two hundred credits and locked it back up. Then he slid the hidden panel back into place, as Wes moved past him and into the cabin. Colt followed.

"You can read any of the books in my library," Wes told him. "I'm pretty sure there's one up there about Readers. That's how I learned about the ranking system the GA uses to qualify you. Just take one out at a time."

"Thank you," Colt said. "I'll take you up on that."

"That's what the ship is for," Wes said looking around the bare cabin. "It's our home. You can decorate this space up however you want. Just keep it clean. You wouldn't want to attract any of the rodents Saide keeps."

"No sir," Colt said, looking at his unmade bed. "I overslept today, but I'll do better."

"Good enough," Wes said. "Let's go get ready for the supplies. Once that's done, and we've helped Di with whatever she found in the salvage yard, you can do a little shopping. You could stand to get some new clothes."

Colt felt another thrill of excitement at the prospect of getting new clothes. He might need more credits, but he would start small. He didn't know how often they might get paid and he didn't want to blow all his money right away.

When the supplies arrived, Wes showed Colt exactly how to attach the refueling and water hoses to the ship. They watched the big tanks fill. They only needed half a tank of water, but the hydrogen was nearly completely empty. Wes had to pay nearly three thousand credits to refill the ship's fuel and water. Then came the crates of food. It was mostly dry goods. Bags of rice, beans, pasta, flour, and sugar. There were boxes of canned goods too, mostly vegetables, but some meat and sauces as well. One of the large chest freezers was reserved for prepackaged meals. Colt helped Wes get it all stowed neatly away and was folding up the cargo nets when Diana returned. Zora was riding on a cargo cart, using the hand held controls to steer it down the street toward the ship. Inside was what looked to be an engine.

"What is that?" Wes said.

"It's an engine," Di said. She sounded excited, like a child on their birthday who had just opened the present they had been hoping for."

"How did you afford an engine?"

"It doesn't work," Di said. "The block is cracked. I think the old ship we took it from had a water leak in the cooling system. Anyway, I got it for cheap."

"You mean you paid for an engine we can't use?" Wes asked.

"It's not to be used, it's to be salvaged," Di said. "Almost all the components on it work. We can use it to overhaul the engines we have. Odds are good it will have all the parts we need to get our engines in tip-top shape."

"Wonderful," Wes said.

"Looks heavy," Colt said. "How are we going to get it up to the engineering bay."

"We'll have to rent a crane," Wes said with a sigh. "There's no telling what that will cost."

"We could leave it down here," Di said. "I can break it down over the next week or so."

"We need this space for cargo," Wes insisted.

"Do we have cargo?" Di asked, knowing full well they hadn't gotten a new job yet.

"Not yet," Wes said. "But I don't want a bunch of engine parts scattered around my cargo bay. Especially not while we're in atmo."

Colt had an idea. He had used his Reader ability to levitate the cards when Wes tested him. He wondered if it was possible to lift something heavier.

"Maybe we don't have to," Colt said.

"What?" Wes asked.

"Let's get it inside," Colt said. "I have an idea."

"See, the kid has an idea," Diana said. "Stop worrying."

"The two of you are the cause of my worry," Wes said, rubbing his stomach.

Zora drove the cart into the cargo bay, and Colt closed the door. Once they were hidden from sight by people who were passing on the street, Colt reached out with his mind. He could feel the engine, not just the big heavy object, but all the interlocking parts. It was like seeing a puzzle and holding it without the little cardboard pieces falling apart. He imagined it rising out of the cart, but nothing happened.

"What's the idea?" Wes asked.

"Just wait," Di insisted.

Colt closed his eyes and willed the engine to move. It was

like trying to wake up from a dream, to escape a nightmare, but he didn't give up. He insisted that the engine rise up, not just willing it to, but insisting it obey him. He pushed his mind into the space where the engine sat on the cart, forcing it to move.

And it did.

CHAPTER 33

Hussain was awake and had just finished washing up when the private communication console beeped at him. It was an alert that he had a message waiting. Hussain, dressed in his usual dark suit, with the long syntha-silk jacket that hung to his knees, and his hair slicked back and bound into a little bun at the base of his skull, moved to the closet sized room. He stepped inside, closed the door, and activated the unit. An image appeared on the screen, once the system had completed the decryption process. Director Emmitt Turkov appeared. He was a small man, his hair buzzed short, with deep lines around his eyes and mouth.

"Hussain, your message is timely," the director said. "We must find and acquire this new Reader that you have discovered. Interestingly enough, I am aware of the ship it is traveling on."

The director paused, almost as if he knew that his announcement would shock Hussain. And it did. The director was a man of great knowledge. The clandestine service was at work in every system of the galaxy, and yet the fact that he would know about the nondescript Hyborian freighter was difficult to fathom, even for Hussain.

"It is a blockade runner we have some interest in. Fortunately for us both, I know exactly where that ship will go next. Take your team of hunters to the Gerber system."

Another pause and Hussain wondered why the *Jolly Rogue* would go to the Gerber system. Gerber three was being terraformed but was far from being habitable. The system was known instead for the Heaven's Trail Resort and Casino space station. It was a place where criminal elements could meet and plan their nefarious business, but the freighter wouldn't find a cargo there, unless they were possibly moving food for the resort. Still, Hussain knew that food deliveries were almost always done by the Freight Haulers Guild and the *Jolly Rogue* was an indie ship. They would never get a contract to deliver provisions to the resort. It made no sense to Hussain, but he trusted his mentor.

"You'll have no trouble blending in there. Let your team enjoy themselves, but stay alert. The *Jolly Rogue* will come to you. When she does, you must capture the target quietly. Take the entire ship if need be. I have sent orders to the Farm to prepare for a new arrival with extreme power. Keep me informed, Hussain. If this target is as powerful as you say, we must bring him under our control. There are plans in motion that will bring the clandestine service to the height of power in the universe. Do not fail me."

The message ended abruptly. Hussain felt both a thrill, and a spark of resentment. Capturing a Reader was never easy. And if Hussain was right about the target's power, if he was really an L5, then it would be an extremely dangerous mission. Not that Hussain would give up. He didn't fear the readers he pursued, but like any seasoned hunter, he respected the abilities of his prey.

He left his suite of rooms and was met by one of the artificials who maintained the ship. This particular android was female, and responded to the name Chi.

"How may I serve you?" Chi asked.

The voice was human, her skin flawless, even the eyes seemed real, but to Hussain she was a void. There was no mental energy, no life inside, just a machine following its programming.

"Is the rest of my team on board?" Hussain asked.

"No sir, you are the only passenger on board at this time," Chi replied.

"Fine, I'll get them. We're leaving. Have Ho prepare for take-off."

"As you wish," Chi replied.

Her voice sounded almost seductive, as if carrying out his commands gave her an emotional response. But there was no emotion. Hussain could swim in the minds of people, and he often felt their emotions if they were strong enough. Chi was no different than a chair, just another part of the ship, with no feelings, no emotions, and no original thoughts. But she was reliable and that made her useful to Hussain. He had programed the artificials on his ship to maintain things the way he preferred them. It was one of the perks of his office, and another reason why working in the GA clandestine services was worthwhile.

Walking from the ship, with the tails of his dressy coat flapping around his knees, Hussain crossed the wide hangar. He didn't have to look far to find his team. Horace, the Feringian was getting a full body grooming. Troy and Kurt were his Reader counterparts. They were busy drinking at the bar that had been constructed where a maintenance crew had once kept their equipment and tools.

"We have work," Hussain said.

"What? We're on break," Troy complained.

A deep throated growl rumbled from Horace. The team of barbers backed away, and Hussain felt a whisper of fear from them.

"Can't say no to the man," Kurt said, after tossing back a shot of some dark liquor from a tiny class.

"Director Turkov has given us an assignment," Hussain said.

"Did you even bother to tell him we just got finished with the last one yesterday?" Troy asked. "We haven't even had twenty-four hours off yet."

Hussain ignored their complaints. He didn't care what they thought. As the team leader, he commanded them and they obeyed. If they didn't, they would be sent back to the Farm for reconditioning. Besides, he knew they wouldn't balk when he told them where they were going.

"We have a target," Hussain said. "Possibly an L5."

"Are you kidding me?" Troy asked.

"What, like a real live L5?" Kurt asked. "What cartel is this target with?"

"We don't believe he is with a cartel," Hussain said. "He is part of the crew of an independent ship. A blockade runner. The director believes the target will go to the Gerber system soon. And we will be there waiting."

"We talking Gerber Three, or Heaven's Trail?" Kurt asked.

"We shall go to the resort," Hussain said. "We leave as soon as the ship is ready."

"Well why didn't you say so," Kurt said with a grin.

"You should lead with that kind of information," Troy added. "Save us all some grief."

Hussain turned to Horace. The Feringian preferred to be naked, but wore battle gear when on duty. He was already pulling on a flight suit over his thick fur.

"We've been ordered to blend in," Hussain continued. "But we must remain alert."

"I don't have to drink to gamble," Troy said.

It was illegal for a Reader to gamble, but if they were going to blend in they would have to take part in the gaming carried out by the casino. Beside, in Hussain's mind, Hunters were above the law.

"Or have a good time," Kurt added.

The two men high fived one another as they left their barstools and headed for the ship. Horace was collecting his weapons. The Feringian was incredibly strong and fierce in a fight. Horace was also a weapons expert, from knives to explosives and everything in between. He was the force segment of their team.

"We're agreed then," Hussain said. He turned quickly and began the walk back toward their ship as the engines hummed to life and his team hurried to keep up.

CHAPTER 34

"Unbelievable," Di said.

"Kid, that's something," Wes said.

Colt was trying to catch his breath. He had levitated the engine from the cart to floor of the cargo bay. It was hard work, but he had managed it. And the truth was, he felt good afterward. It was like using a muscle he had never exercised before.

"I think," Colt said. "I can get up to the engineering bay if I can take my time."

"We don't want you to overdo it," Wes said. "There's other work to be done."

"But we're not in a hurry," Di said. "He can do a little bit here and there."

"Alright, but only with supervision," Wes said. "You drop that thing on your foot and you're toast."

They unloaded the rest of the cart which had dozens of small parts and components stacked inside. When they were finished Wes took them all to lunch. It was odd eating in a restaurant on a real world in what seemed like the dead of night.

Brighthaven was one of the three main cities on Kellar Nine and had several large farms nearby that provided fresh meat and vegetables. They had fresh salads, with cold strips of chicken, nuts, fruit, and freshly baked bread. Colt had never eaten such fresh produce in his life.

After lunch, they did some shopping. Colt bought three pairs of pants, four shirts, a puffy vest, and a new jacket. By the time he was done he had spent nearly two hundred credits, but felt like a king. When they got back to the ship the sun was just starting to rise. Music was filtering down from the Bridge, a pounding beat and distorted guitars. A raw voice bellowed the lyrics: *Stand up, you don't have to be afraid. Get down, love is like a hurricane. Street boy, no I never could be tamed - You better believe it!*

"You gave Stu the CD?" Colt asked Zora.

She smiled.

"Wonderful," Wes said. "Maybe avoid the heavy metal next time."

"Oh come on," Di said. "A little variety never hurt anyone."

They left Brighthaven early the next morning. Colt spent the first part of the flight scanning for anyone who could possibly be Celeste Pierre. There were amazing things he could do with his gifts. He had even managed to move the salvage engine up to the main deck, but he still felt like a failure for not finding the woman they were looking for. It didn't help that he really had nothing to go on. He had no idea what she looked like, or who took her. It was like swimming in a sea that was filled with fish and he was looking for one but he had no idea what it was.

It only took them a few hours to reach Harrisburg, They landed at the space port and Colt went looking for a game system. He had always wanted a video game system, but there was never enough money. Unfortunately, things like game systems and large screen PA were hard to come by in Alliance space. The embargo from the Galactic Authority kept the latest tech from the people they considered rebels.

The search was really more of a front. Wes and Colt went from store to store, browsing, but not for things to buy as much as the people in the town. Colt let his mind move from person to person. Some they encountered, others were far away. He focused on females, close to his age, but after a few hours they seemed no closer to finding Celeste Pierre.

"Maybe this isn't a good idea," Colt said, as he slumped onto a park bench.

He was sweating a little, partly from the exertion of searching for Celeste, but also from the heat of the sun. Kellar Nine was a warm place and Colt was wearing his new clothes. He pulled off the vest and was thankful that he had left the new jacket in the ship.

"Well, we had to try something," Wes said. "I searched the local networks. I had no luck either."

"Where does that leave us?"

"No worse off than before," Wes said. "I've feelers out to my people on this side of the blockade, but so far no jobs worth taking."

"So we stay here," Colt asked, "and keep looking?"

"Might as well," Wes said.

They were headed back to the ship when they passed a tiny shop. It was nothing more than a doorway that led to a set of stairs between two larger businesses. On the door was a sign that read - Madam Stella - Fortune Teller.

"Can you believe that kind of hocus-pokus still exists," Wes said.

Colt shrugged his shoulders. He had seen fortune tellers on television and in movies, but most of the time they were con artists. There were even fortune telling programs on the GA net, all for a nominal fee of course. Colt had never been tempted to find out what his future held. But he did let his mind wander up to the tiny room at the top of the stairs. There was a woman there and he felt her mind, but was repulsed by her own mental barriers.

Colt stopped walking. Wes turned and looked at him.

"You okay?" Wes said.

Colt pointed at the tiny shop. "We should go in."

"No way," Wes said. "Those people are all crooks. They don't have any kind of powers. It's all a con job, kid."

"I know," Colt said. "But she's a Reader."

Wes frowned. Colt probed the woman's defenses and felt her sudden surge of panic.

"She's running," Colt said.

"She probably thinks you're the GA," Wes pointed out.

"On an Alliance world?"

"Okay, then she's afraid of getting caught."

Colt turned back and went into the shop. He bounded up the stairs, but the girl was gone. He looked around but there was no obvious exit, but reaching out with his mind he found her going down a hidden hallway.

"This way," Colt said.

He followed and it didn't take long for Colt's insistent probing to break through into the woman's mind. Unlike most people, who's thoughts and feelings were clear to him, the woman's mind was murky. There were what appeared to be gapping holes.

"Who the hell are you?" a gruff voice asked as they reached the end of the narrow hall and entered a larger room.

Colt had been so intent on the girl, that he hadn't really been paying attention. The room was smokey, and smelled of unwashed bodies. There was a heavily padded reclining chair that looked like someone sat in it all day, perhaps even slept in it. And there was a cot in the corner. A young woman in a colorful outfit was on the cot, huddled in the corner. The man with the gruff voice also had a blaster, which was pointed right at Colt.

"Sorry, sir, we aren't looking for trouble," Wes said as he slowly moved out from behind Colt.

There was fear mingled with anger coming from the man with the gun. *They finally found us,* the man thought. *Took them long enough.* Colt plunged into the man's mind, swimming deep, searching for an answer about the girl. It came to him like it was his own memory. Colt saw a woman approach the man. She was older, with streaks of gray in her hair, and noticeable wrinkles at the corners of her eyes. *We need help,* the woman said. *And protection. We'll pay.* Colt saw a little girl hugging tightly to the woman's legs. *Protection from who?* the gruff man asked. *From everyone. She's gifted,* the older woman said, patting the toddler on the head. *No one can know.* Colt felt the man's discomfort. *I don't want nothing to do with kidnapping,* he said. *It's not like that,* the woman said. *Her father sent her away. He doesn't want her sent to the GA's Reader program. Will you help us?*

Colt pulled back. He hadn't seen or heard anything that revealed the girl's identity, but he felt certain it was the PM's daughter. He looked at the girl in the corner. She was a few years older than he was, and attractive, but clearly not okay. He could feel the fear coming off her in tremendous waves. Colt held up his hands.

"We're not going to hurt anyone," Colt said.

"Damn straight," the gruff man replied. "It's best if you just turn around and leave."

It's her, Colt thought, pushing the words to Wes' mind. *Okay, don't push it,* Wes replied.

"We made a mistake," Wes said out loud. He pointed at the girl in the corner, "This woman took our money. We just wanted to get it back."

"Well, that's too bad, ain't it," the gruff man said. "The sign out front says no refunds. The only thing you'll get back here is a blaster beam to the chest. You want that?"

"No," Colt said.

"No, we don't," Wes agreed.

"Then start moving," the gruff man said. "And don't come back."

I'm a friend, Colt thought, pushing the words to the girl. Her eyes grew wide, but it was clear that she was paralyzed by fear. *I would never hurt you. My name is Colt.*

Wes had a hand on Colt's arm and was leading him back down the narrow hallway. Colt could feel the fear from the girl. The gruff man was pushing her along, rushing her out a back exit.

"Tell me you can track her now," Wes said.

"Yeah," Colt said. "But it's taking a lot of concentration."

"I got ya, kid," Wes said.

They went back down the stairs and out into the front of the little shop. People were passing by, oblivious to what had happened upstairs and who the fortune teller really was.

"Where are they going?" Wes asked.

"I'm not sure," Colt said. "That way."

He pointed and Wes looked around, getting his bearings.

"There's a long term storage facility that way," Wes said. "Odds are they've got a ship there. Come on, Kid. We don't have much time."

They rushed back toward the dock where the *Jolly Rogue* was moored. Colt got glimpses into the girl's mind. He didn't know whether to think of her as Stella, or Celeste, or someone else. She was riddled with fear, and there were gaps in her mind. Colt couldn't be sure but it seemed like she had holes in her memory. He didn't know if it was from trauma or danger, but there were scars in her mind, places his abilities couldn't penetrate.

"Diana, drop what you're doing," Wes said over the com-link. "Get the ship ready to fly."

"You got it," Di replied.

"Saide, do you copy?" Wes asked.

"I'm on my way back," the Hyborian pilot said.

"Good, we made a breakthrough, I want everyone ready to go ASAP."

It took Colt and Wes ten minutes to reach the ship. The fortune teller and her gruff counterpart were faster. Colt could feel her moving away from the city. Saide was back on board by the time Colt and Wes arrived. They shut the airlock and gave the order for lift off.

"We're grounded," Saide said as Colt and Wes rushed onto the bridge. "There's a ship inbound and we're having to wait."

"What happened?" Di asked from her console.

"The kid found her," Wes said. "And get this... she's a Reader."

CHAPTER 35

Wes was busy doing a search on fortune tellers. It didn't take long to find Stella's website on the local network, but there was no picture of her. The search did produce social media hits from clients though, and some of them had taken pictures. Wes picked one and put it on the main display. The girl who called herself Stella was thin, wore too much make up, and had streaks of silver in her hair. Wes wasn't sure what was real and what was simply part of the persona she was trying to create, but to him she looked like a frightened pet, the kind seen on animal rights commercials and in rescue shelters.

"That's Celeste Pierre?" Di asked when the picture popped up.

"Yeah, she's been working as a psychic," Wes explained.

"Makes sense if she can read minds," Saide said. "Who's got her?"

"That's hard to say. Looked like a cartel guard to me," Wes said.

"No," Colt countered. "He's private security, hired years ago by a woman who I think worked for the Pierres."

"She was taken by the help?" Di asked.

"Not taken," Colt said. "Sent away. She exhibited signs early on. Enough that someone realized she was a Reader."

"And her politician father didn't want her sent to the GA's off the books program for Readers," Wes said. "If that doesn't prove the Galactic Authority is no good I don't know what does. How much longer, Saide?"

"Ten minutes maybe," the pilot replied. "The port control is in no hurry."

"You still got her kid?" Wes asked.

"There's a lot of interference, but I think so," Colt said. "If we get closer I'll be able to lock on again, or find her. I'm sure of it."

"So they've been hiding her from the GA, pretending she was kidnapped," Di said. "I suppose being the victim of such a horrible crime helped his career."

"Makes me sick just thinking about it," Wes said. "But I can't say I'm surprised."

"So if he sent his daughter away," Di continued. "Who is Evon working for? Not the PM."

"No," Wes said. "But if they find her and break the real story, it would be a huge scandal. Pierre would almost certainly have to resign."

"Maybe that's the point," Saide said. "It's probably some political rival. Odds are they know the story, but they need to find her to prove it."

"So what do we do?" Di said.

Wes understood the question. Part of him wanted to out Celeste Pierre just because it would embarrass the GA. He couldn't stand politicians and the GA was so heavy handed it made him ill just to think about the way they tried to control everyone and everything. The galaxy was full of people, hundreds of worlds and thousands of space stations. There was plenty of space for people who wanted to different things to spread out and live life on their own terms. But the GA didn't see it that way. They wanted power and control. If a planet didn't want to be in the GA, it was sanctioned, the trade routes in and out of that system would be blocked by military vessels. It was a classic bully tactic and Wes hated it.

But if Celeste was innocent, was it right for him to turn her over to someone who would just use her as a pawn in their political games? They weren't searching out of concern for her well-being. And that meant they wouldn't protect her from the press, or even from the GA itself. Once it was known that she was a Reader, the clandestine service would come for her. Wes didn't like the thought of that either.

"We need more information," Wes said. "We need to find out who's got her and what they're doing with her."

"She's terrified," Colt said. "I've never felt such complete fear. She's probably been told that bad people are searching for her for years. When we showed up, when she felt me with her mind, she assumed the bad people had finally found her."

"So we need to convince her that we're not the bad people," Wes said.

"That means you won't turn her over to the people who offered you that universal shipping pass," Di said.

"Not if she's being protected," Wes said. "But I want the full story."

"And what if they're criminals using her for their own plans?" Di asked.

"We'll cross that bridge when we come to it," Wes said, feeling the burning sensation in his stomach again.

"We're cleared for lift off in three minutes," Saide said.

"Are we... leaving the s-s-system?" Stu asked, craning his head to the side in an effort to get the words out.

"No, not yet," Wes said. "There's some big players involved here. We need to make our next move carefully. Kid, do you still have her?"

"Just a trace," Colt said. He pointed behind him. "She's that direction."

"Stu?" Wes asked.

"South... west," he said. "Nothing for eight hundred k-kil-kilom... meters."

"Russelbrook," Di said. "They'd be taking the long way to get there, but eventually they'll reach Russelbrook."

"Or maybe that's what they want us to think," Wes said. "There's a lot of empty space on this moon."

"It should be easier to find her away from the city," Colt said. "There's a lot of mental noise here."

"Alright, Saide, take us southwest. Cruising speed. Colt, if we get closer can you talk to her?"

"Yeah," Colt replied.

"Then we'll get close but not too close," Wes said. "I don't want to spook them into running again. Let's see if we can convince her that we're on her side."

"I agree," Diana said.

"Sounds reasonable," Saide added.

"I'm... in," Stu said as he rocked back and forth in his seat.

Wes was glad it was Stu's excited rock and not his afraid motion. Wes wanted to do something, but all he could do was sit down at his console and wait. The ship was rising into the air, but Saide had control. Colt would find the girl. All Wes could do was try to figure out their best move. He stared at the picture of Stella the Fortune Teller as he thought about their predicament.

If he went back to Evon's people and denied finding Celeste, perhaps they would believe him. But if they didn't, would they feel the need to take Wes and his crew out of the picture? If they knew that he had discovered the truth they certainly would. He hadn't asked for the job, yet he had taken it and that meant he knew about the group looking for Celeste. They might think that he knew too much. If the people Evon worked with were dirty enough, they wouldn't think twice about having the *Jolly Rogue* vaporized with all hands on board. He didn't like that thought at all.

The fear in the girl's eyes was unmistakable to him. And it seemed contagious. What had he gotten them into? He wanted to think he didn't have a choice, but it was the temptation of the universal shipping pass that had tipped the scales. Normally, he didn't take jobs from people he didn't know. There were too many unseen motives, too often jobs were part shady deals that if they fell apart would leave Wes and his people holding the bag. He had broken his own rule and if he wasn't careful it might cost him more than he could afford to pay.

"I've got her again," Colt said. "We're gaining on them."

"They must have stopped," Wes said. "We're not going that fast."

"Can you tell how far out they are, Colt?" Di asked.

"Still a long way," Colt said. "Forty or fifty kilometers I think."

"Saide," Wes instructed the pilot, "look for a place to set us down. I don't want them seeing us."

"How could they see us if they're fifty klicks out?" Di asked.

Wes pointed at the display screen. In the distance a volcanic mountain rose up. There was snow at it's peak. Wes guessed that meant it was dormant.

"If they landed up there, and they're watching their trail," Wes said. "They'll see us coming a long way off."

"Touché," Diana said with a wink.

"Looks like there's a clearing near that lake," Saide said. "I can put us down there."

"I haven't been camping in a long time," Di said. "Looks like fun."

Wes hoped she was right. He rubbed his burning stomach. He was ready for a break from the stress. Finding Celeste Pierre should have been a major victory for his crew. Instead, it was turning out to be a dangerous turn of events. He felt like he had wandered into a trap and needed to find his way out, before it was too late.

CHAPTER 36

Heaven's Trail was a high end resort. From a distance it looked like a crystal ball floating in space. Beyond it, the golden glow of the Heaven's Trail nebula was a spectacular sight.

"Gerber flight control, contacting approaching vessel *Pakhet*. Do you copy? Over."

Hussain was on the Bridge of his yacht. The vessel flew itself once the destination was put into the navigation computer. And Hussain would let the resort's automated docking program take control of the ship and maneuver it into the resorts hangar. But he liked being on the Bridge. The rest of his team rarely bothered to go there. Yet it gave Hussain a feeling of control, while also allowing him to think and plan for the mission they were on. He pressed a button on his large chair that looked out the yacht's view ports.

"Gerber flight control, this is the *Pakhet*," Hussain said. "We copy. Requesting permission to dock at the resort. Over."

"Copy, *Pakhet*, please forward your reservation documents."

Hussain didn't have a reservation. Normally he would

simply forward his GA credentials, but they sometimes needed to blend in to an environment, which was one of the reasons their official vessel was a yacht and not a military cruiser. For this mission, Hussain would use a different resource. One of the perks of the GA clandestine service was access to nearly unlimited funds.

"Flight control, we do not have a reservation, over," he transmitted.

"Roger, let me transfer you to the resort booking agent, standby *Pakhet*," the flight controller said.

It took a few minutes, which didn't surprise Hussain. When another voice finally spoke up he could hear the skepticism in the booking agent's voice.

"*Pakhet*, this is Heaven's Trail actual. Flight control informs me you are interested in booking a stay at our resort. Over."

"That is correct," Hussain replied. He let his mind connect to the booking agent. It was a simple matter to see into the man's mind. Hussain could even see through his eyes. The agent worked in a tiny, dirty little office that was smaller than Hussain's closet. *Why can't people just book online in advance,* the agent thought. *I'm so sick of these rich pricks. I hope this guy loses a fortune.*

Hussain chuckled. He didn't gamble, but if he did he would win. Losing wasn't something he experienced very often. Occasionally, his quarry evaded Hussain, but rarely for long. The hunter had never not gotten his man or woman eventually.

"The resort requires a deposit for rooms, and gaming. What type of accommodations are you looking for, *Pakhet*. Over."

"The best four suites you have available," Hussain said. "We will gladly put down whatever deposit is required."

"Four rooms, let's see. I've got suites available, they run

fifteen hundred credits per twenty-four cycle. I'm assuming you're human, *Pakhet*. Over."

"Negative," Hussain replied. "Three humans, one Feringian."

"Oh, well, we have xeno-specific rooms. Let me check on Feringian..." There was a slight pause and the tap of the agent's finger nails on his touch screen. "We have a Feringian room available for eighteen hundred credits per twenty-four hour cycle. Is that acceptable, *Pakhet*? Over."

"That is fine," Hussain replied. "Hold those accommodations for two weeks, please. You can put a deposit of half a million credits on our account. The name is Landry, H. K. Capital Bank, system number GA - zero seventeen, routing number two - eight - seven, nine-zero-zero, five-five-one. Account number twenty-four hundred, seventy-seven, ninety-four, double zero, nine. Over."

Hussain felt the shock from the booking agent as he casually dropped half a million credits into the resort's coffers. The man repeated the banking information and Hussain approved it. He was then transferred back to flight control. The *Pakhet* was still an hour from the resort at thruster speeds, but the automated landing sequence had begun.

Hussain got to his feet and moved back down from the Bridge, through what was traditionally the crew's quarters. The artificials who kept the ship didn't need sleep and could recharge in tiny docks that were recessed into the wall of the engineering section. The crew quarters were converted into holding cells. Hussain glanced into one of the small, austere cabins as he passed it. There was no carpet, just metal deck plating a recessed bunk with a rubber mattress, and a heavy door on the hatch with a spinning lock on the outside. He wondered how long it would be until his new quarry, the L5 that had slipped through their fingers near the Farm, was sedated in one of those cells. The thrill of the hunt made Hussain's heart rate increase. Most of their targets had barely any powers at all. And of those few that did rarely knew how to use them. Hussain knew that some of the criminal organizations had Readers that they employed to help carry out their nefarious business, but they were adept at hiding their gifted accomplices. The L5 he was after was both powerful and dangerous. He relished the challenge as he walked into the main salon. It was a long room with view ports on either side. There were comfortable chairs for each of them, and a glossy round table for meals. A movie was playing on the display wall. Kurt was watching it with large headphones over his ears, but he paused the movie and removed the listening device when Hussain entered.

"Are we there yet?" Kurt asked.

"On approach," Hussain said. "We'll use alternative names. If you wish to gamble and keep your winnings, please use your own funds."

"We're paying for this vacation?" Troy asked.

"You will have your own rooms," Hussain said, wondering if the resort was as plush as his cabin on the *Pakhet*. "Meals and drinks have been taken care of. But this is not a vacation. We're on assignment."

"What does that mean exactly?" Kurt asked.

"We'll make a formal plan once the target arrives," Hussain said. "Until then, blend in, but keep your senses open. The target is powerful, perhaps an L5."

Horace grunted. The Feringian was capable of speaking, but he rarely did.

"That much mental power would be hard to hide," Troy said.

"You would think," Kurt agreed.

"Once he is in the system, our job will be to bring him in," Hussain said. "Until then, have fun. Just don't get impaired. I have no idea how long our target will be in system or what his goals are."

"There's only one reason to be in the Gerber system," Troy said.

"To party," Kurt said. "I'm ready to get started."

"Once we dock the ship, you can sign into your rooms and do as you please," Hussain said.

"My kind of assignment," Kurt said. "Let's hope the target takes his time getting here."

Hussain didn't care how long it took. He knew it wouldn't be easy to capture an L5. Most Readers that powerful were taken as children and very few survived in the field. They went insane, or betrayed the service. But Hussain thought that maybe their new target was different. It might be a long hunt, but Hussain didn't mind. He was ready, and with a Reader powerful enough to take control of a person's mind, there was no limit to what might be accomplished.

CHAPTER 37

Colt was outside, standing on the shore of the lake. He hadn't pressed into Celeste's mind yet. Instead, standing at the water's edge, his boots off, his feet in the warm, black volcanic sand, he let the peace of Kellar Nine fill him. It was quiet, the only sound was the lapping of the water nearby. In the sky, the gas giant planet that held Kellar Nine in it's gravitational grip, was starting to rise. Colt didn't think he'd ever seen any place as beautiful. Around the shore large trees with bright green leaves stood and rustled in the breeze. The air smelled clean and inviting. Colt thought that he could stay in that place for a lifetime and never get tired of it.

"You okay, kid?" Wes asked quietly.

Colt nodded.

"Alright well, no rush. We're going to stay here a few days while we figure out our next move. You take your time with Celeste, but let me know if they move."

"Yes sir," Colt said quietly.

Behind him he could hear the others setting up camp. When

Colt looked over his shoulder he was surprised to see that the cargo hatch was down, and a tarp had been hung like a canopy over a group of camp chairs. Zora was gathering fire wood, and even Stu was out of the ship. He and Saide were collecting stones for a fire pit.

Colt had never been camping before. But he knew the moment he saw the others preparing to spend a few days in the woods that he would sleep outside to see the stars and feel the night breeze. It was something he'd never dreamed of before, perhaps because it never occurred to him that something like camping, an activity he had only seen in movies, was even possible for him.

He sat down on the sand. It was coarse, but had soaked up the sunlight. Even though the system star was far away, the light reached Kellar Nine and raised the temperature significantly. When the sun set, the thick atmosphere and the volcanic activity kept the surface temperature above freezing.

It was finally time to send Celeste a message. He thought of her, and could feel her anxiety, even from a distance. She was older than he was, perhaps as much as five years older, and yet she seemed like a child. He focused all his attention on her and said her name in his mind. *Celeste?*

Her fear spiked, but he pushed the sense of calm and peace he felt by the lake toward her. Surprisingly enough, he felt her worry decrease. Normally, the very thought of manipulating a person's feelings made him feel like a creep. But knowing that he could help Celeste not be so afraid gave him a boost of confidence. He realized his gifts could be used to help people, not just manipulate and con people, or steal their secrets.

I'm not going to hurt you, he thought. *I'm going to take you away. I just want to help you.*

He could feel the turmoil that Celeste was feeling. She

didn't trust him but that was to be expected. Yet she was surprised and even a little curious about him.

You can hear my thoughts? she replied.

When I try to, he responded. *I hope that's okay.*

Another pause while she consider this new information. He could sense her mental defenses hovering at the edges of her conscious mind. She had left them cracked open, just a sliver. It was enough for him to get through and he knew she had done that on purpose. She knew he could batter down her defenses, so she hadn't tried to keep him out.

What do you want? she finally asked.

Colt considered his own answer. He didn't want to say something that would make her angry or afraid. *I want to know what happened to you. Why are you on Kellar Nine?*

It's safe, she replied more quickly than before.

Safe from who?

The chasers. I thought you were one of them.

No, Colt admitted. *I'm trying to avoid them too. How long have you been here?*

I don't know. I have trouble remembering.

Colt thought of the gaps he had felt in her mind and realized that her guardians, or captors, had used some type of chemical agent to destroy parts of her memory. He felt her sadness and couldn't help but feel it too. She was lonely, scared, and sad.

Who is taking care of you? he asked.

Orin, the man with the gun. There was someone else before, but I don't know what happened to her.

Do you remember your family?

A surge of fear hit Colt. He wasn't sure if it was because of his connection to her, or if she was so afraid that he could feel the emotion from dozens of kilometers away.

It's okay, he thought, trying to sooth her. *You are safe.*

Family isn't safe, she replied.

I'm sorry about that. Are you in a safe place now?

Orin says so.

Good. Why don't you rest. We can talk tomorrow.

You'll still be there?

Yes, I promise. You can trust me, Celeste. I'm not going to hurt you or let anyone else hurt you.

You want to be my friend? she wondered, sounding more and more like a little child.

Yes, Colt replied. *I'm your friend. My name is Colt.*

I'm Stella. No one calls me by the old name anymore.

Okay, Stella. It's nice to have a friend.

For the first time he felt a different emotion from her. It was excitement, a kind of hopeful expectation. Colt got up, brushed his pants off, and walked over to where his friends were sitting around a bright little fire.

"How'd it go?" Wes asked.

"I talked to her," Colt said. "She's pretty messed up."

"What do you mean?" Di asked.

"Scared, confused. I think she's been abused."

"I though her caregiver took her," Wes said. "Why would she abuse the girl she was trying to protect?"

"I don't know," Colt said, wondering the same thing himself. "There are gaps in her memory and these places in her mind. I felt them when I was closer. They were like scars or something. I think maybe they gave her some type of treatments to make her forget things."

"Sounds like she wasn't really better off," Di said. "I've heard rumors about how Readers are treated when the GA gets hold of them. But I've never heard of memory treatments."

"How long has she been here?" Wes asked.

"She doesn't know," Colt said. "In some ways she's like a little child. She remembers having been in other places, but not moving."

"They wiped her memory of the times they were forced to run," Saide said. "Trying to keep her from understanding what is happening to her."

"So what's their plan?" Wes asked.

"She says they're hiding," Colt said. "The guy with the gun is named Orin. He's the only one looking after her now. Something happened to the woman."

"I feel like I don't know what we're talking about," Di said. "Who are these other people?"

"We followed her and ran into a big guy in the back room of their fortune telling shop," Wes said. "It looked like they may have been living there."

"A Reader would make a good fortune teller," Saide said. "But that isn't a lucrative business I wouldn't think."

"Just something to keep them going," Wes said.

"I dove into his mind," Colt explained. "There was a memory that I think was Orin being hired."

"He's a hit man?" Saide asked.

"No, a protection guy," Colt said. "He was hired by a woman, and I think Celeste was with her. Maybe she was the nanny. Anyway, she's gone now. It's just Celeste and Orin."

"Odds are good they've had a run in with the GA a few times," Wes said. "Maybe even some cartel people. They look for Readers too."

"So maybe the caretaker didn't make it," Di said. "And the girl is brainwashed."

"Not brainwashed," Colt said. "Traumatized."

"We should help her," Zora said. It was the first time Colt had heard her speak to the group.

"Help... her," Stu said, nodding.

"Hold on," Wes said. "We've got to really think about this. Most people believe that Celeste Pierre is dead. If they knew she was alive she would be the most wanted person in the galaxy."

"Plus she's a Reader," Di said. "The poor girl's between a rock and hard place."

"We could do something," Zora said.

"No one is saying we won't," Wes said. "But we have to consider what's best for everyone here. We don't want to put her in danger and we don't want to get ourselves in trouble either."

They all sat staring at the lake and wondering what that really meant. Colt felt bad. He knew his presence with the crew of the *Jolly Rogue* put them in danger. Wes had mentioned cartels and there were stories of organized crime on every world in every system. Some were localized, others stretched the length and breadth of the galaxy. And there were rumors that many of the criminal groups actively looked for Readers. If the GA didn't get to him, the criminals probably would. The only question in Colt's mind was what would happen to his friends when that day came.

"I'm going to start a pot of stew," Wes declared. "I think better on an full stomach."

"I'll help you," Di told him.

"I think I'll look around for something a little fresher than canned meat," Saide said. "I haven't been hunting in a long time."

Wes and Di went into the ship, and Saide moved off into the woods. Colt was sitting next to Zora and Stu.

"I'm thinking about sleeping out here tonight," Colt said.

"Might get... cold," Stu said.

"Maybe," Colt said. "But I've never been on a world like this. I don't want to miss a chance to do something I may never get another opportunity to do. Want to join me?"

The question was directed at Zora, but it was Stu who answered.

"Sh-sh-sure!" he said stammered.

"Okay," Colt said. "It will be fun."

They lounged by the fire while Wes made stew from canned meat and vegetables. It bubbled over the fire for a long time while Wes added seasoning and dried herbs. Di worked on a component for the hyperdrive, taking it apart and keeping the pieces balanced on her legs while she cleaned and checked each one.

Colt sat as close to Zora as he could get and watched the lake. It was almost hypnotic. Part of him wanted to take off his clothes and dive into the water, but of course he would never have the courage to do that in mixed company. And he wasn't sure that swimming in a lake was a good idea. He was used to a more sanitized environment. The moon was in its second phase when they went to sleep. Half of the sky was dark, but the other half was filled with the glowing gas giant Hapsis Five. Colt, Zora, Stu, and eventually Saide, laid blankets out on the sand near the lake. It wasn't as comfortable as his bed on the ship, but Colt soaked in the experience. He was alive, and free, on a real world with clean air and open spaces. For a while he morned the fact that his mother wasn't there too. She deserved a better life than the one she ended up with, being stuck on a space port with a child and no partner. It made him sad that she couldn't see the beauty he was surrounded by, and not just the environment but the people. She would be happy to know he was safe and with good people, good friends.

As he drifted off to sleep he thought about Celeste. He

wondered if she'd ever had a friend before. If he was her first, he wanted to be a good one. And he wasn't sure what the future held, but as far as it was up to him, he would do right by her. With that thought in mind he reached out and found Zora's hand. She didn't pull away, and Colt fell asleep thinking he had never been so happy.

CHAPTER 38

It took two days, but eventually Colt convinced Stella to trust him enough to plan a meet. Her guardian, Orin was skeptical, but Colt could feel the weariness he felt. And it didn't take long to discover why.

"Thirteen years?" Wes asked.

"She can't take care of herself," Orin said. "What was I supposed to do?"

Diana spoke up, "It's admirable."

"I couldn't let the GA have her, and she wouldn't be any good to a cartel either," he said. "The memory purges were Winnie's idea. She thought it would protect her mind, but instead it sort of froze it in time. She'll never be alright on her own."

Orin was a big man, and Colt could tell that he had once been strong and fit. But there was gray in his thinning hair, and his muscle had gone to fat. He was still big, but his clothes were dirty, his hair was oily, and there were dark circles around his eyes. It made Colt realized that running was no way to live. He too would be looking over his shoulder all his life. The thought of it made him nervous. Ending up like Orin was frightening. Worse than that, what if his presence made those around him feel the way Orin did? Colt could feel that Orin had affection for Stella, who sat on the ground working out a hand held puzzle, but he was also at his breaking point.

"So what now?" Orin asked.

"Now?" Wes replied, still uncertain. "We have to figure out a story that the people looking for her will believe."

"You want to turn her over I'll kill whoever comes for us," Orin said. *At least I'll try and when they kill me this will finally be over.*

"We don't want to do that," Wes said. "But the closer to the truth that we get the more believable it will be."

"You can't say here," Diana said. "They might search Kellar Nine for you."

"We'll tell them we were too late," Wes said. "That we found your fortune telling shop but you had already left. I can sell that story. There are pictures of her on the net. I'll pull a few, along with the website."

"You should take her to Adair," Diana said. "In the Ulton system. It's just been terraformed and there are a lot of people migrating there. You'll blend right in."

"Sure, but how do we manage that?" Orin said. "This little camp was our back-up plan. When Winnie died we lost access to the funds she used to keep us going. Stella can work telling fortunes but we barely make enough to buy food."

"The nanny had access to money?" Wes asked.

"Yeah, more than we would ever need," Orin explained. "At least that's what she always said. She never trusted me enough to give me the account numbers. I was the hired help, you know. I liked her well enough, but she was arrogant, thought the rest of humanity was beneath her." Orin looked at Saide and said, "I won't tell you what she thought of other species."

The Hyborian gave a snort. Colt still kept barriers between himself and the crew of the *Jolly Rogue,* but he felt the pilot's rueful humor. Humans, Colt knew, could be elitist. There were far more space faring humans and human colonized systems than any other species.

"Did she talk about it in front of Cel... I mean Stella?" Wes asked.

"I suppose," Orin said. "She was hyper protective of Stella and refused to let anyone else look after her. I told her that she was the wrong person to look after the poor kid. Anyone with access to the networks could do a check for who had worked for the Pierres when their child went missing. She said that Guy Louis Pierre scrubbed her from their finances and that no one would know that she had ever been their nanny. But I knew that was impossible. Nothing is private and nothing get's deleted."

"And they found her," Wes said.

"You're damn right they did. Every six to nine months we were moving, but eventually they caught us. She sacrificed herself to give me a chance to get Stella away. She had guts, that woman, and no one can say she didn't love Stella, but we've been all but destitute ever since. No more salary for me, no more money to care for Stella. Worse still, there's no money for us to go anywhere. Even if we wanted to, we couldn't get off world."

"How'd you get out here?" Diana asked.

"I got us a hover cart second hand, but the range is limited. This is just about the max. And my solar charger is on the fritz. Otherwise we'd be gone already. No offense, but trusting people that are looking for Stella isn't something I do."

"Colt," Wes asked. "Do you think that it's possible you could get the account number from Stella?"

"She doesn't know it," Orin said. "We tried a couple of times, but it's no good. She can't remember it."

"I think it might be possible," Wes said. "To her it would have been a senseless string of numbers and words, but if you can tap into that memory and repeat it, we might be in business."

"I could try," Colt said.

Stella's mind was occupied by the puzzle she was working on. It was a set of wooden blocks in a frame. Each block had part of a picture on it and she was sliding the blocks around inside the frame to line them up, but it wasn't as easy as it looked. Colt didn't bother asking her permission. He didn't need her help with the task. He could hear her thoughts, *but if I move that one, how do I get the face into that slot?* He pushed past her present consciousness and dove deep into her mind. Normally, finding a memory was easy. He could just think about what he wanted, and it would appear. But Celeste was just a child with no under-standing of what her guardians were talking about it. He probed for the banking information but nothing appeared.

He swam deeper, and saw memories floating past him. Some were warm, like a hug from the woman she thought of as nannie. Most were more traumatic, like being questioned about what she said exactly, or who she had seen. There were memories of Orin complaining or fussing at her. He didn't hit her, but he wasn't patient either. And yet Colt could feel her love for him. He was the only constant in her life and she clung to him desperately.

Finally, as Colt probed the memories that Celeste had of the woman named Winnie, he found one that she was especially fond of. Celeste was fresh from a bath, wrapped in a thick, warm robe, and nestled into Winnie's lap while she did some work. Celeste could see the screen of Winnie's PA, but it meant nothing to her. Colt on the other hand noticed the banking logo at the top, PRUDENTIA FINANCIAL.

"I think I've got it," Colt said. "Prudentia Financial.

"Look for the bank's routing number and their account number," Wes said.

Colt found the bank's routing number easily enough. It was listed right on the page. Winnie was typing in a username and password.

"Username is first guardian, spelled with the number one, and capitals S and T," Colt said, hoping someone was taking down the information.

Winnie then typed in the password, but the screen only showed asterisks for each digit, not the letter or number. He had to back the memory up and strain to see what her fingers were typing. Winnie's hands were visible, but her fingers moved quickly and Colt could only make out a few of the letters.

"Something, something, U, G, H, T, something, R," he said, double checking the number of characters typed into the space listed as password. "Something, then O or P, it's hard to see what letter she's hitting. V, something R, maybe E-R, I can't tell."

The screen changed, and he saw their account number at the top. It was sixteen digits, which he relayed to the others. And below the account number was the balance, just over twenty five million. As he watched, she sent a payment of eight thousand credits to a company called Pendergraf Security & Investigations. Then she turned off the PA and began to tickle Celeste. It was a sweet moment, but it ended quickly. Colt felt sorry for Celeste. There had been so little love and affection in her life. He had been raised by a single mother who was forced to work long shifts to pay for their second hand belongs, and yet he realized she had always made him feel safe, loved, and important. Winnie was quick to move away from the affectionate moment, as if she couldn't allow herself to care too deeply about the child, even though it was clear to Colt that all she wanted was her nanny's love.

"Anything else?" Wes asked, as Colt pulled back from Celeste's mind.

She never even realized he had been inside her head. He knew she had thought of the memory, there were tears welling in her eyes, but she didn't know that he was the reason it had come to mind. Colt felt his own eyes stinging with tears. Stella was a full grown woman, yet she had the yearning of a child to be loved by someone. It wasn't romantic love that she sought, but rather the unconditional love of a parent and Colt knew she would never get it.

"I saw the balance," Colt said, wiping his eyes.

Zora was standing on the other side of the group of people, closer to the ship than to Colt, but she was looking at him with compassion. He nodded to her, hoping she understood that he was okay.

"What was it?" Orin asked.

"I'm just guessing, but Celeste was only five or six at the time," Colt explained. "But the balance back then was over twenty-five million credits."

Diana whistled a single, low note. But Orin shook his head.

"No, that's not right," he insisted. "She had money, sure, but she was miserly that woman. She insisted that it had to last Stella her whole life."

"Twenty five million would do that," Wes said.

"You probably saw a dream," Orin said. "It's not reality."

They'll take it all, the worn-out security man thought. *That's all they're after. I should have known it.* Fear and anger came rolling off Orin. Colt didn't have to see the man's hand moving toward his blaster to know he would rather shoot it out with the crew of the *Jolly Rogue* than be taken for a fool.

"Wait," Colt said, raising both hands. "We aren't here for the money."

Wes and Di looked confused, but Colt didn't pay them any attention.

"We only want to help," Colt said. "Give him the banking information."

Di handed over her PA, and Orin took it, before stepping back and drawing his pistol. It was old, but still looked deadly.

"Okay," Wes said. "I see how this looks, but we're trying to work out our own problem here. And we don't steal."

"And I'm just supposed to take your word for that?" Orin snapped. "You hunted us down and pilfered her mind for this information. People don't do that. I'm no fool."

"We were commissioned to find you," Wes said. "I'm not sure by who, but I'm guessing they aren't looking out for your best interests."

"No," Orin said.

"If we go to them and tell them the truth, they'll come and take her away," Wes continued. "But if we aren't careful, they'll see us as a loose end. We're just trying to find a way out of this mess for both of us."

"Twenty-five million credits would be a good start," Orin complained.

"And whoever sent us probably already knows about that account. Even if they don't know about it they'll be watching us. If we suddenly turn up with that kind of money they'll know we were bought off and that means they'll torture and kill us."

He said the last few words under his breath so that Stella wouldn't hear him. She was still occupied with her puzzle and hadn't picked up on the sudden tension between Orin and the crew of the *Jolly Rogue*. Colt tried to summon up a sense of calm and send it to Orin. He wanted the man to believe they were trust worthy.

"You can't access that money from here," Di said. "That's a GA affiliated bank and the embargo won't allow them to have dealings with Alliance banks."

"Then we'll run the blockade and get it," Orin said. "We need that money."

"I know you do," Wes said. "But that's dangerous for you. Let me pay your way to whatever planet you want to go to. We'll report to the people who sent us, and then find a way to help you. That's the kind of work we do."

"Or you'll steal the money and I'll never hear from you again."

"We don't even know if we can get access to it," Colt said. "The password wasn't clear."

"If you think I'm going to trust you," Orin growled, "then you're out of your mind. I'll just take your ship and do as I please."

Colt sent another wave of calm toward the angry man. Wes held his hands up to mimic Colt, as if he were surrendering.

"You can't take our ship," Wes said. "We're independent and without our guy you can't engage the hyperdrive. But maybe there's another way."

"We'll leave a crew member with you," Di said. "That way we'll have to come back."

"Hold on a second," Wes aid.

"It's okay," Di said. "He doesn't trust us, and this way he doesn't have to. I'll go. I'll pay for passage to Adair or whatever he wants to go. Once you deal with this Evon, you can come and get us."

"And what if the ship breaks down?" Wes said. "We can't make interstellar jumps without an engineer on board."

"I'll stay," Colt offered.

"No," Wes said. "If we're going to check on the funds will need your memory. This is a crazy idea."

"I'll stay," Zora said.

Colt felt a crushing feeling in his chest. The last thing he wanted was to leave Zora behind, especially with someone he didn't know or trust."

"No way," Colt said.

"I'm the only one," Zora said.

Wes looked uncertain, but Di nodded her approval.

"She can handle herself," Diana said, looking from Wes to Colt. "She's ready."

"Two weeks," Orin said. "You don't come back in two weeks I sell her to the highest bidder."

"No!" Colt said, his heart thundering. There was a sick feeling in the pit of his stomach. He wasn't sure how the entire conversation had gone so wrong.

"You hurt her and I'll make you pay," Wes said. "You'll wish you were never born."

"Are you seriously considering this?" Colt asked.

"We've got to do something, kid," Wes said. "We need to deal with whoever sent us here. And if we can help these people it helps us."

"You get me the funds and you can keep ten percent," Orin said. "The rest is Stella's. And back pay for thirteen years of watching out for her."

"This is insane," Colt said.

"No," Wes said, shaking his head. "It's just business. Get what you need from the ship, Zora. And don't tell us where you're going. Just in case things go south when we cross back to GA space, it's better if we don't know."

CHAPTER 39

Colt was trembling with anger and fear. It felt like someone was ripping his world apart and forcing him to watch. Zora hurried onto the ship and Colt went after her. She was in her cabin, but the door was open. Colt had never seen her private space. It was the same layout as his own, and yet she had painted the walls, even the ceiling. There were small chairs, neatly arranged, and a colorful blanket covered her bed. In the corner, where boxes and junk had once been stacked in his cabin, Zora had rolls of canvas, an easel, and a shelf full of paints.

There was so much about her he didn't know. She was a beautiful mystery to him, captivating and precious. The thought of leaving her with Orin was physically painful. But she was already stuffing her clothes into a duffle bag.

"Don't do this," Colt said. "You don't have to."

"It's a job," Zora said softly.

"That guy's on the ragged edge," Colt said. "You can't trust him."

Zora zipped up her duffle bag and walked to the door. Colt hadn't entered her cabin and was standing by the open door.

"I trust you," she said softly. "You'll come for me."

"I will," Colt said. "No matter what."

She leaned into him. She wasn't as tall as he was and her head rested lightly against his chest. He wrapped her up with both arms and bowed his head to smell her hair. It had the slightest fragrance of apples and vanilla.

"You ready?" Diana asked from the stairs nearby.

"Yeah," Zora said.

"Use the blind account to leave us a message about where you are," Diana instructed her. "We won't access it until we've dealt with things on our end."

Zora nodded and Di gave her a hug. "You're part of this family, and we look after one another."

The three of them went back down to the cargo hold. Wes already had Orin and Celeste on board. And Colt felt the engines spooling up.

"We're taking them to a port where they can get passage out of the system," Wes explained. "Then we'll go our separate ways. You sure you're okay with this, Zora?"

She nodded.

Colt could feel the anxiety coming off Orin. The man still had his blaster and one arm around Celeste. The only thing that Colt could say for certain was that Orin hadn't hurt Celeste. He wasn't abusive, or perverted. There were no inappropriate feelings coming from Orin at the thought of Zora staying with him. In his mind, the entire plan was outrageous, but he was still the newcomer. And the truth was, he had no right to tell Zora what she could and couldn't do, just as he had no right to tell Wes that the plan was insane.

"I going to the Bridge," Orin said, his hand on the grip of his pistol. It was holstered but easily accessible. The older man knew he couldn't take them all out, but he was willing to die trying if they were tricking him. "I want to know exactly where we're going."

"Russelbrook," Wes said. "The Bridge is this way."

Zora dropped her backpack by the pile of cargo netting and sat down. Colt stayed with her, and so did Celeste. Diana handed Zora a stack of credit markers.

"That should be enough to get you wherever he wants to go," Di said. "And you can pay for a place to stay. Have you got everything?"

Zora nodded and discretely patted her left boot.

"Good," Di said.

She left the cargo bay which looked forlorn without the stacks of supplies. Colt felt mixed feelings. Celeste was sitting beside Zora, still working on the wooden puzzle and completely oblivious to the tension around her.

"I wish you didn't have to this," Colt said.

Zora took his hand and leaned her head on his shoulder. She never talked much, and he didn't mind. It was part of what made her a mystery and he liked that about her. But the temptation to know what she was thinking was high. Part of him wanted to peer into her mind and discover how she really felt about him.

"Two weeks isn't that long," she said softly, her voice almost startled him.

"Feels like an eternity to me," he said.

She laughed. It was a quiet laugh, almost silent, but he felt her shoulders shaking and she gripped his hand tighter.

"I can't do it!" Celeste said in a loud, angry voice.

She threw the puzzle against the metal bulkhead. The frame broke and the pieces flew out in all directions.

"It's okay," Zora said to her.

She let go of Colt and settled closer to Celeste, who was four or five years older. Where Zora was slim, with a girlish figure, Celeste had the curves of an adult. And yet they both had similar features. They could have been sisters. Colt felt Celeste's anger subside as Zora moved close.

"I could have helped if you had asked me," Zora said as she picked up one of the wooden puzzle pieces that had landed near her feet.

Colt reached out with his mind and lifted all the different puzzle pieces into the air. They were lightweight and lifting one wouldn't have been taxing, but there were eleven pieces and holding them all up in the air made him feel as if he were lifting a heavy weight. They floated in front of Zora and Celeste, who was thrilled. She laughed and pointed, the way a child might. Zora pointed to one piece and Colt moved it closer.

"Now that one," she said, pointing to another. Colt moved it toward the first but Zora shook her head. "No, the other side."

He moved the pieces, just as she told him until the picture painted on them came together. It was a mountain scene, with a river, and evergreen trees.

"Beautiful," Celeste said.

"It is," Zora said, looking at Colt and giving a smile that made him feel like fireworks were going of in his chest.

He levitated the blocks down on the floor in front of Celeste. When he released them he felt almost light headed from the strain, but it also felt good to exercise his power. Each time he did something it wore him down a little, but he felt like he was getting stronger too.

Zora got up and picked up the pieces of the puzzle frame. It had broken at the joints on the corners. She walked over to a storage locker, found some glue and began putting the puzzle back together.

"I like fixing things that are broken," she said softly.

Colt wasn't even sure if she was speaking to him, or to Celeste, or just talking to herself.

"Whenever I feel broken, it reminds me that I can put things back together again," Zora said.

Colt had never heard her talk so much. And yet there was depth to her words that moved him. He knew that she had overcome horrors in her past. To him she didn't seem broken, but people often felt inadequate. He certainly did. But she seemed perfect to him.

By the time they reached Russellbrook the puzzle was back together and Celeste held it like a treasure. They landed at the space port and Colt watched as Zora left with Orin and Celeste. He felt as if someone had reached inside him and pulled out his heart. How was he supposed to go on as if everything was okay, when it felt like it might never be okay again?

"She'll be fine," Wes said, as he and Colt watched the trio leave the ship. "That girl's tougher than you think."

"I don't get it," Colt said. "Why are we taking such a chance?"

"Two point five million credits, that's why," Wes said.

"It's not worth it if we lose her," Colt said.

He had already lost sight of Zora. Russellbrook was a busy city and the space port was teaming with people. They were standing just outside the ship's airlock, and Colt felt a heavy weight descending on him. It was impossible to protect the people he cared about from every danger, and yet he didn't like the idea of sending Zora off with strangers. It seemed reckless and unlike the captain of the *Jolly Rogue*.

"We won't lose her," Wes said.

"That money is probably gone already," Colt pointed out.

"Even if it's still there and we can get it, that doesn't mean the entire twenty-five million is still there."

"We just did a job and earned a little over fifty thousand credits," Wes said. "We were all pretty happy about that. But this job could easily be worth ten times as much, kid. We could fix everything on the ship three times over and still have more money than we would earn in months, maybe even a year."

"So, we're all about money," Colt asked. He knew he wasn't being fair, but he was angry.

"No," Wes said. "It was your idea to help the girl."

"Sure, but I didn't think we would be risking so much."

"Like I said, that girl can handle herself. Let's go get ready for launch. The sooner we deal with the people looking for Celeste, the sooner we can get back to Zora."

It was the first positive thing Colt had felt since the idea to leave Zora with Celeste and Orin had been brought up. He couldn't stop her from going, but he would do everything in his power to make sure they got her back as quickly as possible. The first part of that work would be cracking the password to the Prudential Financial account.

CHAPTER 40

_ _ U G H T _ R _ _ R _ V _ R

The puzzle was perplexing to Colt. He had never been very good with word games. He had the password pulled up on his display screen. He was on the Bridge with everyone else, but he could feel Zora's absence as if he were missing his right arm.

They had just broken out of atmo and were in orbit around the moon. They would have to wait until their trajectory was clear of the huge gas giant before moving out and making the jump to hyperspace.

"Do we have a jump calculated?" Wes asked.

Stu lifted a hand. It shook as his body moved. Working through the calculations in his mind his body often moved like a fighter bobbing and weaving, looking for an opening and preparing to strike.

"How are we looking, Di?" Wes asked the engineer.

"Colt moved the engine to the upper deck and levitated it

straight into the engineering bay," she said. "You should have seen it."

"I meant the ship," Wes said.

"Oh, I know," she replied with a chuckle. "But I thought you should know."

"Thank you for sharing."

"He's a talented kid," Di said.

"I'm aware. How's the ship? Are we ready to make the first jump?"

"All systems are green, captain," she said in a dramatic tone. "Fuel level is ninety percent. Fusion reactor is functioning at optimal levels. We're good to go."

"Outstanding. We'll make several jumps to reach the Gerber system," Wes said. "Once there, if we aren't contacted immediately, we'll get a day pass to the resort."

"No complaints about that," Saide said. "They serve live prey in the Hyborian restaurant."

"That's fine," Wes said. "I want everyone to leave the ship and be seen around the resort."

"We're just going to take a vacation?" Colt asked, not sure what resort they were talking about. He looked up the Gerber system on the ship's computers. He didn't have access to the navigation net, or the GA interplanetary networks, but the ship's computer had basic info on most systems. There wasn't much to learn about the Gerber system. The one outstanding facet about the system was it's clear view of the Heaven's Trail nebula, and the fact that there was a luxury resort and casino there taking advantage of the view.

"No, not a vacation," Wes said. "We're banking on the fact that Evon and whoever she works for doesn't know about you. So once the rest of us are off the ship and being seen around the resort, you can sneak off and use the resort's computers to log into the banking account."

"You want me to take the money?" Colt asked.

"No," Wes said. "We just need to find it and make sure it's there. Perhaps you can get a copy of the activity on the account to show Orin."

"Alright," Colt said, looking at the password again. He still had to figure it out before he could get into the account.

"They don't know about Colt or what he can do," Diana said. "So when we meet with Evon he should be able to find out who she's working for and what they really want."

"I've thought about that," Wes said. "And it's possible she has a Reader on her crew. It would explain how they knew what we had on board and where we were going."

"We'll have to be careful," Di said.

"Got... it!" Stu shouted triumphantly.

"Jump point is set in the computer," Saide said. "Ninety-seven minutes to transition point."

"How many jumps are we making, Stu?" Wes asked.

"Th-th-three," the navigator stammered.

"How long?"

"Th-thir-thirty-nine... hours. Not counting... com-com-computing... time."

Stu bounced in his seat. He enjoyed the challenge of his job. Colt wished he could be happy, but all he could think about was Zora. He couldn't help but worry about what she was doing. What if there were other people looking for Celeste? If they found her while Zora was there she might get hurt by the people trying to capture Celeste. It wasn't something he could stand to think about.

"You should have Stu help with that," Diana said when she got up and looked at what Colt had on his computer screen.

"That's a good idea," Wes agreed. "Stu, we're trying to decipher a password."

"How many... letters?" Stu asked.

"Fifteen," Colt said.

"Blank, blank," Di added, "U-G-H-T, blank, R, blank, blank, R, blank, V, blank R."

Colt knew that Stu was a savant with mathematics, but he didn't have much faith that the navigator could solve the riddle of the missing password. He had gone over his memory of Celestes, but it was like trying to remember the details of a dream. The emotions lingered long after the details had slipped away. It was a marvel to Colt that he could see another person's memories so clearly. He remembered seeing a movie where a detective used an ancient technique to bring a person's memories back into clarity. It was called hypnosis and he had thought it was just an urban legend, but since his Reader abilities allowed him to swim in other peoples minds he had discovered that their memories were not just accessible, they were highly detailed.

"D-d-daughter," Stu exclaimed. "F-fo-for... ever!"

"Unbelievable," Di said with a grin.

Colt quickly added the letters and realized it fit. That didn't mean it was the password, but it fit. And, if Orin's story was true, and the nanny had taken Celeste at her father's behest, it made sense that the money stashed away for her, would have a password that described a parent's feelings for the their child.

"That makes sense," Wes said. "Dollars to donuts that's it."

"You really think the PM sent his own daughter away?" Di asked. "It's pretty fantastic when you think about it."

"Or hypocritical, depending on your point of view," Wes replied. "He didn't want his daughter taken, but other people's kids were fair game."

"Maybe he wants to change that," Di said.

"He's the Prime Minister, don't you think he would be able to?"

"The GA is a giant bureaucracy. Every division and department is fighting for more funds, more influence. And the clandestine service is so secret it's not even officially a division of the government. We all know about it, but they never admit that it's real. Maybe in all the murky business he's just as helpless as everyone else."

"I don't buy it," Wes said. "But either way, if we tread carefully, we should be able to get free of this mess. That's all I want."

"And get Zora back," Colt said.

"Of course, kid. She's part of this crew. We never give up on a member of the crew," Wes said.

"Let's go fix some dinner, Colt. It will take your mind off things."

CHAPTER 41

They had been at the resort for three days. Hussain found his accommodations adequate. They were posh in an obvious sort of way. The furnishings were imitations, the fixtures were polished brass to look like gold. But the suite of rooms were clean, and the food was top rate. Of course it all came at a premium price as well, but money didn't concern the hunter. He had laid his trap carefully, and all he needed was patience. Hussain had learned the art of waiting long ago and was rather good at it.

Troy was at a poker table, slowly cleaning out the other players. He had an advantage in knowing the other players cards. But he couldn't control what cards he was dealt. He folded often, and even lost a few hands, always when the betting was low. But when the cards were right, he won big.

Kurt was at the bar, when he wasn't taking someone up to his room. The man had voracious appetites. He could drink for hours, loved gourmet food, long massages, and beautiful women. The bar where he wiled away the hours overlooked the casino floor and Kurt had an excellent view of every person moving through that part of the resort.

After getting a Feringian grooming, Horace took a spot at one of the slot machines where he could see into the shop that lined the mall. There were hundreds of stores along three levels, with an open atrium down the center of the mall. Horace couldn't see everyone, but he was in position to monitor their target once Hussain, Kurt, and Troy had spotted him. Or her, Hussain wasn't sure what gender their target was. He assumed male, but that was more of a gut feeling than anything he had discovered during his brief encounter with the powerful Reader.

Hussain was in a cigar lounge with a clear view of the hotel's lobby. There were people checking in and out, or waiting for their companions in the posh seating. Hussain couldn't see clearly through the pall of bluish cigar smoke that hung in the air. The walls to the lounge were glass, and a powerful ventilation system sucked the smoke out as fast as it could, but it really only succeeded in keeping the smoke from leaking out to the rest of the resort. But Hussain didn't need to see the people with his eyes. In fact he kept his eyes half closed, and let his mind wander among the individuals. Many were trying to hold themselves together after losing more than they could afford. A few were walking away winners, but none where Readers.

Cigars were one of Hussain's vices. He loved the rich taste of the smoke, and the feeling of the tobacco as he rolled it between his thumb and forefinger. As he hunted through the minds of the people in the hotel lobby, he considered their plan. They would let the target enter the resort. Once they had spotted their quarry, the next step was to contact the other members of the team and ensure everyone had a firm grasp of their target's identity. That was easily done with Kurt and Troy. They were moderately powered L2 Readers, capable of hearing Hussain's thoughts and receiving the mental images he would send to them. They would have to use their PA's to keep Horace in the loop, but the Feringian's skill was with weapons. He was used to intimidate people and when dealing with criminals, to fight for the team of hunters. Once their target was comfortable in the resort, they would formulate a plan for capture. Taking on a powerful Reader in the middle of a crowed casino wasn't a good option. Hussain had no qualms about innocent people getting hurt, but he didn't like to draw attention. The best course of action was to sedate their target in a place with few or no witnesses. Perhaps, if they were lucky, the target would head to the bar and sedate himself with copious amounts of alcohol. It wouldn't be the first time. Liquor could dull the senses and block the onslaught of thoughts and emotions that bombarded a Reader.

Since reaching the resort, Hussain had received a message from Director Turkov regarding the crew their target was traveling with. A second team was on route to the casino. If they arrived in time, Hussain was to work with them to gain intel on a separate mission. The clandestine service was compartmentalized, and while his work as a hunter was obvious, the other missions within the service were classified. Hussain had no idea who the other team was, other than their point person, a female named Evon, or what their mission with the crew of the *Jolly Roger* was. And, truth be told, Hussain didn't care. As long as he got his target, what happened to the crew of the little indie ship was of no concern.

This is starting to get boring, Troy thought. *Any sign of the target?*

Not up here, Kurt replied.

Negative, no sign yet, Hussain added. His associates had not been in the field for all that long. A few years for Troy, only two years for Kurt, and both were impatient. It seemed odd to Hussain that they were anxious to complete the mission, since they were doing whatever they wanted in the meantime. They had unlimited access to every vice, and yet they still weren't happy. He didn't see them lasting much longer. At some point they would run, as if they would be happier on their own. When that happened Hussain would hunt them, and when he found them he would terminate them with extreme prejudice. It wasn't personal, just a simple fact. They had not adapted to the service, despite years of training to develop their gifts and prepare them for the important work they were currently involved in. Somewhere, deep in their stunted minds, the belief that freedom was real still lingered. The harsh training of the Farm system was supposed to stamp that out, but it was rarely a success. And when the rigors of hunting wore down that training, the spark of an ancient idea — that a person would be happiest if they could make the decisions about their lives without a government or outside entity's input — often flamed to life. When that happened, there was no chance of retraining. The only thing to do was put that hunter down.

He took another draw on the cigar. The tobacco had burned down and the heat was harsh in his mouth and throat. He exhaled sharply, took a sip of the water on the little table by the buttery soft leather chair he was sitting in, and placed the stub of the cigar into the ash tray. His body was buzzing with the nicotine dump from the cigar. He stood up, stretched, and started for the door. He would go the deluxe fitness center, which also overlooked the hotel lobby, and work out the drug that was pumping through his system. His quarry would arrive sooner or later.

They always did. And when that happened, Hussain would close the trap. It didn't matter how powerful the Reader was. They all had the same weaknesses, and Hussain was an expert at exploiting each and every one.

CHAPTER 42

Hussain's PA vibrated. He had just sat down to a meal in the resort's best, and most expensive restaurant. No one would call Hussain a glutton. He preferred a few bites of finely cooked gourmet food to a feast. The chef was preparing a tasting menu just for him, and before he could even enjoy it there was an interruption.

Before he could check the device his server hurried over with single plate on a round tray. He carefully set the plate in front of Hussain. On it was an ornate spoon with a thick, green liquid. Floating on the liquid was a tiny little wafer.

"To start your dining experience," the server said, "the chef had prepared a split pea reduction, with a pork belly infused diamond, dusted with pepper, garlic, black truffle, and a single drop of olive oil. Bon appetite!"

Hussain didn't have social media accounts. There were no friends that might contact him. The Readers on his team would simply send him their thoughts. The Personal Access device he kept on his person was for work purposes, and therefore any message he might get was important. But he took the time to taste the amuse-bouche. He put the spoon in his mouth and slowly withdrew it. The warm split pea reduction seemed to expand, filling his mouth and delighting his senses. The different flavors were all clearly delineated, and yet they formed a cohesive whole that Hussain found delicious.

After taking the time to savor the single bite of food, he took a sip of the wine in his glass, followed by a deep breath to ensure that he was able to bask in the wonderful flavors. Only then, did he pull the PA from the pocket inside his jacket pocket. The device was small, but lit up as he gazed on the glass surface. A text message appeared. Hussain read it in a fraction of a second, and then stood to his feet, slipping the device back into his pocket.

The server, seeing his patron getting up from the table hurried over with a concerned expression. "Is something wrong, sir?"

"Work has come up," Hussain said. "Please tell the chef that his meal was sublime."

"Of course," the server said, looking distressed. "But surely you'll want to stay for the entire experience. There are six more courses. I was just about to open the next bottle of wine."

Hussain gave the man a piercing look.

"But you've already paid," the server pleaded.

The meal had cost over a thousand credits, but Hussain didn't care. His quarry was approaching, and the hunt superseded every other desire. Turning on his heel Hussain moved toward the exit and sent a mental missive to his associates.

The Jolly Rogue has entered the system and will dock at the station in just over an hour. Someone get Horace. It's time to spring the trap.

I'll find him, Troy thought, *and I can have my winnings added to my personal banking account along the way.*

Kurt didn't respond, which meant he was either sleeping or dead. Hussain would have to send someone to his room. They had time, but he didn't like his associates hedonistic desires, or their need to see to their own interests before joining Hussain in their preparations for the hunt. It was what made them second rate and would eventually cause them to fail. Hussain didn't love the clandestine service. He didn't feel an obligation to director Emmitt Turkov. What he lived for was the challenge. Facing off against another person with supernatural abilities. They were surrounded by people with weak, ordinary minds. Hussain could have been a titan of industry. He could have led a cartel. For that matter, he could have risen to the rank of PM in the Galactic Authority with his mental abilities. But he felt all of that was beneath him. It was like an adult beating a child a chess. It was too easy, and all the advantages were on his side. But hunting other Readers with the same mental abilities that he possessed was a task worthy of his time.

Unfortunately, most Readers were lower level, and didn't have the experience to really bring their abilities to bear. But every once in a while Hussain encountered someone he thought of as his equal. Nothing, not the finest food, the most beautiful women, or any amount of money, would ever distract him from the hunt. And the target he was pursuing had more potential than any that had come before. Hussain had captured more Readers than he could remember. And yet, he had never faced an L5. If the target had been evading capture long enough he could have abilities that no hunter had ever faced before. Capturing the Reader onboard the *Jolly Rogue* would be the highlight of Hussain's career.

I've got Horace, Troy sent via mental message.

Send him to get Kurt, Hussain replied as he moved through the crowded mall area. *We'll meet in the lobby.*

Roger that, Troy replied.

Hussain knew his team and not because he had scoured their minds for thoughts of sedition. They were understandable because they were like the rest of humanity. Spreading out through the stars hadn't changed things. They weren't enlightened, but rather occupied. Mankind was occupied by the pursuit of things, from the young and poor, living paycheck to paycheck, to the rich and powerful. They all were all occupied with the pursuit of something else, something new, something they needed, or something they wanted. Hussain didn't judge them, for he too was occupied, and his pursuit was of the thrill of battle. He never felt more alive than he did just after a dangerous operation. And he knew he would pursue that thrill until it killed him.

Troy would take care of his financial concerns, and Kurt would be summoned from whatever activity had him occupied at the moment. His compatriots were predictable, but also capable, and they had the time. Hussain glanced at the message again. It was from the booking agent deep in the bowels of the station. Hussain had found the man easily enough and bribed him to report on the *Jolly Rogue's* approach. Another message came through on his PA.

— Docking slip J: Day pass —

It seemed almost too easy. They knew when and they knew where the *Jolly Rogue* would be. Hussain's only concern was that his quarry might not still be on board. Knowing he had been encountered when the *Jolly Rogue* was caught in the GA interdictor field near the Farm installation, a person trying to avoid the clandestine service would have changed ships. But Hussain would find his target. The galaxy was a big place but he had all the advantages. No one could stay hidden forever. If nothing else, Hussain would detain the crew of the *Jolly Rogue* and find out where his quarry went. The noose was tightening, and that reality always made Hussain's pulse increase. He couldn't wait to get his hands on the L5 and turn him into a human weapon.

CHAPTER 43

"Alright, let's do this right," Wes said.

The ship had just settled into a slot on the resort's day hanger. Wes transferred the minimum twenty-five hundred credits to get in, which just about cleaned out their operating funds in the GA banking system. It was impossible to avoid having some funds in the system, even though Wes hated everything about it. Fortunately, there were many online banking companies that were easy to create false accounts with. Wes operated one such account for the *Jolly Roger* and her crew to use with harbor masters and system tolls.

"I'm not sure there's a wrong way," Diana said.

"Just stick to the plan," Wes said. "Keep your com-link active."

Colt fiddled with the little device in his ear. Com-links weren't allowed on the gaming floor, which also had signal blocking that made PAs worthless. But the Heaven's Trail resort was much more than just a casino.

"You know the plan, Colt, just stick to it," Wes admonished him. "And we'll be out of here soon."

"What if this Evon isn't here?" Di asked. "What if the whole thing was just a set up?"

"There's nothing we can do about that," Wes said. "We did our part. Colt, give us half an hour and then make your move. There should be banking kiosks all over the place."

"Got it," the kid replied.

"Okay," Wes said, leading Diana and Saide down the stairs. "We're off. You reading me Stu?"

"Loud and... clear," the navigator said.

The airlock opened and Wes lead the way into the dimly lit hanger. Unlike the rest of the resort, the hanger was grimy, and crowded with ships. The paint showing the directions to and from the bay was faded.

"Make sure you know how to get back," Wes said as they walked down the narrow aisle between ships toward a bank of elevators.

"This is a busy place," Di said, looking out the atmospheric shielding into space.

Wes didn't like open hangers. He knew a simple glitch in the power would result in sudden and total vacuum that would kill anyone not in a fully sealed space suit.

"Lots of money wasted," Wes said. "People will do just about anything as a diversion from their normal lives."

"That's a pretty grim view of humanity," Diana said.

"He's a pessimist," Saide said.

"Yeah, and I've seen the places he usually does business in," Diana said. "This is a big step up."

"We'll be on video the entire time we're here," Wes said. "We probably already are."

"There are worse things," Di said.

"Not for us," Wes replied. "The less the GA knows about us the better."

They got onto the elevator. The doors closed and Wes felt the familiar weight in his stomach as they rose upward.

"We should get one of these for the ship," Di said.

"I'll talk to the chief engineer about that," Wes said in sarcastic tone.

The doors opened and the trio entered a world of glitz and glamour. Gone were the rusty deck plates and faded paint. They stepped onto polished marble floors and looked across the lobby toward a massive window with a spectacular view of the Heaven's Trail nebula.

"I could get used to this," Di said.

"I smell food," Saide said.

He walked away from Wes following a sign that said Multi-Species Dining.

"I'm going shopping," Diana said.

"Be careful," Wes said. "That can be dangerous."

"Don't I know it," Di replied with a mischievous grin.

She sauntered away, and Wes couldn't help appreciate her figure. Normally she wore bulky coveralls, but she was wearing a classy looking pants and vest outfit that was form fitting and left her arms and shoulders bare. She had her hair undone and wavy. Wes felt his heart beat harder at the sight of her.

Eventually Wes moved over to a short line of people waiting to speak to someone at the resort's information desk. Unlike most places, the resort used people instead of artificials or self help kiosks. A young woman in a resort uniform greeted him with a smile when it was his turn at the information desk.

"Welcome to the Heaven's Trail Casino and Resort. Is this your first visit?" she asked.

"It is," Wes said.

"Then you're in for a treat. We have the best gaming, dining, shopping, and entertainment in the galaxy. All at your disposal. How can I help you make this the best getaway of your life?"

Wes hoped they could get away, and soon. He felt uncomfortable in fancy places. As if he didn't belong and everyone could see it. He cleared his throat, trying not to seem too nervous.

"I'm looking for Evon," Wes said.

"Evon?" the woman asked, still smiling, but Wes could see the judgement in her eyes. "Is she part of our hospitality services?"

"No," Wes said quickly. "It's not like that. We were supposed to meet her to talk business."

The concierge at the help desk typed in the name on her console. It was hidden on her side of the desk and Wes couldn't see it, but the look on the woman's face told him what he needed to know.

"I'm sorry, sir. I don't have any information on an Evon. And it's against resort policy to share guest information."

"That's okay," Wes said. "I'm sure she'll make contact sooner or later."

Wes left the information desk and made his way to one of the many sitting areas in the lobby. He settled into a chair that gave him a view of the elevators. The resort was a large place, with a massive tower where overnight guests had rooms with views of the nebula. Most of the tourists were on the far end of the lobby, mesmerized by the shining, glittering nebula that looked like a curving trail or river of light. Wes pulled out his PA and checked for messages. There was nothing from Evon. Wes hated waiting on people. In many places his contacts preferred to make him wait, but he had never gotten any more comfortable with it. He felt like he was on display.

"Can I offer you refreshments sir?" a woman with a tray of drinks asked. "They're complimentary?"

Wes knew that liquor had a way of loosening a person's inhibitions. A drunk would throw caution to the wind, and lose their shirt in the process. But he took one of the drinks. It was an exotic cocktail, with what looked like glitter floating in the sweet beverage. He took a sip and had to admit it was tasty, but he didn't want to dull his senses. There was too much at stake. He glanced instead at his PA and saw that half an hour had passed. Colt would be on the move. The kid had skills and with a little seasoning would make a good addition to the *Jolly Rogue*'s crew.

"That won't happen," a deep voice from behind Wes said. "Your friend is coming with me."

Wes was on his feet and turning, expecting trouble, but found a plain looking man in a dark business suit. He was sitting in a chair, his fingers steepled together.

"Who the hell are you?" Wes asked.

"That isn't important," the man said. "I'm here for the Reader."

"I don't know what you're talking about," Wes said.

He knew there were people and cameras everywhere. If he drew his hidden blaster and killed the man, he would be wanted for murder. On the other hand, if Colt got captured he couldn't live with that either.

"I know everything about you, Wes Hanzor, captain of the *Jolly Rogue*," the strange man said. "You're a blockade runner and I could take you in for that alone, but at this point in time you have something much more valuable to me."

"You have me mistaken, friend. I don't know you," Wes said.

There was a sickening dread spreading through Wes. He had no idea who the strange man was, but he knew exactly what he was. A hunter, a GA agent with the clandestine service tasked with bringing in Readers. How they had gotten to the Gerber system so quickly was a mystery. But there was no time to solve it. He had to warn Colt.

Kid, if you can hear me, stay on the ship and get her ready to launch.

"Or, I'm sure he can hear you. But he's not on the ship," the strange man said, rising to his feet in a distinctly snake like motion, as if his very bones were flexible. "My man has him at the banking kiosks.

Wes? What's wrong? Stu got the password right. You've got to see this.

Hearing another person in his head made Wes feel strange. He could hear the excitement in Colt's voice, and recognized the feeling. The poor kid had no idea everything in his life was about to come crumbling to pieces. The only thing left to do was to make a run for it.

Wes tapped his thumb to his pinky. It was a tiny movement, and most people never even saw him do it. The sensors on his thumb and pinky, when touched together, activated his hidden blaster. The barrel of the weapon silently extended just over the back of Wes' hand.

"That wouldn't be wise," the strange man said, as if he knew exactly what Wes was thinking. "My compatriots have the woman and your Hyborian pilot."

Kid, run! Wes thought urgently.

There's nowhere for him to run, the strange man's voice was in Wes' mind and he suddenly realized just how hopeless their situation was. The man was a Reader. He would know what Wes was planning before he did it. *You may be fast with a blaster, Wes, but not faster than thought. That's all it would take and my companions would kill your friends. We're taking the boy.*

Nothing can stop that. And we'll take your crew and your ship too.

Wes was trapped. He would fight, even where there was no hope of winning, but it wasn't just his life on the line.

"Let her go," Wes said, silently retracting his hidden blaster. "You have me. You don't need her."

"I have you all," the man said with a smile that Wes could see and feel was pure evil. He would kill Diana and Saide just because he enjoyed it. "And soon I'll have your friend too. It's simple, really, and if I'm being honest a complete disappointment. For someone of such power to be enslaved by petty emotions like compassion is just a waste. But that's okay, I'll teach him better. You can count on that. Now come with me, I have a room ready for you on my ship."

Wes had one last chance. He could run. But how many other agents were in the crowds around them? He couldn't be sure. And Wes was certain the psycho would murder Di and Saide. He wasn't giving up, Wes would never give up. But he would have to bide his time and wait for the right opportunity.

"The elevators?" Wes asked.

"Precisely," the man said. "Your cooperation is appreciated."

Wes was about to tell the man where he could shove his cooperation, when the crowd parted and leaning casually against the elevator was Colt.

CHAPTER 44

Colt felt Wes' shock of fear. He knew his captain feared that he was trying to get back down to the ship, but Colt had felt the agent in Wes' mind. A quick search for Di and Saide revealed their fear and the fact that they were also in trouble.

"Hello, captain," Colt said. "I was just heading down to the ship. You want to join me?"

There was confusion on Wes' face and in his mind, but Colt didn't have the time to explain what he was going to do. In fact, he didn't really know if it would work, but he had come with an idea on the fly and was going with it.

So, we meet at last, the agent's voice entered Colt's mind. It felt strange and out of place, like putting on a shirt backward. A quick look into the agent's mind revealed his name and confirmed what Colt thought. The man was a clandestine service agent who hunted Readers.

You should let my friends go, Colt thought back.

Don't be naive, they broke the law. Harboring a Reader is a felony. Their days running the blockade in their pathetic little ship is over.

Oh, Colt thought. *You're taking all of us?*

Of course I am, the agent thought with just a trace of glee.

Then you'll want Stewart as well, Colt thought. He closed his eyes and held onto the frame around the elevator's door as he reached out mentally. There were three readers in the resort. Colt had felt them as soon as he opened his mind fully. Wes had warned him that there might be people waiting for them. Colt's job was to avoid those people, and get the banking information about the account for Celeste Pierre. He had accomplished his part easily, but he had also discovered the agents and their plan to catch him using the crew of the ship. As he reached out, he formed a chain, touching each of their minds with his own, while at the same time reaching out to Stewart.

The elevator dinged and the doors opened, just as Stu's mind connected with Colt and subsequently the other Readers. Even though he was ready for the onslaught, it was still a shock. Only his hold on the elevator kept him from falling down as a screaming onslaught of sensory overload hit. Colt held the connection as long as he could, perhaps two seconds, before moving away from Stu. His heart was pounding and his legs felt shaky. Wes grabbed him and pulled him into the elevator just as a savage, beast like roar made everyone in the lobby of the resort turn.

Colt opened his eyes. Hussain "the Hunter" was on the floor, holding his head, his eyes squeezed shut. The plan had worked. The agents, completely unprepared to touch Stu's autistic mind, were shocked by the sudden influx of the navigator's hypersensitivity to everything around him. But there was another agent, not a Reader but a hairy, ape-like Feringian, charging toward them. Beside Colt, Wes raised his arm. The

Feringian was drawing a blaster, but Wes was faster. A bolt of yellow light flashed from Wes' hidden blaster and hit the Feringian in the chest. The savage creature was knocked backward, just as the doors to the elevators were closing.

"Di?" Wes said.

"She's okay," Colt replied, as the elevator began to descend. "Saide too."

"Stu," Wes said, activating his com-link. "Get the ship ready to launch."

"Aye, aye... captain," Stu replied.

"Di?" Wes said.

Colt could feel the fear and worry for her safety coming off the captain in waves. Unfortunately, he could also feel Hussain and his henchmen getting their bearings again. Even the Feringian was back on his feet. Colt pushed his way into the alien's mind. It was different than anything he had experienced before. There were strong instincts like the beams of a building running through the creature's mind, but Colt forced his will onto the alien.

"Colt?" Wes asked.

He knew he was hunched over, feeling every bit as much of the Feringian as the alien was feeling him. The elevator had disappeared and Colt could see through the Feringian's eyes. People were crowding close to Hussain, who held up his identification.

Galactic Authority business, he said. *There's nothing to see her—*

Before he could finish Colt forced the Feringian to leap upon Hussain. He felt the hunter's mind pushing him back, trying to stop Colt's control of the alien who he had learned was called Horace. But Colt pushed back, forcing his will onto the Feringian. They were on the floor and the powerful alien raised a fist. It hovered there for a moment as Hussain fought to restrain Colt, but the younger man was stronger. The fist dropped with all the strength that Feringians were known for. Colt felt Hussain's nose shatter under the blow, and several teeth was bent inward. And then a group of resort security agents grabbed Horace and pulled him from his boss.

Colt pulled back and slumped into the wall. His legs felt like lead weights and he was trembling all over. Wes grabbed Colt's left arm, pulled it over his shoulders and wrapped his own arm around the younger man's waist.

"I don't know what you're doing, kid, but I hope it's working."

The elevator door opened, and they were back in the dingy day hanger where the *Jolly Rogue* was docked. Wes pulled Colt along. He was doing his best to walk, but he couldn't feel his legs, and his mouth was suddenly so dry. His tongue felt swollen. Over the com-link Di's voice called out.

"Wes, they've got me cut off," she said. "There's two of them."

"Leave me here," Colt said as he grabbed onto one of the massive steel girders. "I can get to the ship on my own."

"You sure?"

"Yeah," Colt said, pointing back toward the elevator. "There's an emergency staircase over there. No cameras."

"Thanks kid," Wes said.

He tapped his com-link. "Hang on, Di, I'm on my way."

Colt leaned onto the girder and let his mind float free. Hussain had been knocked senseless by the blow from Horace. The Feringian was in a rage, fighting the security people. Fear was so thick on the resort level above that Colt felt it pressing down on him. Higher up, at the second level of the mall shopping complex, Colt found the two Readers. They had cornered Diana inside a boutique that sold handbags. Di was on the verge of panic. The two Readers were hurling threats via their mental telepathy. With the last of his strength Colt levitated a thick hand bag and swung it at the nearest of the two Readers. It caught him by surprise, but wasn't heavy enough to do any damage. It did however, break the man's concentration, and his companion's too.

Di shook her head as the mental bullying abruptly stopped. And to Colt's satisfaction, she sprang into action. She wore decorative shoes for her shopping trip, but landed one squarely on the closest Reader's groin. Colt felt a shiver of pain from the man as he dropped to his knees.

The other Reader, one named Troy Colt realized, took a swing at Di, but she ducked under it shoved him backward.

Where is she? Wes thought.

The handbag boutique, Colt sent back, as he slumped onto the ground. He needed to get to the ship, but he couldn't abandon his friends. The elevator dinged at the far end of the corridor and Colt looked up, hoping to see Saide. Instead, two of the resort's security personnel came out. They had weapons drawn, stun pistols Colt hoped, and not deadly weapons, but it was impossible to tell. He could feel their suspicion upon seeing him slumped on the ground.

Upstairs in the boutique, Di picked up a hand bag and imitated Colt's attack, hitting the Reader name Troy and driving him back. Colt could feel the other man's intentions. He was hurting, but not disabled. His name was Kurt and his mind was full of menace.

Touch her and I'll kill you, Wes said.

The threat worked only for a few seconds, but it was long enough. Kurt got to his feet and put his hand on a blaster at his hip, just as Wes dashed into the store. Colt felt Kurt's attention shift to what he considered the greater threat.

"Don't do it," Wes said.

"I'll kill you then take my time with her," Kurt replied.

Colt tried to force his will onto Kurt, but he was too weak. His efforts had all but exhausted him. The Reader drew his blaster but Wes was faster. The stun blast hit Kurt and his consciousness winked out almost as if someone had simply flipped his switch.

Confident that Wes and Di could take care of the last Reader and get back to the ship, Colt switched his focus to the two security guards approaching.

"You alright sir?" one asked.

Probably just another drunk who couldn't find his way back to his ship, the other guard thought. *He's young though.*

"I'm sorry," Colt said, doing his best to sound frightened. "I knew I shouldn't have drunk it."

"Drunk what?" the second security guard asked.

"They just left them sitting on the table," Colt said. "My head is spinning. Can you help me to my ship."

"Dumb kid," the first guard said. "You're too young to be drinking."

"My dad is going to kill me," Colt said.

"It's no more than what you deserve," the second guard said.

They pulled Colt up to his feet. He didn't have to pretend to be unsteady.

"You aren't going to be sick are you?" the first man asked.

"No," Colt said. "I don't think so."

"You start tossing your cookies and you're on your own, kid," the second guard said. "They don't pay us enough for that."

"What ship?" the first guard asked.

"The *Jolly Rogue*," Colt replied.

He knew it was a mistake the moment he said it. The alarm in the two men's minds were like gongs ringing out to Colt. He felt the bodies tense and their hands on him tightened.

"The *Jolly Rogue's* on lockdown," the first guard said. "You'll have to come with us."

"No," Colt said, pushing the thought into their mind. *The Jolly Rogue is a fine vessel. Nothing wrong with her.*

He could sense the confusion in the two guards. Colt leaned forward and retched. It wasn't real, but it didn't take much to fool the two security officers. The first let go of him and jumped back, the second shoved Colt away. He staggered forward, caught himself on a shinny little ship and pretended to be sick.

I'll be fine, I can make it to my ship on my own, Colt pushed toward the security guards. *You don't need to help me.*

"You're on your own, kid," said the first man.

"We warned you," the second added.

They turned away and Colt thought he was in the clear, but then the elevator opened and Saide stepped out. It was easy to spot a Hyborian with their red skin and thick hair braids. Colt felt the suspicion of the security officers spike again.

"You there," one of them shouted. "Stay where you are."

Colt knew he didn't have the strength, but he shoved his thoughts at the men. It reminded him of movies he had seen where children break into food fights. He had never done it. Food on Helix Prime had been dull, gray, mostly tasteless gruel, but the thought of wasting had never entered his mind. But in a last ditch effort to save his friend, Colt pushed a bundle of thoughts, throwing everything he could think of at the two security officers. Then his world went dark. He felt himself falling, but he was out before his body hit the metal deck plates.

CHAPTER 45

Di finished the man with a swift blow to his chin with the palm of her hand. His head flew back and he dropped to the ground at almost the same time that Wes' stun blast took out his companion.

"Sorry about this," Wes said to the terrified woman behind the sales counter as he grabbed Diana's hand.

"Lovely bags," Di called out.

She dropped the bag she had pummeled her attacker with onto the sales counter and let Wes drag her from the shop by the hand.

"You okay," Wes asked at they hurried for the moving staircase that led down to the main floor of the resort.

"Fine," Di said. "I think Colt did something."

"Yeah, he saved all our bacon," Wes said. "We have to get out of here."

"Were they the people who sent us after Stella?"

"I don't think so," Wes said. "They wanted Colt. GA hunters."

"How did they get here so fast?"

"They had to have been here waiting," Wes said. "I don't know how they knew we would be here."

They hurried past the gaming floor. It was one of many with loud machines and flashing lights. It was a playground for adults, only one with a heavy price for those without the self control it took to walk away.

"Where's Saide?"

"Headed to the ship I think," Wes said. He tapped his com-link activator. "Saide?"

"I'm here," the Hyborian said, his words coming in a puff that sounded as if he were out of breath.

"You okay?"

"I'm almost to the ship," Saide said. "I've got Colt."

"Is he okay?" Di asked.

"He passed out. There were a couple of security guys down here. He must have done something to them."

Wes pulled Di into an open elevator. It was going up, but he didn't want to wait for another. He stepped in and hit the button for the day hanger.

"We're on our way," Wes told him. "I want us out of this place the moment the airlock closes behind us."

"Roger that," Saide said. "Watch your back."

"We're going up," Di said.

"I know," Wes replied.

The elevator went up to the eighth floor and opened. Wes and Di moved to the back corner of the elevator as a group of women crowded on board. One wore a pink tiara and had a sash around one shoulder that hung to the opposite hip that said *Bride To Be*.

The women were loud and more than a few gave Wes appraising glances, but Diana crossed her arms and glared back.

They were obviously on a bachelorette trip and looking to make bad choices. When the elevator returned to the main level, they hurried off and Wes hit the button for the day hanger again. Fortunately, no one tried to get on before the doors of the elevator closed.

"The security officers are on high alert," Di said. "There were a bunch in the lobby."

"I saw them," Wes said. "Coming here was a huge mistake."

"You couldn't have known that," Di said.

"We almost lost everything," Wes replied. "What happened to you?"

"I was shopping at that creep flashed a badge at me. He said I was under arrest for crimes against the GA."

"How'd you get away?"

"One minute he's poking a blaster in my ribs, the next he grabs his head and topples over," Di explained.

"Yeah, same here," Wes said. "Colt was saying something about Stu."

"Whatever it was worked. I was on the top floor and headed down when the other guy showed up. They cornered me in that boutique."

"Looks like keeping Colt around has paid off," Wes said. "You were right."

"You act surprised."

"I'm just glad I've got the sense to listen to you."

The doors opened and they were back on the day hanger. The space was gloomy and intimidating, but Wes knew the *Jolly Rogue* was nearby and that bolstered his spirits. They ran down the aisle until the Hyborian ship came into view. The large cargo area looked like a skull and the quad engines stuck out like the cross bones of ancient pirate ship flag.

"It's good to be home," Diana said.

"Sometimes I wonder why I ever leave," Wes said as he slapped his hand onto the bio metric lock reader.

It beeped and a green light flashed as the airlock opened. Di went first, then Wes right behind her. She pulled the lever to close and cycle the airlock. After a moment the airlock opened into the cargo hold with a swish.

"We're here," Wes said. "Let's go."

"That's going to be a problem," Saide said over the com-link. "Gerber flight control is denying our request to leave."

Wes sprinted up the stairs and down the corridor to the bridge. Colt was slumped into his chair, Stu was rocking at his station nervously, and Saide was in the pilot's seat.

"Did they give a reason?" Wes asked.

"Negative," Saide replied. "But I'm pretty sure the GA agents won't let us go."

Wes walked over to Colt and started tapping the young man's face. Colt's eyes fluttered open but he wasn't sure where he was or what was happening.

"Colt... Colt, can you hear me?"

"Yeah," the kid replied.

"We made it back to the ship but the flight control is denying us the chance to leave," Wes said. "We're sitting ducks if we can't get out of this space station."

"Okay," Colt said in a groggy voice.

He closed his eyes and Wes felt his hopes sink. The kid was too exhausted. He remembered how Colt had passed out after the encounter with the GA's interdictor ship. If they took off without clearance they ran not only the risk of a collision, but they would be black listed in every port in the galaxy.

Suddenly a voice came over the bridge speakers.

"*Jolly Rogue*, this is Gerber flight control. You are cleared for take off. Come to heading two-four-seven by three-one-niner and proceed out of the system."

"Yes!" Wes said. "Go! Go! Go! Before they change their minds. You did it kid!"

"Is he okay?" Diana asked moving to Colt's side.

"I hope so," Wes said. "Stu, get us a jump plotted and put into the computer."

"O... kay!" Stu said.

"I won't relax until we're in hyperspace," Wes said.

"Where are we going?" Saide said, as he piloted the ship out of the day hanger and away from the resort.

"I'm going to get him something to drink," Di said. "He's dehydrated."

"Back across the embargo line," Wes said, speaking over Di. "We'll find somewhere to wait to hear from Zora."

"*Jolly Rogue*," the voice boomed over the bridge speakers again. "This is Gerber flight control. Something's come up. Please come to heading one-one-seven and enter a holding pattern. We've got a security issue on the resort."

"Repeat," Wes said, as he repeatedly tapped the transmit button to break up his reply. "Flight control, I say again, repeat. You're breaking up. Must be interference from the nebula."

"What's happen?" Colt said in a croaking voice.

"We're going to make it if we jump soon," Wes said. "Are we past the gravity threshold?"

"We'll be clear in—"

Before he could finish the flight control operator repeated his orders for the ship to return to orbit. Wes hit a switch that would transmit static.

"Stu?"

Stewart was rocking in his chair and held up a hand. His mental computations weren't complete. Wes didn't think Gerber control had any way of stopping a ship from leaving the system, but that didn't mean the GA agents on the space station didn't.

"We don't have much time," Wes said. "If we don't jump soon they'll find a way to keep us in the system."

Di returned with a shaker bottle. She unlatched the lid and helped Colt get a drink.

"*Jolly Rogue*, this is Gerber Flight control. You are ordered to return to the Heaven's Trail resort for security questioning."

"They don't really expect us to go back do they?" Di asked.

"Got... it!" Stu announced.

"I don't give a damn what they expect," Wes said. "Saide, as soon as the jump is in the computer, we run."

"Roger that," Saide replied.

"We'll be in trouble," Di said.

"Won't be the first time," Wes said. "Besides, we're never coming back here again."

"But those GA agents won't give up," Di pointed out.

"No," Wes agreed. "But the next time, we'll be ready."

"Preparing to make the transition to hyperspace," Saide said.

Wes breathed a sigh of relief as the ship jumped into hyperspace. He dropped into his chair and rubbed his face. They weren't in a great place. Having Colt on board had brought them more attention than Wes had expected. And that would make it hard to get work, but at least they were all together. They were on the run again, but that's what they were: smugglers, outlaws, independent freighters. It was all the same to him. They were runners, and they were doing what they did best.

EPILOGUE

They were ten hours from the Gerber system and on their second jump through hyperspace. Diana had made pancakes with bacon flavored protein strips. Colt was eating as if his stomach was a bottomless pit.

"Say that again," Wes said, trying to wrap his mind around it.

"The last entry was thirteen years ago," Colt replied around a mouth full of pancake that was saturated with syrup. Wes had no idea where the kid was putting it all. "Since then, the interest has been growing."

"I understand the basic economics," Wes said. "But the total was how much?"

"Fifty eight million," Colt said. "I didn't have time to read it all, but I got a picture on my PA before all the excitement started.

He slid the hand held Personal Access device across the table toward Wes, whose own plate of pancakes had been completely forgotten. The readout showed the total, last withdraw, and average interest of 10.29%. Wes knew that if money was invested and the interest compounded, that an interest rate of 10% would effectively double every seven years. The last withdraw thirteen years ago had left the total balance at sixteen million. And thirty years later, the total was nearly sixty million.

"No wonder the rich just get richer, huh," Di said.

"Yeah," Wes said. "That's incredible."

"Orin will be happy," Colt added. "That's way more than he's expecting."

A plan began to form in Wes' mind. Orin had said he would pay them a ten percent finders fee and Wes meant to hold him to it. With five million they could buy a new ship, but Wes wasn't thinking of getting rid of the *Jolly Rogue*. He loved her too much for that. But with enough money a man could buy a new registration for a ship. A new ID, new name, maybe a few cosmetic changes to the hull, and they could travel back into GA controlled space as if nothing had ever happened. It was their ticket back into the game that he loved. He looked at Colt who had just woken up after sleeping for nearly ten hours. The kid had saved them at the resort, and was proving to be a worthy member of the crew. Wes felt a tickle of excitement deep down inside. Colt was more than just a crew member, he was a game changer. And if Wes played his cards right, he knew their adventures together were only beginning.

"Good work, kid," Wes said.

"Thanks," Colt replied with a grin.

"And just what are you up to?" Diana said. "I know that look."

"Just thinking about the future," Wes said. "And things look bright."

AUTHOR'S NOTE

Thank you for reading Runners. As an author and publisher, it's my job to make sure my books are as perfect as they can be when I put them up for sale. Unfortunately, Runners was first published after my editor failed to get the manuscript into shape. I then made the mistake of putting it up without going through a proper beta testing. Hopefully, this new edition has corrected the mistakes. Please know that I am reworking my entire publication protocol and will strive to raise the level of professionalism in all my future books.

In the meantime if you could leave an honest review on Amazon and/or Goodreads it would help these books tremendously.

Below I've added an excerpt of one of my all time favorite books - Kestrel Class. If you liked Runners, I'm sure you'll love the Kestrel Class series.

For the latest news on what I'm writing sign up for my mailing list and be the first to hear about new books!

www.TobyNeighbors.com

KESTREL CLASS 1

Ben Griminski pushed his body back into the shadows, scarcely daring to breathe. The Salvage Scalpers were climbing over the junk heap Ben was hiding in. There had been just enough time to scramble into a burned-out escape capsule before they caught sight of him with his treasure. He couldn't help but notice the bloodstains inside the rusty wreck he was hiding in. It had been the last resort of some poor soul during the war, only to find it wasn't enough. Either the passenger died when the pod crashed, or it had been discovered before the occupant could escape. Ben didn't want to share the former passenger's fate.

The Scalpers were loud, which was the only thing that had saved Ben. If they had been moving quietly, he would have been caught out in the open. Not that he was doing anything wrong. On Torrent Four, no one owned the scrapyards. The vast fields of ruined tech, crashed and shattered aircraft, broken weapons, and scrap metals stretched for miles. Occasionally an unfortunate salvage hunter came across a bomb or an undiscovered load of explosives. With so much metal, it was almost impossible not to set off the dangerous ordnance. So far, Ben had been lucky. He had found nearly everything he needed without getting hurt or caught by the Scalpers. But he didn't believe in pushing his luck. The sooner he could find a way off Torrent Four, the better.

The Scalpers thought they owned the place, which worked in his favor. They were only interested in the salvage that came easy to them, rarely digging past the top layer of junk. What they really wanted was to catch a knowledgeable junker, raid their victim's cache, and put them to work finding more valuables in the expansive scrapyards. Ben would never work for the Scalpers, and he would die before he gave them his ship. He had worked too hard and too long to lose her to the Scalpers, who would only rip her apart and sell the pieces.

Ben watched with a sense of relief as the filthy Scalpers moved away. He didn't dare show himself, not until he was certain no one would see or hear him. He had a fine piece of triple-insulated shielding, which he'd pulled from the hulk of an old Osprey class transport vessel. Most of her fusion core was melted to slag, but what remained was in perfect shape for Ben's needs. He had cut it loose with an ancient angle grinder and was making his way back to his own ship when the Scalpers came tromping toward him.

Crawling out from the crashed escape pod that was mostly covered with junk, Ben felt a renewed sense of fear. It was impossible to move through the mounds of metal, carbon fiber, ceramic heat shield panels, and jumbled wires without making noise. He wasn't a coward, but the thought of losing his ship was more than he could bear. He moved quietly out from hiding and was just getting to his feet when a whistle sounded.

Ben turned and saw a straggler pointing at him. The Scalper was dressed in rags, his hands so dirty they looked like he was wearing dark gloves. The Scalper continued blowing the whistle, and Ben didn't wait to see the rest of the Scalpers come running. He knew they would follow him, and the only hope he had was speed. If he could be far enough ahead of the thieves, he might be able to hide again.

Running across a field of scrap metal, junk, and old space ships was difficult under any conditions, but Ben didn't have time to watch where he was going. His boots slid and fumbled across the shifting mounds of metal, which clanked and scraped loudly behind him.

As Ben topped a small hill of junk, he risked a backward glance. Just as he feared, the group of Salvage Scalpers was running to catch up. Fear mixed with desperation pushed Ben forward. He jumped down the small hill and landed on the cracked window of an ancient land vehicle. He could feel the glass giving way beneath him, and he flung his body forward, barely escaping the trap in the mounds of junk on the massive scrapyard.

He scrambled to his feet and kept running. Ben knew the section of scrapyard he was in. His ship, an old Kestrel class vessel, was buried in junk not far away, but he couldn't risk hiding there. He needed to lure the Scalpers away from his prize, so he turned to the right, racing around an old aviation tower that was leaning precariously over the junk field. He ran so hard, it felt as if his heart would break through his ribcage and leap from his chest. Eventually, he found the cab of an old transport and looked back over his shoulder. The Scalpers were nowhere in sight, so he climbed through the broken window and huddled on the rusted out floorboard.

The seats of the transport were gone, as was most of the old analog dials and gauges. Retro tech was in high demand. The dashboard had been torn away, leaving loose wiring hanging down like the grotesque entrails of a giant robot. Ben pressed himself against the door, lodging his head under the vehicle's steering column. His breath came in ragged gasps as he tried to calm himself down, and he listened for any sounds of the Scalpers.

It was quiet for a long time, and Ben liked to think that he had simply outrun the thieves. The Scalpers weren't known to be in great shape, but then neither was Ben. He only ran when he was being chased. Building was his forte, not strength or speed. He was a master at restoring things, and he marveled at the ingenuity of his ancestors.

Torrent Four was a junk world, but it hadn't always been so. Long ago, before the war, before Ben had been born and abandoned by his parents, Torrent Four was a thriving world full of industry and art. The citizens were proud and stubborn. Even in the face of the Royal Imperium's overwhelming forces, they had refused to give in to the big government's demands. And in return, the Imperium Fleet had slagged the entire planet. None of the towering buildings from before the war still stood. Vast junk fields covered most of the landmasses. Clean water was hard to come by. Food was handed down by the Royal Imperium in the form of tasteless protein bricks. And the air was choked with debris and the effects of heavy bombardment.

It made Ben sad to think how far the planet had fallen, but it didn't hamper his desire to leave. He wasn't the type to stick around and try to rebuild from the ashes, even though rebuilding was like art to him. His heart was in the stars. Nothing could be better, at least in his mind, than the freedom of his own ship. And the *Modulus Echo* was his ship. He didn't own her, simply because she was scrapped decades ago. But he had found her, and spent years restoring her. His sweat equity had, in his mind, given him the rights to her, and he was almost finished with the restoration.

As the sun began to set and the shadows grew long, Ben ventured a glance out the broken window. There was no sign of the Scalpers, but Ben feared they were simply waiting for him to appear. He decided to wait until full dark before coming out of his hiding place. After squirming quietly for a few minutes just to get the blood flowing through his legs and numb backside again, he settled to wait for nightfall.

KESTREL CLASS 2

Darkness didn't bother Ben. There was just enough starlight that he could navigate the mounds of rusted metal. Torrent Four's shattered moon hung like a ghostly reminder of the terrible losses of war. A large chunk of the moon had been blasted away, but the debris was caught in its orbit to form a luminous ring around the disfigured celestial body.

Ben took it all in stride. He was born after the war, his parents disappearing before he was fifteen. With no prospects, Ben had turned to the salvage fields, teaching himself how to build things and learning his craft from the ruined tech that littered the planet. Slowly, over a decade, he had discovered that the old gear spoke to him. There was a logic and order to the way things were made. He could disassemble a device, find what was broken, and put it all back together again. It was almost second nature to Ben, just like the mounds of trash and trails that made up the section of the salvage yard he called home.

Eventually, he came to a ridge of junk, a long mound that

ran hundreds of yards in either direction. He climbed to the summit, which was forty feet from the surface of the salvage yard. From there, on a clear day, he could see a mile in every direction. At night, he could only see a short way, but it was enough to ensure he wasn't being followed and there were no other scrappers nearby.

He made his way down the other side of the ridge and slipped between two old water containers. Both had cracked like dried-out egg shells over time. From between them, Ben saw the hatch of his ship, the *Modulus Echo*. He had to climb up several feet and then slip down through the crack to get inside, but as soon as his feet hit the deck, a light came on beside him. It was a motion-activated lantern he had picked up and put back together. He walked through the cargo bay and up the stairs to the main level of the ship. Nancy Josslyn sat at a computer terminal. Not a holographic, gesture and voice-activated, bio-computer, but an old-fashioned binary computer with a keyboard. The display was built into the ship's console station and showed a diagnostic of the ship's systems.

"Evening, Nance," Ben said.

"Is it?" Nancy replied. "I've been working and lost track of time."

"Well, that's good, I suppose."

"Where have you been?"

"Hiding from Scalpers," Ben replied. "I finally found the shielding I needed to complete the fusion containment chamber."

"So we can bring all systems to full power?"

"If we can get the Zexum. Once I finish the fusion reactor, all we have left is to get the hydro-generator up and running."

"And find a pilot."

"I've got a lead on that."

Nancy leaned back in her seat and stretched. She wore thick, bulky clothing that hid her diminutive figure. Her hair was tied neatly back in a bun, and she wore no makeup. Nance, as Ben preferred to call her, was a no-nonsense type of person. She lived through her computers and was just as talented at hacking and programming as Ben was at restoring machines.

"Better not wait too long. Running power from the auxiliary batteries isn't optimal. They could go kaput at any time, you know."

"So you keep telling me," Ben said. "Anything else go wrong while I was out?"

"No, I got the solid state drives wiped and debugged the operating system. The system is slow, but fully functional. Navigation, coms, and engineering can all be accessed from here."

"We're close," Ben said excitedly. "I can feel it. Are you hungry?"

"I could eat," Nance said, turning back to her computer screen.

Ben grinned. His partner was nothing if not predictable. He might have hoped for a more active sidekick, but Nance was fully invested in the project. She was quiet, almost a recluse, but that didn't bother him. Like Ben, she wanted desperately to escape Torrent Four, but her skills were different from his own. Getting up and preparing a meal for the two of them simply wouldn't occur to her. There was work to be done at her computer and she would spend every waking hour doing that work, even to the detriment of her own health.

He walked up the stairs to the upper level of the ship, which was open in the center with a food prep station and long banquet table. Above the kitchen and mess area, the hull was made of transparent steel so that the open space on the upper level served as an observation deck. It was surrounded by small cabins, which Ben hoped to refurbish one day, but the crew quarters were a higher priority to him.

He unwrapped the vacuum seal on a protein brick. The protein was manufactured and tasteless, just a lump of moldable food that would stay good for decades if the vacuum seal wasn't broken. They were the main food source on Torrent Four—cheap, easy to get, transport, prepare, and keep. The difficulty came in obtaining spices or flavor packs. They were much more rare and exponentially more expensive. It was rumored that with the right spices and seasonings, a chef could turn a protein brick into a gourmet meal. To Ben and Nance, it was simply fuel their bodies needed. He had artificial seasoning packs, which didn't taste like real food, but did give the protein brick flavor. He cut the brick in two, sprinkled it with a powder that claimed to be pizza flavoring, and stuck them in the processing unit.

While the protein warmed, Ben checked their water stores. They had just under ten gallons left of potable water. Once they had enough pure oxygen and hydrogen, they could manufacture drinking water. But the hydro-generator needed a magnetic coupler, which he had yet to find in the vast scrapyard. Once he had it, they would be ready to take the *Echo* into space. All they would need was a supply of Zexum, which would serve as fuel for the fusion reactor, and Ben had a feeling he knew exactly where to get the rare element. He forced himself not to look ahead. They still needed the hydro-generator working and a competent pilot they could trust. Only then would Ben consider uncovering the ship from the mounds of scrap that hid her in the vast salvage yard.

The processor chirped, signaling that their meal was ready. Ben grabbed their clean sporks, filled two steel water bottles, and put all the food on a tray. He carried the meal down to where Nance was working, and they ate without talking. When they finished, there was more work to do, then they could get a few hours of sleep before they made plans to do it all over again the next day.

KESTREL CLASS 3

"You flying today, Kimbo?"

"I fly every day, Squatter," Kim Beaudry said.

They were in the canyons in one of the taverns known to cater to kite flyers. Squatter wasn't a flyer, but he made a living organizing races.

"Mavrik's back. And looking for revenge," Squatter said. "I could set up a head-to-head if you're interested. There should be some heavy action with your history."

"I'll race anybody, any time, you know that," Kim said.

"Good, I was hoping you'd sign on."

He walked away, and Kim looked back out the large windows. The canyons were beautiful in a way, but all Kim saw were the dangers. Deep, narrow channels that funnel winds that made flying difficult under normal conditions. Racing through the canyons took nerve, skill, and a healthy dose of luck. Kim had the skill, and nothing could keep her from flying, but she knew that sooner or later her luck would run out. One bad crash would be enough to cripple her for life, or worse yet, kill her. Still, she would rather die flying than live a long life but never leave the ground.

The footsteps approaching were unmistakable. Kim felt her skin begin to crawl even before she heard the deep, gravelly voice or smelled Ray Gan's perpetually sour odor.

"Hello, Kimberly," the fat tavern owner said. "It's good to see you."

"My name is Kim, not Kimberly."

"Why do you despise being a woman?" Ray Gan asked. "A girl as lovely as you could make a good life for herself."

She had expected the fat man to make his pitch. He did every time she went into his tavern, and each time she rejected him. It was familiar, but not welcome. Kim wished the dirty, smelly man would go away and leave her alone, but if she wanted to fly in the canyon races, she couldn't insult him.

"You know, I think you're good enough to fly for the Imperium Fleet," he said.

"I know I am," Kim said, feeling unnerved.

Joining the Fleet Academy was her dream. She wanted nothing more than to leave Torrent Four and spend her life flying fast attack craft for the Imperium Fleet. She wasn't a patriot, and could care less about politics. All she wanted was to fly.

"I have some contacts," Ray Gan said. "You know, I might be willing to put your name forward for consideration. Maybe even pay for your entrance exams."

"Yeah, and what would I have to do for you?" Kim asked.

"Is it too much to ask that you show a little appreciation?"

"You mean be your lover?" Kim whirled around to face the fat tavern owner. He had a huge stomach and fat rolls around his neck. His thin hair was greasy, his teeth were coated in something that Kim didn't recognize, and his small, piggish eyes ran up and down as he stared at her.

"There is a lot to be gained, Kimberly. I ask for so little in return."

"No," Kim said. "I'll get to the Fleet my own way."

"Perhaps," Ray Gan said. "If you don't end up dead in the canyons first."

She turned away as tears suddenly flooded her eyes. The futility of her life galled her. She was young, talented, ambitious, and hardworking. But she didn't have the connections, or the money, to be considered for the flight academy. Even so, she would never give herself to Ray Gan or anyone else for a chance to chase her dreams. If that was the cost, it was too high and Kim refused to pay it.

"Well, if you change your mind, sweetheart. Just come find me," Ray Gan said as he heaved himself back onto his feet. "My door is always open to you."

Kim raised her hand to acknowledge the offer but knew she would never accept it. A horn sounded, signaling another race. Behind her the patrons grew rowdy. They were watching the high-resolution hologram displays that showed the views from the race cameras mounted onto each pilot's kite.

Kim watched through the windows as a second horn blasted away, signaling the start of the race. Five pilots leaped from a platform over the tavern and dropped into the canyon. The kites were large gliders, built from aluminum with silk sails stretched between the frame to catch the wind. The pilots hung beneath the kites, some fifteen to twenty feet below the gliders. Kim watched as the air currents in the canyons propelled the fliers away and out of sight.

Somewhere, Squatter was taking bets on the race, holding markers and wads of credit slips. Kim felt as if she might be sick. The odds were against the pilots. If they didn't get injured, or wreck their kites, they only made money if they won the race. Sometimes the fliers got desperate, and that often led to bad choices with deadly consequences.

www.ingramcontent.com/pod-product-compliance
Lightning Source LLC
Chambersburg PA
CBHW051958240626
47153CB00005B/1802